# BLUE LIGHT IN THE SKY
## & OTHER STORIES

# CAN XUE

# BLUE LIGHT IN THE SKY
## & OTHER STORIES

**TRANSLATED BY**
**KAREN GERNANT AND CHEN ZEPING**

**A NEW DIRECTIONS BOOK**

Book design by Sylvia Frezzolini Severance
Manufactured in the United States of America
First published as a New Directions Paperbook (NDP1039) in 2006.
Published simultaneously in Canada by Penguin Books Canada Limited
New Directions Books are printed on acid-free paper.

Library of Congress Cataloging-in-Publication Data

Can Xue, 1953-
  [Short stories. English. Selections]
  Blue light in the sky & other stories / Can Xue ;
translated by Karen Gernant and Chen Zeping.
      p. cm.
  Translated from various Chinese sources.
  ISBN-13: 978-0-8112-1648-7 (alk. paper)
  ISBN-10: 0-8112-1648-9
  1. Can Xue, 1953—Translations into English. I. Title.
  PL2912.A5174B58 2006
  895.1'352—dc22

                                    2006009091

New Directions Books are published for James Laughlin
by New Directions Publishing Corporation,
80 Eighth Avenue, New York 10011

**FOR LU YOUNG**

# TABLE OF CONTENTS

# TRANSLATORS' ACKNOWLEDGMENTS

We are grateful to: the author for reading our English versions and making sure they were faithful to the originals; translator Herbert Batt for introducing us to Can Xue's stories and offering suggestions for revising a few of the translations; Jin Jianfan, of the Chinese Writers' Association, Sun Shaozhen and Lin Benchun, professors at Fujian Teachers' University, and Xie Youshun, literary critic, for generously giving their time and recommendations; editors Chen Haiyan (*Chinese Literature*) and Frank Stewart (*Manoa*) for being supportive of our translations early on; and editors Bradford Morrow and Martine Bellen for publishing Can Xue's "Helin" (*Conjunctions: 40*), "Scenes Inside the Dilapidated Walls" (*Conjunctions: 43*), "Blue Light in the Sky" and "Night in the Mountain Village" (both in *Conjunctions: 45*). The first English version of "Mosquitoes and Mountain Ballads," translated by Chen Jie as "Mosquitoes and Folk Songs," appeared in *Conjunctions: 36*. We thank these editors, as well as William Ryan and Jack Heflin at *turnrow* and Pat Matsueda at *Manoa*, for their receptivity to our various submissions. We are also grateful to Han Lei for allowing us to use his photograph "Shanshui" for the cover. Thanks are also due to the Aura Gallery in Shanghai. Finally, we thank Declan Spring and Barbara Epler at New Directions for their enthusiasm for Can Xue's innovative work and Declan Spring for the expertise he's brought to editing this volume.

KAREN GERNANT AND CHEN ZEPING

# BLUE LIGHT IN THE SKY
## & OTHER STORIES

# BLUE LIGHT IN THE SKY

**W**HEN SUMEI WAS PLAYING A GAME OF "CATCH THE ROBBER" IN the yard, a piece of sharp glass cut her foot. Blood gushed out. She began crying right away and limped toward the house. Behind her, the other kids went on playing like crazy. No one noticed that she had left.

As soon as she went in the house, she stopped crying, opened the wardrobe, took a rag out of the drawer, and bandaged her foot. As the blood continued seeping out, she added another rag. She pricked up her ears: she was afraid her father, who was in the backyard repairing a wooden tub, would come in and see her. The bleeding soon stopped. Sumei took off the two blood-soaked rags, and bandaged her foot with a clean cloth. Then she stood up, intending to throw the two dirty cloths into the garbage can. As soon as she got up, the door opened. But it wasn't her father who came in; it was her older sister Sulin.

"What's that?" she asked aggressively. She was quite pleased as she pointed at Sumei's foot.

"Don't tell Pa," Sumei pleaded.

"So much blood! Your foot! What a catastrophe!!" Sulin was shouting loudly on purpose.

In a flash, Sumei thought the whole sky was falling. She lost no time in hiding the two rags in the burlap bag behind the door. A frightened young rat glided out of the burlap bag and fled in desperation. Because of her hurried, vigorous movement, her foot started oozing blood again. Sulin observed her little sister carefully for a while, then turned and went into the backyard. Sumei knew she was going to report this to Pa, and—terror-stricken—she sat down on the bamboo chair to wait. She predicted a storm would soon descend on her. But she waited and waited. Pa still hadn't made a move. So she thought, *Could Pa be too busy* (that morning, she'd noticed that three people had come to ask him to repair their tubs) *to come and discipline her?* Thinking this, she felt a little better. She decided to spend the day in the woodshed. As she left, she took the two dirty rags out of the burlap bag behind the door. She limped down the steps and threw them into the garbage can. She also grabbed two handfuls of dried leaves to cover the rags.

The woodshed was more than ten meters from the house. Living inside it was Sumei's old friend, the big gray rat. As soon as she saw the nest made from bits of grass and rags, warmth surged up inside her. She knew that there were a few baby rats inside. They'd been born a few days earlier and hadn't yet opened their eyes. The day before, she'd taken advantage of the time when the big gray rat was out hunting food to steal a look at those little things that were almost transparent.

Sumei sat down far away from the rat's nest. From the woodshed, she could hear Sulin's voice. What on earth was she saying to Pa? Maybe they were discussing how to discipline her. And in the front yard, the kids playing "catch the robber" were shouting with glee the whole time.

When it was almost afternoon, Sumei was so hungry she couldn't stand it anymore. She intended to slip stealthily into the house and find something to eat. When she walked into the kitchen, she saw Sulin in the midst of washing dishes. Sulin was staring at her full of suspicion.

"Your food is in the cupboard. Pa kept talking about you. We thought you'd had an accident!"

Sulin's voice had become really soft. It was even a little fawning. Sumei felt truly flattered. Sulin made quick work of bringing the food to the table. Sumei sat down, and as if in a dream began gobbling down the food. At the same time, she heard her sister talking on and on beside her.

"Sumei, Pa says you could die from tetanus. What do you think? You know Mama died from tetanus. I've never approved of your playing with those wild kids. Why don't you ever listen? Actually, I've known for a long time that there was a lot of broken glass by the fence. Last year, I smashed a few wine bottles there. I just never imagined that you would get hurt so soon. Now you've been hurt. I'm so jealous of you. This morning, I saw that your foot was very swollen, and I ran over to Pa. He was putting a hoop around a barrel, and without looking up, he just asked me if it was the broken wine bottles that had hurt you. He also said that those wine bottles had all held poison;

there'd be no way for you to escape with your life. His words upset me. As soon as I calmed down, I remembered those stencils that you used for drawing flowers. Why not just give them to me to save? You won't be able to use them anyhow. I know that you get along well with Little Plum—she gave you those patterns; but if you hadn't asked her for them, she would have given them to me. Right? What can you do with those things now?"

Sulin frowned. It seemed she hadn't thought this through. It also seemed she was up to something. Sumei washed her dishes and was about to go back to the bedroom. She noticed that Sulin was still standing next to the stove and smirking. She ignored her and went back to the bedroom by herself. She and Sulin shared this bedroom: the two beds were opposite each other, with a wardrobe in between. It was from a drawer in the wardrobe that Sumei had found the cloth to bandage her wound. Now she opened the wardrobe again, took out a key, opened a locked drawer, and took out that set of stencil blocks. They were made of peach wood, a smooth red color. Altogether, there were four of them. One could draw four floral designs to embroider pillows. Little Plum had told Sumei that she had swiped them from her mother. In the last few days, her mother had looked everywhere for them. Sumei didn't know how to embroider flowers yet, but the magical blocks enchanted her. When she had nothing to do, she drew flowers in pencil on old newspapers—page after page of them. She felt this was incredibly wonderful. After holding those floral blocks for a while, she carefully put them back in the brown paper bag, then locked the drawer. Her wound was hurting a little, but it had stopped bleeding. Sumei recalled what Sulin had said, and all at once she felt a little afraid: was it possible that she would really die? Just now, she had thought that Sulin was making a mountain out of a molehill. Sulin had never lied. And Pa—whenever she or Sulin did something wrong, he slapped them twice. This time, though, had been an exception. Was it because Pa was giving her special treatment that Sulin had said "I'm really so jealous of you"? And why in the world had Pa discarded wine bottles with poison in the vicinity of the house? Sumei couldn't figure it out. She didn't even bother to think it through. Her policy was always to wait for the trouble to go away. "It'll turn out all right"—that's what she always told herself. Sometimes, when something bad happened, she hid out in the woodshed and slept there. After she woke up, it didn't seem nearly so bad. But today perhaps what Sulin had said wasn't so trivial. For some reason, at the time, Sumei hadn't been at all worried; but now remembering what Sulin had said back in the bedroom, she began to feel vaguely worried. She was also afraid that Sulin would see that she was concerned. She sat on the bed, took the bandage off, and looked at her foot. There wasn't anything unusual about her wound. She thought, *Maybe that piece of glass wasn't from the wine bottle containing poison. Pa and Sulin were both too decisive about this—really oddly decisive.* Sumei decided she would walk to the other end of the village. If she could walk that far, it would mean there was no problem. How could anyone who was about to die walk to the other end of the village?

By the time her father caught up with her, Sumei had left the woodshed behind, and was almost at Little Plum's door.

"Are you asking for trouble? Go back and lie down!" her father roared ominously.

"I, I'm doing my best . . . ," Sumei said in a small, pleading voice.

"Your best! Soon, we'll be watching your finest drama!"

Through it all, her father's expression was stern. Not daring to look at him, Sumei glided to one side like a mouse.

"Where do you think you're going? Do you want to die? Hurry up and go back to bed and die there. If you die outside, no one will pick up your corpse!"

Chased and scolded by her father, Sumei didn't feel that her foot was lame at all. She rushed back home. As soon as she went in, she saw that Sulin was trying to open the drawer where the floral stencils were kept. She was using a wire to open the lock. When she heard the door open, she chucked the wire at once and blushed.

"You can't even wait for me to die."

Slamming the cupboard shut, Sulin left in a huff. Sumei knew that she was going to look for Pa again. It was strange: Pa didn't even like Sulin. Of the two sisters, he liked Sumei somewhat better, but from the time she was little, Sulin had always done her best to please her father. Even if Pa was mean to her, she was never discouraged.

Sumei lay in bed, closed her eyes, and forced herself to go to sleep. She was a little worried about sleeping. After a while, she felt dazed. In her dream, she went into a forest by accident, and couldn't get out. It was cold in the forest, and there were huge trees everywhere. She sneezed a few times in a row, and suddenly as she bent her head, she noticed that her foot had been perforated by a sharp piece of bamboo. She'd been nailed down and couldn't move. Feeling an indescribable stabbing sensation, she screamed. She woke up. Her hair was drenched with sweat, but her foot didn't hurt. What was this all about? *Could it be that it was someone else who stepped on the sharp piece of bamboo in her dream? And that person was the one who would soon die?* Although her foot didn't hurt, the feeling of pain she'd had in the dream was deeply embedded in her memory. The poplar tree outside the window was whispering in the wind. Sumei was afraid she'd go back to the same dream, but—without knowing why—she also really wanted to go back to it so that she could understand some things better. She shilly-shallied back and forth between sleeping and waking. Finally, she woke up, because of the tremendous sound of Sulin shattering a bowl in the kitchen.

Sumei went into the kitchen to help Sulin. Just as Sumei was about to start cleaning the rice out of the pan, Sulin suddenly turned polite. She snatched the pan out of her hand, and said repeatedly, "Go and rest. Why don't you rest?" Her behavior again made Sumei suspicious. Sulin kept busying herself, while Sumei watched from the sidelines. She admired Sulin's skillful way of working that she could never learn. Now, for example, Sulin was absorbed in using tongs to roll damp coal dust into little balls. She stacked them up next to the stove. It was as if her right hand were joined with the tongs in a single entity. She looked rather proud of herself.

"Sulin, I had a strange dream. I dreamt I was dying." Sumei couldn't keep from saying this.

"Shhh! Don't let Pa hear you."

"But it was just a dream," she added. "Weird, huh?" Sulin looked at her speculatively, and then buried her head in her work.

At dinner, their father didn't say a word. Only when they'd finished eating and Sulin had stood up to clear the table did he say abruptly, "Sumei mustn't go out."

"I'm okay. There's nothing wrong," Sumei argued, her face flushed.

Father ignored her and walked away. "You're so stupid—so stupid!" Sulin said as she grabbed the bowl out of Sumei's hand. "Go off and rest!"

Lights were on in Little Plum's home. The whole family was just wolfing down their dinner. After Sumei went in, Little Plum just nodded at her, indicating that she should wait, and then didn't look at her again. They were eating pumpkin porridge and corn bread. Their faces were covered with perspiration. Little Plum's two little brothers buried their faces in the large bowls. Little Plum's father and mother didn't look at Sumei, either. They both looked a little angry. Sumei stood against the wall for a long time. When the family finished eating, they all went into the other room, leaving only Little Plum to clear the table. Sumei thought, *Little Plum is really strange. Neither her pa nor her ma is here now. Why is she still not even glancing at me?* Little Plum piled up the bowls and carried them into the kitchen. Sumei followed her, not guessing that she would snatch up a cloth in the kitchen and come back to wipe off the table. And so Sumei collided with her.

"Leave now—now! Later on, I'll go to see you," she said in annoyance. She actually forcefully pushed Sumei outside.

Sumei fell down the steps of Little Plum's house. After sitting up, she inspected her foot. It was still okay. The wound was no worse. As soon as she looked up, she saw Little Plum motion to her anxiously, shouting softly, "Leave now—now!" Then she shrank back into the house and didn't emerge again.

Sumei felt it was really a little dangerous now. Recalling her father's orders and his expression, she couldn't help but shiver. All around, it was very dark. In the dark, two people carrying lanterns were in an urgent hurry. Soon, they went past Sumei. She heard one of them say, "We need only get a move on and we'll be in time. In the past, people in our family . . . " Sumei was about to get up and go home, but Sulin had caught up with her. Out of breath, Sulin said to Sumei, "I don't dare stay home alone."

"Is Pa going to beat you?"

Sulin shook her head vigorously.

"What's going on?"

"I was at home thinking about your situation. The more I thought, the more I felt afraid. Why do you always have to go outside? I guess it's great outside. It's so dark that it seems there's no point in being afraid."

She took Sumei's hand solicitously, and strolled around with her on the path. All at once, Sumei felt greatly moved. She had always thought that Sulin just talked rubbish. She'd thought that she stirred up their father to be against her, but at this moment, she felt puzzled.

Maybe Sulin really was more sensible than she was, and knew some things that she was in the dark about. Why had she taken on all the housework Sumei was supposed to do? Sumei had learned through repeated experience that Sulin was a smart person and had always had a clear head ever since she was little. With this thought in mind, Sumei felt she could rely on Sulin, and she held her hand tighter. She whispered to herself, *I can count on Sulin no matter what happens. She is so good, kind, and gentle. She helps me take care of everything. I should rely on her.* Then Sumei suddenly found that she had been following Sulin all along. They hadn't gone far at all; they were just circling around Little Plum's home. Now no one was on the street. The wind blowing from the mountain was like a song. All the while, Sulin was silent. What on earth was she thinking about? Or wasn't she thinking of anything?

"Let's go see Pa over there."

After walking around several times, Sulin finally suggested this.

When they went into the backyard, their father was splitting firewood in the dark. The sound he made was rhythmic. Sumei was very surprised: she didn't believe her father could see in the dark. But the fact was that Father was clearly working in a systematic way—just as if it were daylight.

"Pa, Pa, we're afraid!" Sulin's voice quivered.

"What are you afraid of?" Father put down his work, walked over, and spoke amiably.

Sumei couldn't see Father's face well, but it was a relief to hear his tone. She thought to herself, *Pa isn't angry anymore.*

"Sumei isn't afraid, is she? Sulin, you should learn from Sumei. As I split firewood here, my whole head is filled with things having to do with the two of you. Ever since your mother died, I've been fearful. Sometimes I'm so scared that I get up at midnight and split firewood. Talk about being afraid, I'm the one who should be afraid. What do the two of you have to be afraid of?"

With that, he bent down again and resumed his work.

That night, once Sumei fell asleep, she saw that forest, and she saw herself located in it again. At first, she noticed just one scorpion. Then she noticed scorpions hiding everywhere—under the dried-up leaves, on the trunks of the trees. As soon as she found some, they disappeared and others appeared. They were everywhere.

Time after time, she screamed and woke up with a start. In fact,

it was worse than death would be. When Sumei woke up, she saw
Sulin standing motionless on the bed across from her: it was as if she
was observing the night. Finally Sumei didn't feel like sleeping. She
turned on the light and, drenched in sweat, sat up in bed.

"Sumei, you're really brave." Sulin's voice held jealousy.

Sulin jumped down from the bed, approached Sumei, and gave
her a handkerchief to wipe away the sweat.

"When Pa threw away the broken glass from the wine bottles
that held poison—threw the glass along the fence—I was off to the
side. He wouldn't let me get in on the act. He's always like this.
When I told you today that I was the one who threw away the broken wine bottles, that was just my vanity making mischief."

Sulin was deep in thought. Sumei suddenly thought that, under
the light, Sulin's face had become a shadow. She couldn't stop herself
from stretching out her hand to touch her face. But the thing she
touched let out a sound like the rustling of dried leaves. Sulin moved
at once, and reproached her: "What the hell are you doing? You're
really insensitive. I've told you repeatedly that you should cut your
fingernails, but you just don't listen. What do you think Pa is doing?
Listen!"

Sumei didn't hear anything. But Sulin was terribly tense. She
crept to the door, opened it, and slipped lightly outside. Sumei did-
n't feel like going with her. She just turned the light off, and sat on
the bed and worried. She thought again that if she woke up from a
really sound sleep, maybe everything would change. But she was also
afraid of sleeping and seeing the scorpions. Her mind was really con-
flicted. But finally in a haze, she couldn't ward off sleep. She entered
that forest again. This time, she shut her eyes tight and didn't see
anything. When she woke up, it was already broad daylight.

Another day passed, and she found that her foot had healed. It was
obvious that her father and Sulin had made a mountain out of a
molehill. Even so, she didn't feel the least bit relieved. She couldn't
ever forget the dreams she'd had of the bamboo and the scorpions.
Those dreams were linked with the wound where, each time the
wounded foot was punctured or bitten, it was exactly on the spot
where the wound was. It was really strange. All right, then, go outside, and look for Little Plum and other people. Maybe Little Plum
had to chop grass for the pigs. Well then, she'd go with her to chop

grass for the pigs. While they were doing that, she could sound her out and see if she had changed her attitude toward her.

After chopping grass for the pigs at home, Sumei went over to Little Plum's house.

"Little Plum! Little Plum!" she shouted as she craned her neck.

Nobody inside the house responded. After a while, though, she heard Little Plum's parents cursing—calling Sumei "a bad omen." All Sumei could do was retreat and walk discontentedly back along the path. After a while, she came to Aling's home. Aling was in the vegetable garden out in front. Sumei called her several times before she looked up slowly. She looked all around in alarm. With a gesture, she indicated that Sumei shouldn't come any closer. But just then, Aling's mother came out and walked over to Sumei. Taking hold of her shoulders, she looked at her carefully. She said, "Lambkin, lamb—." Sumei was uncomfortable and really wanted to break away, but that woman's grip was very tight. Without listening to any protests, she forced herself on Sumei.

"Sumei, your father is quite good at his craft. He must have made a lot of money—am I right? But I don't think it's all that great to make money, and I don't want my children to get close to someone like that. I'm not so shortsighted. Let me tell you, if a person sets himself up too high and also knows things that a lot of ordinary people don't know, then he's heading for a major fall. Actually, my Aling is a lot better—quite ordinary and without any cares or worries. As the saying goes, she's 'content with her lot.' How's your foot?"

"My foot? It's fine." Sumei was surprised.

"Haha. You don't need to hoodwink me. This is an open secret in the whole village. Could someone like Sulin keep this quiet? You don't look at all happy about this. . . . So I say, it's still better to be ordinary. I always wonder: What's your father up to? Aling! Aling! What the hell are you doing with the hoeing? Have you lost your mind? Run off and feed the pigs—now!"

Suddenly she relaxed her grip on Sumei, and began bellowing at Aling. Aling threw the hoe down at once and started running toward the house.

Sumei wanted to leave, but the woman gripped her by the shoulders and wouldn't let her go.

"Your sister Sulin is much too curious. She's brought herself to an emaciated state. I don't admire her one bit. And I don't let Aling have any truck with her. But you're different. I adore you. Let me see you smile. Smile! Ah, you can't smile. You poor child. That guy has been too strict with you. I can't ask you in. After all, Aling has her own life. Everyone knows what kind of trick your father is playing. Everyone wants to know what the end result will be. We say this is an instance of 'wait and see what happens.' Understand?"

"I don't understand! I don't!" Sumei was struggling with all her might.

The woman held her shoulders even tighter, and pressed her mouth against her ear.

"You don't? No wonder! Let me clue you in. Listen: you mustn't walk around outside aimlessly. And when you're home, you mustn't sleep in. Prick up your ears. Spy on your father's activity. You won't be used to doing this at first, but as time goes on, you'll get used to it."

Sumei twisted around and looked over the woman's shoulder. She saw Aling talking with Little Plum in the doorway. They were both excited and gesturing a lot. Sumei recalled the good times when she had played with them. She felt miserable. "Little Plum! Little Plum!" she shouted in despair.

Little Plum was dumbstruck, and then pretended that she hadn't heard and went on talking and laughing with Aling.

"You little girl, you're rotten through and through," Aling's mother said, gnashing her teeth.

All of a sudden, the woman scratched her hard on the back, hurting her so much that everything turned black and she sat down on the ground.

When she opened her eyes again, the woman had disappeared. So had Aling and Little Plum. It was as though they hadn't been here just now. Only the pain in her back reminded her of what had just happened. Sumei thought back on what the woman had said about her father. Although she didn't quite get it, she still knew it wasn't anything good. After going through this, she gave up the dream of finding companions. She was weak all over. Only after struggling hard did she manage to stagger to a standing position. That woman had definitely hurt her back. This was truly sinister. Weeping, Sumei walked slowly to the other end of the village. No matter what, she still felt that perverse desire: she had to walk to the other end of the village. It was as though she was struggling against her pa and Sulin.

Taking breaks to rest, she walked ahead. No one else was on the street. At the doorways to the homes, everything was quiet. If she weren't walking in the village she knew so well, she would have suspected she had come to a strange place. Now, even on the hill where cattle used to graze, she didn't see even one cow. At last, Sumei reached the old camphor tree at the other end of the village. Leaning against the tree trunk, she thought she'd rest for a while, but the deathly stillness all around began to terrify her. A long brown snake was swaying back and forth on the tree, hissing at her. The frightening scene in her dream suddenly recurred in its entirety. Holding her head, she ran away crazily. She ran a long way before stopping. She sat on the ground and took off her shoe. The wound had split open again, and there was a little red swelling.

"Sumei, let's hurry on home. There isn't much time."

Looking up, she saw her father. This was really weird: was it possible that Pa had followed her?

"I can't walk any farther," she whimpered timidly.

"Come on. I'll carry you." Father bent down as he said this.

Sumei straddled her father's broad sweat-covered back. She was feeling myriad emotions. She glued her small, thin ear to her father's body, and heard clearly the sound of a man's sobbing. But her father surely wasn't crying, so where was this sound coming from? Father was rebuking Sumei, and talking, too, of the wine bottles that had held poison. Sumei was absorbed in identifying that sound of weeping, so she couldn't care less about what her father was saying.

Carrying Sumei, Father walked on and on. Sumei realized they weren't heading home; instead, they'd taken a fork in the road leading toward the river. At first, Sumei was a little scared, but the sound of weeping coming from her father's back was like a magnet drawing all of her attention. She forgot about danger, and she forgot about how she hated her family. Everything seemed more and more distant. At the back of her father's neck, she said lightly, "My foot doesn't hurt anymore."

Father began laughing. They were already in the river now. The water came up to Father's neck. Supporting herself on Father's shoulders, Sumei managed to get her face above the water. But her father gently pulled her back down. She heard the sound of Sulin's resentful sobbing being blown by the wind along the river. She thought to herself, *Is Sulin perhaps jealous of me?* She closed her eyes and in her dream, she drank lots and lots of river water. She felt it was strange that, even with her eyes closed, she could see the blue light in the sky.

The next day, when Sumei woke up, the sun was already shining on the mosquito net.

Sulin stood motionless at the head of the bed watching her. Her face was as fresh as pumpkin blossoms opening in the morning.

"Sumei, you've completely recovered. Get up now and chop grass for the pigs. I've exhausted myself with work the last two days. I need to rest. Yesterday, Little Plum came looking for you. She wanted to take those floral blocks back. Since you were sleeping, I took the key out of your pocket, opened the drawer, and gave them to her. It never occurred to me that, after thinking about it a moment, she would turn around and give the stencils to me. God only knows what she was thinking. But to tell the truth, what good would it be for you to have them? You don't know how to embroider."

"I guess you're right." Sumei's voice was buoyant.

# THE BIZARRE WOODEN BUILDING

THIS MULTI-STORY BUILDING IS REALLY TOO HIGH. ITS OUTER WALL is made of long wooden planks piled up horizontally, and the inside is also made completely of wood. These boards with their exposed wood grain have already turned black from the passage of time. If you look at it from a slight distance, it's just one blurry expanse. The building is of ordinary design. In just one small point is it different from others: it's so unexpectedly high that people can't believe it. Considering its construction materials—ordinary wood—we find it hard to imagine that it was possible to build such a high structure. Standing here, even craning my neck, I can't see its roof, because the top half has completely disappeared into the mist. It's very foggy in this region. This must have been the evil design of whoever designed this building—the work of an extremely suspicious person who didn't know his place. Perhaps he started planning it with just the general outcome in mind and without any consideration of its daily use. Later, he didn't examine it closely, either, and left things unsettled. When you went up the stairs, shaking and squeaking sounds accompanied each step—and even the groaning sound that one associates with carrying a heavy load of wood became more and more intense the farther up you went. As I was hesitating, the master issued a cheerful invitation from the top of the building. The voice came down from above, like an echo in a deserted valley. He'd seen me from so far away, and had finally shouted to me. Had my reply reached the top?

Somewhat relieved, I started climbing up. On each floor were residences for two families. All the doors were tightly closed; it seemed they were locked from the inside, but it was also possible that there weren't any people inside. I was dizzy. When I finally reached the last floor, I looked up to see the master smiling and standing at the entrance of the open door. He was dressed cumbersomely in a black down jacket—even though it was late in the spring. Yet after climbing up the stairs, I—wearing only a wool shirt—was dripping with sweat. Not until I walked up to him did I see that the man's face bore the marks of having stayed up all night. His face was puffy and his greasy hair covered his pate like a thin pancake. The room was empty but for a narrow bed. On the bed was a quilt that was neither gray nor green, all in disarray. Under the bed was a clothes trunk.

He invited me to sit under the quilt with him, saying that one could keep warm this way. So each of us sat at one end of the bed. Sure enough, after a while, I felt the wintry chill in this room. Although the room had only one small window plastered tight with newspaper, the wind poured in from every crack between the wooden boards. The whole room was whizzing with cold wind. Luckily, the quilt was very big. He told me to wrap myself up in it, and only then did I slowly stop shivering.

"I didn't expect you today, so last night, I worked hard again all night long. Now that I'm in bed, my eyes are fighting to stay open. You won't take offense, will you?" he asked.

"Of course not," I said, wrapping the quilt more tightly around myself.

The room was only dimly lit. Even though he and I were sitting across from each other, I still couldn't see his expression well. His pale face kept wobbling, his teeth all exposed on the outside, bringing terrible thoughts to my mind. It was only his body warmth under the quilt that reassured me. I bent my head to avoid looking at him. I thought, *Hasn't he fallen asleep yet?* He hadn't even taken off his down jacket.

"Most recently, I've started considering how to overcome the obstacle of distance," he said, his train of thought clear, "and last night, I made a lot of headway. My house is the highest building in this area—my ancestors were proud of it, for you know, in the past it was densely populated here and the means of communication were much different from today—but this fact hasn't brought any essential benefit with it. Rather, it's taken the shape of an impassable obstacle. The invasion and attacks of the white ants also give me a headache. Every day, they seem to proclaim that the end of the world is approaching. You also noticed that all of the households here have moved away. So then how did I make headway? This is the problem that I've been thinking about constantly for the last several years. Last night, I finally made an unimaginable breakthrough. But now I need to go to sleep right away. The pitiful child at the door can tell you what the solution is."

Strange . . . I hadn't heard anyone come up the stairs. Was he talking nonsense? Aside from me, who would come here? I hesitated a while, and finally—risking the cold—shuffled over to open the door. Sure enough, a figure stood at the entrance. He turned around: it was a boy of thirteen or fourteen. His lips were trembling from the cold. In his hand he carried a basket.

"Who are you?" I said as I fled back to the quilt.

"I deliver pancakes. He wants me to deliver them twice a day. But downstairs, I saw you coming up, and thought you would probably also want pancakes. This is gratis. Look, there's bottled water, too."

He removed the cloth from the basket, and took out a small bottle of water, a tumbler, and two pancakes.

I took the tumbler from him, and as he bent to pour water for me, I noticed that he was wearing an odd long gown. The front of this gown was all covered from top to bottom with large pockets. When he saw me staring at his clothes, he shrank back, and sniveling in embarrassment, he smiled. This long, pocket-covered gown lent his actions an experience that didn't match his age. Just then, the master was snoring thunderously.

"Actually, what these pockets hold is all the same thing." Watching me eat a pancake, he said, "It's all information from this region that I've gathered for him. When I sell pancakes, with no one the wiser, I grab onto those people's inside stories. They never guess that I'm in the habit of jotting things down. Huh!" He conceitedly patted the pockets on his chest, then asked, "Can you guess what's inside? This room is so cold it's like a tomb. It's lucky I came to pass the time of day with you. Otherwise, you'd be just sitting here frozen stiff, wouldn't you? He's different. He took precautions long ago by wearing such a thick down jacket."

"Are you cold?" I asked him anxiously.

"I'm not afraid of the cold!" He let out a piercing yell, as startling as firecrackers. "You're a villain. You intend to find fault with him, don't you!"

The kid's yelling had apparently disturbed the master. He turned over, and vague moans came from his mouth.

Then it was as if the kid had forgotten what he had just said, for pointing at the master, he assessed him in a mocking tone:

"Look at him. His life is like a pig's. Each time I come up here, he's dreaming. He sits there swaying on the bed and drinks water and eats pancakes, without coming to at all. When I put the news items in the trunk and lock it up, he goes to sleep." In a flash, the kid's expression turned unusually serious, and he asked again, "You aren't finding fault with him, are you?"

"Does he read your jottings at midnight?" I was trying to be ingratiating.

"Why do you ask?" He was on his guard as he glared at me. "He's never read them. All of the materials are in my small wooden box. My small wooden box is then placed in his large trunk. But he has the key only to the large trunk. How could he read them?"

The kid pulled a big bunch of keys out of a large pocket on his chest, and—showing off—he shook them so that they jingled. While he was talking, he came up and sat down carelessly on the bed. Without knowing why, I felt a little afraid of his zeal. As he talked, he massaged the master's back through the quilt. I found this disgusting: it was as if his and the master's positions had been reversed. In short, I felt this kid was too affected.

"Although he has never read the first-hand information I've brought him, I always tell him about everything I've run into. That's the usual situation. Wait a minute! You can pretend to be him, okay?"

I nodded my head.

"Please close your eyes, and lean back against the wall."

Then he climbed up beside me, his rapid breath rushing against my face. I waited a long time. He said nothing. What was he doing? I opened my eyes, and saw that he was dejectedly withdrawn to one side.

"Is this how you interact with him?"

"Exactly. Ordinarily, this is how I interact with him. I actually don't have to say anything. Of course, each time, he's asleep, and those things that I'm thinking of enter his dreams. He says that what I pass into his head nags at him all night, and so he's pissed off at me. He says he won't allow me to come up here anymore. I know he's just talking through his hat. This guy—if I didn't bring him pancakes and water, he'd have starved to death long ago! I discovered that he actually likes to listen to my reports: if a day or two goes by without my reporting to him, he feels wronged and loses his temper. As I see it, this kind of person belongs to the class of people who can't get what they want but aren't willing to settle for less. He can't let go of his pride. All day, he lies in this high place, and depends on the news I bring him of the outside world. Once I've satisfied his wishes, he again considers himself aloof from politics and high-minded things, and then he's exceedingly condescending to me."

I couldn't help laughing at his tone of voice.

"Are you laughing at me?" Sternly, he said, "Did I climb up to such a high place to give you food just for you to ridicule me? I'm telling you: What I just said is not exaggerated in the slightest. He really cannot do without me for even one day. Otherwise, he'd starve to death. Now, though, I have to take a look around the staircase. Someone wants to come up, and that is something he absolutely does not allow." With that, he turned around, bounded over to the door, and went out.

But I hadn't heard any sound at all outside. I was really surprised that the master's, and the kid's, sense of hearing was so acute. Did this building have some kind of mechanism set up somewhere that made it possible for people to sense activity going on below? Or was this building connected with the master and the kid into an organic whole? After a while, the kid came back and told me that he'd thrown a bottle down the staircase to serve as a warning. The bottle would roll straight down to the bottom of the staircase. The many bottles at the entrance to the master's room were all for this purpose. Generally speaking, none of the persons who intended to charge upstairs had much courage. They were all afraid of their own shadows. When they were halfway up the stairs and unable to withstand the cold and then suddenly saw a bottle rolling down from the top, they were naturally scared out of their wits, and took off as if they'd seen a ghost.

"He demands that absolute silence be maintained here," the kid announced solemnly. "One time, I arrived a little late. As a result, a guy had groped his way up the stairs and entered his room. I'll never forget it: that was such an ugly scene. Of course, he immediately lost consciousness. He had no ability to defend himself against this kind of occurrence. I've never been able to forgive myself for this. I know that guy; he's one of my customers. I rushed up and pounded him with a bottle. As he was running away, he pounded me with a bottle, too. He hit his target, and the blood on my face scared him. Without looking around, he ran off and never came up here again."

The kid lifted the hair up from his forehead so I could see his scar—a very deep, sunken, wedge shaped scar, incredibly deep. It was as if you could see through to his brains. The kid smoothed his hair, laughed uneasily, and went on to say:

"Several days ago, he told me that you'd be coming here. I asked him who you were, but he wouldn't tell me. Who are you? Anyhow, you can't be the guy who scurried up here last time. You don't look at all like him. To my surprise, he also invited you to sit under his quilt. It's so cold up here, you should leave." Jealousy appeared on his face.

Since I didn't make any move, he came and sat on my feet. He meant for me to be uncomfortable. I saw through his plot, and stayed persistently under the quilt without moving. When he saw that his little trick couldn't succeed, he stood up decisively and walked over to the window. With a *peng, peng!* he opened the window. A gust of wind blew fiercely into my face. Not only was there wind, but mingled with it was a profusion of fluttering snowflakes. It was really bizarre that there would actually be snow falling in the late spring! Swaggering as they floated in, the snowflakes created a dazzling vortex in the room. The kid stood there as if stupefied by the scene. The cold was beyond the limits of my endurance. I was afraid I'd freeze to death here. I had to go downstairs at once while my legs could still carry me.

I turned over and got out of bed, and—scuffing along because I hadn't tied my shoes—I ran downstairs. But I couldn't run fast. In the severe cold, my body was gradually stiffening. My feet were numb. Clenching my teeth, I stepped forward desperately. Those stairs were endless! I don't remember how many curves I turned, nor do I remember how many stories there were. The whirlwind in the staircase was wrapping around me, and my thoughts were frozen stiff. I walked down the last flight of stairs, and—suddenly dizzy—I slipped down to the ground. I was desperate for a rest! Tears of pain were running down until my whole face was covered with them.

"I thought you could hold up. It never occurred to me that you didn't have even a little patience and willpower. You loser!" In a daze, I heard the kid berating me, "People can't just sit down here anywhere they like. Up there he can hear you clearly."

Supporting me with his slight, skinny body, he helped me walk away. I wouldn't have imagined that he had so much strength. After taking several steps, we reached the street. He abandoned me at the side of the road and went back.

I sat on the ground for a long time before recovering. It wasn't snowing at all. It was still foggy. Pedestrians were wandering around slowly on the street, as though everyone was undecided about something. When I looked up at the wooden building, I could see only as far as the seventh floor. Above that, it was hidden in fog. As I composed myself, I felt terrified by the experience I'd just had: our climate down here could differ so greatly from the climate up there! I couldn't help being filled with hatred for those forebears who had created such a building. Evidently, the master hadn't gone downstairs for more than ten years. Yet, in the past, he and I had often played chess in the vegetable garden—playing continuously until, from the sun shining overhead, we saw stars before our eyes. While I was thinking of this, I saw the kid carrying a basket of pancakes and turning hurriedly into a small alley. I looked up again, and I could still see only as far as the seventh story, but I distinctly heard the depressing *peng! peng!* sound of the window up there being shut. Of course, that might have been my illusion.

# A NEGLIGIBLE GAME ON THE JOURNEY

**M**OST RECENTLY, THE WINDOW HAS BEEN INVARIABLY WHITE—A good sign. For someone like me, whenever the window turns white and there are voices outside, it's hard to escape a feeling of surprise—or of being awakened, if you don't mind my overstating it a bit. Actually, what does the color of the window have to do with me? These last few days, I practiced until becoming quite skillful at manicuring my own nails. A knock at the door couldn't stop me. Opening the door, I'd strike up a conversation with the person entering, but my nail clipper didn't stop. It was a piece of cake. I was calm and serene, my movements nimble.

Without paying any particular attention, I hear the flowing water outside mingled with people's voices. These sounds carry a certain overtone of inspiration. People are washing vegetables by the running water—going about their daily activities in this shining world. Maybe this so-called "feeling of awakening" is a little exaggerated. Twenty-five years ago, when I was swinging in the courtyard, I experienced a similar feeling. Then, too, the willow trees and the stone slabs in the courtyard had an exaggerated effect. Otherwise, now, I couldn't remember it so distinctly. It seems that if one goes all out to capture things intensely, some tiny waves are stirred up in one's head for a while, and one becomes hotheaded. This is usually brought on by something negligible, not itself related directly to the brain's activity. It's like using extra string to tie a slipknot in a fishing net. With a gust of wind, the knot slips out and falls to the ground. With another gust of wind, the string blows away.

My ability to think is declining. Everyone can see that I'm becoming more feeble-minded by the day. In the past, I did some mental exercises: every day, I committed a few numbers to memory. Over a long period, I memorized many numbers. Now, however, because I'm lazy and don't want any bother, I've long since abandoned mental exercise. I'm not so conscientious about trimming fingernails, either. Although I'm very skillful, there's nothing pretty about the manicured fingernails.

For a long while, the window has been that gray color. Once in a while, though, I rouse myself—just stretch my neck out the window and glance out. This time, though, it seems a little different. I hear water flowing and people talking, and I stare for a long time and unwittingly blurt out those numbers: "eighteen, nineteen, twenty. . ." This feels like an abrupt change. I realize that I'm not reciting silently this time, but rather I'm saying them out loud. This doesn't feel quite right. I've no sooner had this thought than I grow aware that it isn't anybody else's business and I can continue as long as I wish. So I go on to recite, "twenty-one, twenty-two, twenty-three!" The person coming in thinks I'm doing mental exercises again; he doesn't imagine that after reciting these six numbers, I won't say another word. He's bored and leaves in embarrassment, and I resume trimming my fingernails. I still pay a lot of attention to the expression of whoever comes here, but this has no power to hurt them; no one has to worry about me. Yesterday, I noticed a person staring greedily at my feet. I smiled, took off my shoes and socks, and stood barefoot in front of him. At this, he blushed and left in embarrassment. I noticed another person's expression; he had circled around from the athletic field. If you want a description, it's best to say his expression was "empty." But I just cultivated my habit of attentiveness.

The disappearance of the monochromatic blocks of color is most unexpected. It's as if it happened overnight. Many withered twigs are pricking my scalp. Stories about the old house drift up to the sky and away from these twigs. I see a flash of ginger-yellow, and everything quickly becomes transparent again like colorless flakes of soap. In the midst of the time I was becoming an entrepreneur, I focused all my energy on pursuing the monochromatic blocks, and—with fiery, torch-like eyes—set fire to the twigs accumulated on the ground. I wanted to see red and yellow flames. Now the blocks of color have faded from before my eyes. All material goods have become colorless.

Old stories keep drifting out. Each time one emerges, my scalp itches a little, as if covered with a heat rash that will heal with time. When I open my mouth, a soundless story is on the verge of exiting.

A peddler of sweet wine lives next door. He has curly hair and a face showing a life of bad luck. On Wednesday, I distinctly saw him pushing a handcart past the door, and distinctly heard him tell me that he had already sold one barrel of sweet wine and half a small barrel of flavored bean curd. He and I even chatted for a while. He spoke of saving money to buy a house, and said he had already saved just about enough. He was just waiting to choose a suitable place in the city. It was then about seven o'clock in the evening. About half an hour later, he pushed his handcart past my door again.

"Are you going out again so late to ply your trade?"

"I haven't been out yet today. I slept straight through from last night until now. When I woke up and realized how long I'd slept—damn it, the sweet wine was all about to turn sour. Luckily, it's a cool day. Otherwise, I'd have no choice but to dump it out."

Words left me.

"Tonight, I have to go to at least three districts and take my chances. Didn't you say that you also hoped to take your chances? Hey! Why not join me?"

A lot of stories are woven into the fishing net. Only a random string is needed—the less related, the better. For example, this sweet-wine seller—one sleep messed everything up. He and I met by accident. When he talked of buying a house, this became a story. It's best not to look for an explanation of this story. It's okay in itself. Explanation often ruins the effect. In the middle period of my entrepreneurial venture, drifting blocks of color could be found everywhere. Nothing escaped my burning eyes. It was really a little like the magical power of the philosopher's stone. Now, whenever I recall this, I'm often surprised. What caused such a miracle?

This story is brand-new. I mean the story of the sweet-wine peddler. When it was finished, the random string fell off. The fishing net is still a fishing net. No marks are left. I love this kind of story, in the midst of good days of awakening.

Another problem is Auntie's letter. Auntie lives in the countryside. All along, she has complained about the humidity, and grumbled that rural people are selfish to ignore hygiene. I tore open the envelope with the familiar writing, a sneer tugging at my mouth. My reply was light: as usual, I played up how my business was growing and how much money I had. The problem wasn't this: the problem was that when she received my letter, Auntie was irritated and stopped writing. Her silence lasted six months. Then another letter came. Looking at it closely, I saw that the new letter was a photocopy of her last one. The old woman was playing tricks on me! There was nothing for it but to write back and find some new reasons to play myself up. After receiving this letter, she fell indignantly silent again. After another half a year, she resumed her tricks.

But, while I'm reading Auntie's photocopied letter, my nail clippers go on working without stopping. I can't say this isn't pleasant. Lots of people are always telling me, *I'd like to trade places with you!* Yesterday, Auntie's son dashed in and suggested, "Trade places with Auntie. It's really tough being a country bumpkin." Frowning, he added, "A morning like this—if you want to sleep in, you can't. The land is waiting to be hoed, and you have to water the squash and beans. What's good about that? Just tell me, what's good about that?" He was too pushy. Then he changed the subject and began singing my praises. Only, he didn't say one word about her trick of sending me photocopies of the same old letter. Like mother, like son.

Of course, I can't swap places with them. They came too late. Recently, I've become very pleased with things here! As to sleeping in, I haven't gotten into that. Other people envious of my position see only the advantage of sleeping in. They don't understand the subtlety of my role. For example, that peddler with the unlucky face—to one's surprise—slept from one evening to dusk the next day before getting up! Although in his dreams, he can interfere with my thoughts, he can't understand the subtlety of my position. People with an insatiable desire for sleep can't appreciate the benefits of my position.

Auntie's letter-writing also counts as a story. I've taken the role of this story's recorder. This will last for years, because Auntie won't stop writing me letters, and she won't die anytime soon, either. As for her overbearing son, he's sure to come back next year. He's been written into the story, too. I've already prepared a pair of boots, which I plan to give him when he next arrives. While people are making a commotion washing vegetables by the running water, I'm pacing back and forth inside, working out a mental draft of a letter to Auntie. Sometimes it takes me a long time to write a single letter, just because I mean to enjoy my good mood a while longer. Everyone has some weaknesses.

After the peddler came over, a clue gradually emerged. Although Auntie's son wants me to change places with his mother, inwardly he looks down on me. Why can't I shout loudly in the daytime? The truth is, as long as I have a sheet of paper and a pen, nothing else matters. To take the truth a step further: even if I have neither paper nor pen, I can still correspond with Auntie. For instance, I can do as Auntie does: go to a shop and photocopy a letter, even photocopy the name and address onto the envelope, glue a stamp on it, and drop it into the mailbox. This is simple enough—nothing mysterious about it.

I can also adopt this kind of tone to tell stories: *As soon as the peddler Wang Gui climbed out of bed in the morning, he discovered that everything around him had changed. First, it was the rooster in the coop. Although it crowed and ate as usual, its round old eyes revealed an indifferent expression.* How's that for a beginning? If it isn't so good, I can change my tone: *The peddler Wang Gui sells sweet wine and flavored bean curd on our street. He roams the streets and alleys. Under the constant influence of his familiar hawking, the people in this town somehow seem to be becoming simple and unsophisticated. No one has wondered before: Where is he from? What if he falls ill and can't get out of bed again? Does he hope someday to sleep in comfort?*

Of course, both beginnings are ordinary and uninteresting, but they're simple and easy to relate. From now on, I'm planning to adopt this handy method for everything. I want to simplify over-elaborate procedures, and come close to purity.

I'm not going to be constrained by any of the threads, either. I want to accustom my head to the miscellaneous ideas coexisting in it. After the colors have been eliminated, a certain tendency toward simplicity will be revealed. I'm starting to leap—just casually jumping on my tiptoes, or landing with my heels on the ground. One step forward, two steps back, and so on. After I finish going through the motions of jumping, I feel pleased that I haven't perspired at all.

The world has so many unexplained riddles. Since even the mighty force that can cause mountains to shake doesn't help one bit to solve these riddles, haste and passion show only essential weakness—that's all. Of course, there are still the monochromatic blocks—that baffling sorcery. Ten years have passed. I am finally close to getting to the bottom of the matter. Of course, ultimately that stage is unreachable. It can just be observed from afar to provide a certain inspiration. When I talk of the road back, it's just my own preconception. The actual circumstances are of course unclear. For example: Is the mountain range still grand? Is the forest still green? The homeward journey is remote, endless. The last image, which no one has ever seen, is printed on a rhombic eye. Just thinking of this is enough to make me lose the courage to explore. The actual circumstances are these: I'm just walking, and I seldom look back to take stock. I also seldom worry about what's ahead of me or what might appear. That would be premature. After walking each course, I've never forgotten to adjust my pace. That's the survival instinct in me, I guess.

A neighbor is trying to teach me the ins and outs of trimming fingernails. Interacting with him, I go on trimming the same as before, thus unnerving him for a while. Because he looks as though he wants to help me, I ask him to go out and photocopy a letter to Auntie. In fact, I still have a lot of photocopies in a drawer.

# HELIN

**W**E WERE SKIPPING ROPE IN THE COURTYARD. TWO PEOPLE swung the rope, while five jumped. We hadn't been jumping very long when Helin took a tumble. She collapsed slowly, her face pasty. The children surrounded her in panic, and someone shouted for Helin's father. Her father was a cooper here. His old face showed the vicissitudes of his life, and his back—bent at a ninety-degree angle—looked as if it had been broken. To look at him, you wouldn't know he was Helin's father; rather, you'd think he was her grandfather. He walked over to Helin, and holding her upper body, headed home. Her lower body dragged along on the ground. It appeared that this old man was already very familiar with his daughter's spasms, for he didn't think this was at all odd. A girl who knew the inside story told me, "Helin is really in wretched shape. Ever since she was born, she's had this malady." I watched from a distance: Helin looked like a corpse being dragged away by her deformed father. The father swayed as he walked.

That whole spring, we played like crazy. When it grew dark, the parents of one of us stood on their front steps and called their child's name. Stamping their feet, they shouted abuse. Just like a mouse, that child then silently stole home for dinner. Every day was like this. Sometimes, the children were also beaten. The children who were beaten strained all their muscles to let out bloodcurdling screams. The parents were annoyed at hearing this, and all they could do was let them go for the time being. I hadn't seen Helin for a long time, but her father's old duck-like figure frequently appeared.

One boy, Little Zheng, asked me if I wanted to go and see Helin. My heart went pitter-pat as I followed him, shuttling among the old houses. At last, we stopped in front of a shabby wooden house. Little Zheng told me to sit on his shoulders, press close, and look through the high window. I saw a glass cabinet in the center of the room. Helin was sleeping in it. When she wasn't sleeping, she often tossed and turned and yawned. I wanted to look more carefully, but Little Zheng was impatient and told me to get down.

"How can she sleep there?" I asked, perplexed and alarmed.

"She's sick. That's a quarantined room." Little Zheng was proud that he knew this. "It's not out of fear that she'll infect others, it's that she herself needs to be quarantined. Otherwise, she won't live another day."

"Yet she still jumps rope?"

"She can come out and play for a little while. I don't think that will hurt her."

In dead earnest, he put out his hand, and I gave him two yuan.

I still wanted to peep through the cracks in the door, but that old duck was visible in the distance.

"Quick! Run!" Little Zheng frantically grabbed me by the hand.

The two of us streaked away together, past those old houses, and came back to the courtyard. On the way, we bumped into dried mushrooms that one household was drying on the patio, scattering them all over.

Whenever I thought of the girl in the glass cabinet, my heart throbbed, and I blushed. I was itching to spill this discovery to someone right away.

Eventually, I had a chance to do so. I invited Xisui to climb the mountain with me to dig up fern roots. We escaped from those boys, and made our way into a shady ditch. After we had harvested some plump fern roots, I lowered my voice and spilled this secret to Xisui. I also embellished the story, describing Helin as a boa constrictor that wandered around at night and devoured small chickens. Xisui cried out and leapt from the shady ditch, scattered the fern roots that we'd collected on the ground and, with her head in her hands, cried her eyes out. Following behind, I apologized to her in confusion. I didn't know how I had offended her to elicit such an emotional response. But all it took was for me to open my mouth and she squealed even more sharply. Downhearted, I chucked the fern roots away, and sullenly headed slowly home. Before I'd gotten there, Xisui's mama caught up with me, and rebuked me in no uncertain terms, saying I had "teased a girl." I wanted to plead my innocence, but she interrupted me peremptorily and threatened, "There are some things that you can't gossip about. Mind your tongue."

To be told off by someone for no reason at all made me feel that

I had dropped into an abyss. This abyss was a bottomless riddle. I wanted to ask Little Zheng about it, but Little Zheng was also avoiding me. Whenever he saw me from a distance, he ran off and disappeared.

At dusk, grown-ups would scold people especially ominously. Lots of grown-ups would point at one but abuse the other. They scolded their own children for hanging around with a thief, and threatened to break their legs. I didn't dare listen, but I didn't dare not listen, either. I felt I'd become a mouse crossing the street. All the children had gone home, and still two women were cursing. Mama saw me hiding behind the door and listening. She walked over and drew me into her arms. Her big hands, roughened by work, were stroking my back. She was sighing a string of sighs, as if I had gotten into big trouble and couldn't be redeemed.

"Mama, I haven't done anything at all," I said unconvincingly.

"Naturally, naturally, how could you have done anything? You are a good child."

Her perplexed, alarmed gaze was directed at that wall in front of us. That told me clearly that disaster was about to befall me. Suddenly, I really hated her. I frequently had this sensation, but this time, I felt she was in cahoots with the outsiders. I yanked myself free of her arms, and she nearly fell over on the ground.

Since all the children were avoiding me, all I could do was play by myself. I played a war game in the mud, and had the warriors of two forts attacking each other. I was busy shouting, "Charge! Kill!" I also had the warriors of the first fort dig a canal that went underneath the second fort and diverted the sewage from the courtyard; thus the second fort was submerged in sewage. While I was absorbed in doing this, I suddenly saw a girl's leather-shoed foot step on my fort. It collapsed. I looked up in astonishment, and saw Helin standing all akimbo above me.

"You weakling!" She said haughtily, "Why do you have to talk so much? Can you really understand all these things?"

"Helin, Helin, they're all ignoring me. If you ignore me, too, what am I going to do?"

I almost wanted to cry. Feeling desperate, I caught hold of her hand.

"Naturally, I won't ignore you." Helin suddenly chuckled.

She let me hold her ice-cold hand. And I—it was as though I had won her approval—brought my face to it. It was odd. As soon as my face came in contact with the palm of her hand, it grew warm. And then it went from warm to hot, as though she had a high fever. Her small eyes, set close together, flashed with confusion. I felt she was going to become critically ill. I immediately disengaged my face from the palm of her hand. She held her chest tight with her free hand, and gasped for breath with difficulty.

"Helin, Helin, you aren't going to faint, are you?" I asked fearfully.

It was a long time before she quieted down. She pointed at the large rock beside her, indicating that I should sit down there with her. Her hands grew icy again, and she looked very sick. I saw several heads flash past the hole in the gate of the courtyard. By all appearances, these were children from the street in front. As soon as they saw Helin and me sitting together, they dodged out of the way. This was really weird. Helin shot a sharp glance at me, and said:

"Now I can't be around people, and it's all because of you. You're self-absorbed, and heedless of consequences."

"I didn't know. I was in the dark. Ah, I dare to swear that if I knew, I would cut off my hand."

When I said this, my face must have changed color. I hoped Helin would go on talking, and thus clear all of this up. Everything would come out in the wash. Holding her hand, I waited and waited, but she didn't say anything. It was as though she was thinking of something else. I thought, *What kind of world is Helin's world? She must think that I'm completely full of nonsense.* Helin's silence was a peaceful silence. It seemed she didn't want me to say anything. It seemed that she had already known ahead of time that I had too many questions and there would be no end to the answers. Eventually she sighed and stood up, saying she had to go. I wanted to see her home, but she checked me with a gesture. She walked the same way her father did—like a duck. I guessed that she was going back to her glass cabinet. I couldn't help feeling afraid. What if she had died beside me just now? That would have been a disaster with no end of trouble.

Those days, I was infatuated. I always wanted to go over to Helin's home. The door was closed, and I didn't dare shout for her. The windows were also too high. Weighed down by anxiety, I loitered outside. As soon as Helin's father appeared, I pretended to be playing a game of "building the fort" under the eaves. One day, after Helin's father went inside, I heard him talking loudly with Helin. From outside, I heard it all. Her father asked, "What's that wild brat up to outside?" The daughter replied, "Probably he's jealous of me." Then they also said some other things—words that I had trouble understanding. Helin's voice sounded as though it was coming from inside a vat. Buzzing echoes accompanied her voice.

One day, Helin finally came out, weak and fatigued from illness. She swept a disparaging glance over the dirt fort that I had built, and lazily sat down on a chair.

"The sun is wonderful, Helin! And the tea plants are flowering! Let's go up the mountain and catch little birds." I was trying to please her.

"I can't be in the sun," she said laconically.

"That's too bad. Too bad. How dreary to hide in that cabinet all year long!"

"You blockhead. It's only in the cabinet that I can enjoy myself. I get sick as soon as I come out. Haven't you noticed? The sun makes my blood turn black, and pollen makes my windpipe swell. And the most awful thing is: I can't think when I'm outside. The things I think of, you would never think through. Someone like you can only play this boring old game that everyone plays." As she spoke, she headed toward the house. I caught up with her right away. It seemed that Helin didn't object to my looking around her house. The glass cabinet was exquisite—a brilliant contrast to the simple, crude furnishings in the house.

The rectangular structure was even a little taller than a grownup. It had a sliding door in front, and brilliant floral designs spiraled around its four sparkling stainless-steel posts. The posts formed supports at the four corners of the cabinet. Those posts really gave the cabinet quite a look of luxury. Embedded in the glass door was a tube, which was connected to a very small machine. Helin said that as soon as this machine was turned on, a vacuum could be maintained inside the cabinet. "That condition is too marvelous for words." As I bent over to look at the machine, the sound of a cough rang out from outside. Helin pushed me out at once, and said softly, "Leave right away, leave now. If your scent is in the house, Father will be furious." She used force, and I tumbled down the steps outside the door. I didn't have time to get up before Helin's father grabbed me by the scruff of my neck. He shoved me roughly onto the muddy ground. He pushed me so hard that my forehead was bleeding. Altogether, he shoved me more than ten times before he stopped. Then I must have fainted.

I don't remember how I got home that day. My spirits hurt much more than the injury to my head. Mama was crying softly beside my bed, saying time after time that she would avenge me.

"How can you?" I interrupted her wearily.

From my swollen eyelids, I looked down at her blank expression.

"That's right. How will I seek revenge?" she whispered hesitantly.

Those days that I lay in bed at home were the very darkest days of all. An old woman who had lost her son wept and wailed all night long outside the gate. It seemed to me that the end of the world was coming. One night, I had just fallen asleep when someone began fiddling with the wound on my forehead. With a quick movement, the person jerked the scab off. This hurt so much that I screamed my head off. And then I saw the old woman's hunched back leaving hurriedly. Blood from the wound covered my face. Next, Mother appeared with a kerosene lamp. She turned me from side to side for a long time before finally getting me settled. She didn't listen to my explanations, but insisted that I must have cracked the wound open in the midst of a nightmare. I closed my eyes, and the wound pulsed with pain. I thought, that old woman must have thought I was her unfilial son. That was probably why she had finally dropped in—to seek revenge. The wound worsened and left a large scar on my forehead.

It was on the tenth day that Helin came to see me. As it happened, it was the very day that I conquered the inflammation and high fever. The girl's face was as white as paper. She glided to the front of the bed, and said over and over, "I'm sorry. I'm sorry." She whispered in my ear and asked if someone had disturbed me while I was sick. I told her about the old woman.

"Did she mistake me for someone else?"

"Impossible. I think this was Father's idea." Her expression was trance-like.

"Was it also your father who arranged for you to sleep in the glass cabinet?" I jeered bitterly.

"Hey! Don't talk nonsense. Now the two of us have become melons on the same vine. It's just because you charged into my home that things turned out this way."

With her talking like this, my anger completely dissipated. I wanted to sit up and hold hands with her. But several heads were flashing past the window. They were the street children. Then, I also heard those grown-ups, pointing at one while cursing another. I shivered with cold and put my hands back under the quilt. I saw that Helin was like a plant that had suffered from frost. It seemed as though the coat she was wearing would press too heavily on her slender shoulders. Her face was anguished.

"I have to go home. I can't take the air here," she said feebly.

I closed my eyes before she'd even gone out the door. In my spare time that day, I kept pondering this question: *Why had she come? Had her father sent her?* The more I thought about it, the more uneasy I felt. And then I thought about her situation. By no means was she her father's accessory, but rather a tool controlled by her father. My view of her was always swinging between the two poles.

While I was recovering, I secretly came up with a plan. I couldn't tell anyone of this plan, including Mama. And as soon as I was well, I dashed out of the house. Without paying any attention to the other children, I ran ahead alone. The odd thing was that everyone stopped in their tracks to look at me: they seemed dumbstruck. I felt a little proud of myself, and as I ran, I lifted my legs even higher—as if riding on horseback. I ran and ran—ran all the way to the foothills. Not until I clasped the big pine tree did I suddenly realize: I had overdone the running. The shouts of the children on the other side of the street could be heard faintly, riding the wind, and this suddenly gave me the illusion of a little peace. I turned around and dashed toward Helin's home. When I had almost reached the fence in front of her house, I stopped. I saw that Helin happened to be sitting feebly in front of the house.

"Helin—Helin!" I called her softly, feeling my hands grow sweaty.

Helin's eyes brightened. She stood up right away and trotted toward me.

"How can you have the guts to come here again? Don't you want to go on living?" she said in a low, solemn voice.

"Helin, I've come to give you an invitation. Let's run off, cross this mountain, and go to my uncle's home. He'll take us in. Nothing ever shocks or surprises him. Let's take off!"

To my surprise, Helin didn't argue. Indeed, she seemed enchanted as she said over and over, "Cross over the mountain—Cross over the moutain. What a good idea. I've never gone to the other side of the mountain. Ah, you little kid!" She patted my head lightly, and then plunged into fantasy again.

"What are we waiting for? Run, run!"

Dragging Helin along, I ran a few steps, and then she shrugged me off and ran on her own. She couldn't have been sick before: she ran as fast as I did, even faster. It was the first time I'd seen her face flush scarlet, so scarlet that it was like two flowers. Beads of sweat appeared on the tip of her nose. It was truly a miracle. We reached the pine tree, and were about to climb the mountain. I was still a little worried.

"Helin, do you really want to abandon your father?" I asked.

Helin began laughing, and said I worried too much. She also said that fathers couldn't be abandoned. How could a person not have a father? "You can't abandon your father, either," she added.

"Then you'll still go with me?"

"I'll go with you, because this is really interesting. You little radish, let's go."

Although I was a little dismayed, Helin and I were after all on the same side. I had successfully bamboozled her into coming away. How hurt the old bastard would be! We started climbing the mountain. Helin was even more excited about this than I was, and kept asking me about my uncle. I told her almost everything I knew, but she still wasn't satisfied and kept pestering me for some details. In the blink of an eye, we had crossed the small mountain. The wind was blowing in the woods, and the black-colored rooftop was like an old tortoise floating in an ocean of woods.

Helin and I were both so tired that we lay on the wooden sofa gasping for breath. Uncle and Auntie were both super big. They were like two houses as they moved back and forth before our eyes. Looking up at them, I couldn't keep from laughing.

"Helin has finally flown out of the old tyrant's hands." Uncle's voice came humming up from his chest.

Later, I sat up and told Uncle that we wanted to stay for a long time in his home, because Helin couldn't put up anymore with the life she'd been leading. In fact, Helin wasn't sick. It was that old bastard who had made her live an inhuman life. As for my mother, certainly she would agree. She had often joked with me, saying that she would take me to live at Uncle's home. As I told Uncle all of this, Helin was at one side kicking my foot, and saying I was just blabbering.

"What does Helin herself have in mind?"

As Auntie asked this, she drew Helin to her breast and let her sit on her fleshy thigh. It was just like a big sofa. This made Helin feel really flattered.

"I don't have anything in mind. Nothing at all!" Helin blushed deeply.

Auntie stroked the girl's thin hair lovingly, and laughed out loud. And then Uncle laughed, too. It was like thunder in the house. I was suddenly rather disgusted. It had never crossed my mind that the two of them would become so loathsome. Why did they have to try to get to the bottom of this? But Helin seemed comfortable on that "sofa." As soon as she inclined her head, she actually fell asleep. Auntie stood up, and—as if Helin were a chicken—clasped her under her armpit, headed to the bedroom, and arranged a place for her to sleep.

At dinnertime, Helin still hadn't gotten up. Auntie said she was sleeping so soundly that she didn't have the heart to wake her up. I felt, however, that Auntie meant something else as well: it was as though she were blaming me. Should I not have brought Helin here? Uncle seemed happy, and patted my shoulder lightly with his gigantic paw. He said I was "brilliant," that I had "actually high-handedly taken on that old tyrant." After saying this, he asked me to spill all the details. So I started with Little Zheng taking me to Helin's home to steal a glance at the glass cabinet, and then talked on and on for a long time.

Uncle listened with relish, frequently interrupting to say, "Truly brilliant!" "Really clever!" This baffled and discomfited me. We went on eating for a long time, and after Uncle had taken in all the details, he announced to me: Helin and I could stay in his home. We could stay as long as we liked. Of course, if I left tomorrow that would also be all right: I had my own legs. Auntie admonished me strongly, "You have to be concerned about Helin's illness. This kind of girl doesn't live long."

That night, Uncle and I slept in one room, and Helin and Auntie slept in the next room. As soon as Uncle got into bed, he snored so thunderously that the bed vibrated with a creaking noise. The moon was bright. From outside came the suspicious, sustained sound of knocking. It seemed that someone outside the window wanted to come in. A long time passed, and I really couldn't take it any longer. I got up and took a look. What I saw greatly surprised me. It was Helin whacking on the window lattice with a stick. Her hair was all disheveled, and she was sitting on the branch of a tree. That branch reached my window.

"You're crazy. You'll catch cold."

"I've always been an invalid."

"No, you are not!"

"You're just looking at the surface."

"I have to go to sleep now."

With that, I closed the window and lay on the tiny camp bed without moving. The whacking sound stopped. Later, I heard a *tong!* sound; probably that was Helin jumping down from the tree. In the dim light, I saw that mountain across from me start to move: Uncle sneezed, and asked, "Is it a little sprite making the noise outside?"

"It's Helin. She isn't sleeping. She's sitting in the tree and playing."

"That's the way she is. Don't pay any attention to her. If you pay too much attention, your head will explode."

Uncle started snoring again. In the midst of that thunderous sound, I slowly fell asleep. I didn't sleep well. Time after time, the squabbling "cock-a-doodle-doo" of the roosters woke me up. I didn't know why on earth Uncle was raising so many roosters. Just about every ten minutes, they made their reports. Perhaps the roosters were confused because some strangers were staying overnight in the house. Their midnight calls were deafening, yet Uncle was blissfully unaware.

Helin didn't show up for breakfast, either. Auntie said that she "was running around outside all night and she still hasn't come back." Uncle bent his head and drank some goat's milk. Smiling a little, he put in a word: "That's the way she is."

Only after we'd finished eating and Auntie was ready to clear the table did Helin return. Her clothes were in disarray, and she looked dreadfully haggard. She staggered as she walked. She rushed over to the table, grabbed a *mantou*, and began to devour it ravenously. It wasn't until then that I remembered that she hadn't eaten dinner yesterday. Auntie was watching her eat with an approving gaze and urged her to eat more. But Helin just ate half a *mantou* and then put it down. She rested her head on the table, and moaned feebly, "I'm probably going to die."

I worried about being with her. I was the one who had urged her to come away. If something terrible really happened to her, her father would probably beat me to death. Or, at best, I'd be disabled. That was for sure. The odd thing was that Uncle and Auntie weren't worried in the least. Maybe they thought Helin was pretending. I knew she wasn't pretending. In just one day, her appearance had undergone a tremendous change. The corners of her mouth drooped; her forehead was all wrinkled. Even the hands that I knew so well had all of a sudden become as withered an old woman's.

Auntie pushed me away, and just as she had yesterday, she clasped Helin under her armpit and headed for the bedroom. I resented Auntie's rough behavior. I was too worried about Helin.

"I've seen this phenomenon many times. There won't be any problem," Uncle said. "She isn't softheaded like you. From childhood, she's been quick-witted, and quick with responses. She knows what she wants. For example, this time, do you think you hoodwinked her into coming here? In fact, it was she who hoodwinked you into coming here. Hahaha . . . "

He laughed until he didn't feel like laughing anymore. Then, turning serious, he said to me, "Today I'm going to take you to see someone, but you mustn't be scared when you see him."

Before Uncle and I set out, we looked in on Helin. She was lying under a thin quilt, having sporadic spasms, and her teeth were clicking noisily. I was really worried about her, but Uncle went out with me in tow. "It's nothing," he said lightly. "The spasms used to be much worse than this. The painstaking efforts of her doting father haven't been for naught, after all."

We went through one paddy field after another. The farmers all put their work down, and stood stock-still in astonishment. Uncle paid no attention, and walked ahead unhurriedly like a camel. Following his example, I—such a small little guy—also held my head high. Head high, chest thrust out, I followed on his heels. Not until we had walked through the small paths in the fields and reached the mountain did I dare ask Uncle:

"Why were those people surprised?"

"Because I hardly ever go out. They have a hunch that something big and unforeseen is about to occur. You and Helin are living in my home: everyone in the village knows this. Helin ran around crazily for a whole night. Probably she visited every single family."

Although Uncle was a heavy man, he was physically powerful in climbing the mountain. He didn't even gasp for breath. I admired him a lot for this. The late-spring mountain breeze blew comfortably over my face. Along the way, I picked some mushrooms. I had nearly forgotten Helin, who was sick at home. Now, Uncle slackened his steps and began to speak of her. He said she would never be content. "After she was born, she cried from morning to night. No one could quiet her. Helin's mother was exhausted by her; she died the year that Helin was two. Then, Helin's father made that weird glass cabinet, and had her sleep inside it. Then she quieted down right away.

"Helin's father and I were partners when we were young. We panned for gold. Neither of us could stand hard work, though, and so we came back soon. Neither of us could have guessed that he would have this kind of daughter. Your auntie and I will never forget that day when the glass cabinet wasn't yet finished—Helin's father was just installing a post—and the agile Helin immediately pushed the cabinet door open and climbed in. Then she closed the door. We were all dumbstruck! What a girl! Alas!"

We walked on and on. The mushrooms I picked filled the basket. Uncle ridiculed me as "a collector for petty profit." When we crossed the second mountain, it was almost noon. Pointing at a small thatched hut in the distance beyond a col, he told me, "There it is." I asked what, and he said I'd know when we got there. Consumed with curiosity, I walked faster. But Uncle didn't go on. He sat on the grass beside the road and said he wanted to rest. So I sat down next to him. Probably I was really tired. As soon as I leaned against Uncle, I fell asleep.

In a daze, I heard Uncle talking with someone—*wengwengweng*, like the sound of working the bellows. It seemed the person was asking Uncle about something. Uncle told him that everything was in order. There was just one tiny obstacle. He would see to it. They also talked of some other things—all weird. The more I struggled to wake up, the more I couldn't. I felt as if I were in a locked vault—Uncle and I in it together. That person talking with him was on the other side of the door. Finally, I put my fingers in my mouth and bit them hard, and then at last I woke up. I was baffled as I looked all around, and heard Uncle say, "This is the thatched hut. We're here."

I was on a simple, crude bed. Someone was lying next to me. I saw the familiar gaze at once. I was so astonished that I nearly leapt up and ran away. Uncle took hold of me with his big hand. He didn't want me to be scared. From head to toe, that person was swathed in gauze bandages. Only one hand could be seen, and pus was running out of its festering sores. I noticed that the back of the hand had already rotted away down to the bones. Could this be Helin's father? Not long ago, he'd thrashed me with so much strength.

"This guy can't even talk. What are you afraid of?" my uncle said.

The odor in the hut was enough to make a guy gag. It seemed to come from the man before us. I recalled that one time when I was digging for worms in the foothills, I dug out a dead cat. Its odor was exactly the same. Now, this living corpse sat on this worn-out bamboo bed, and that hand—too horrible to look at—was trembling slightly. He seemed shy and ill at ease. Naturally, I wasn't afraid of him anymore. Actually, I felt very happy. This was great: he wouldn't be able to interfere with Helin any longer. Helin and I were completely liberated!

My happiness made me blush. Just then, Uncle's eyes caught my attention. Those unfathomable dark eyes seemed to see my selfish calculations. His gaze held reproach. Not until later did I realize that my plan was nothing more than wishful thinking. I was thirteen. I hadn't acted on anything that wasn't entirely my own wishful thinking. I seldom thought through all the angles.

We sat for a while in silence. I couldn't bear it, and tugged at Uncle, wanting to leave. Uncle threw off my hand, and berated me: "Tommyrot!" He said he needed to change the bandages for his good friend. That's what he had come to do. At this, I really felt depressed. In changing the bandages, Uncle started with the stomach, and that person yelled like a pig being butchered—he yelled so much that I really couldn't take it. I had to go out, but Uncle wouldn't let me. I didn't dare look at this person. Just shooting a quick glance at that miserable condition would scare the life out of me. There wasn't one piece of good meat on his whole body. In lots of places, his skin was putrid and purplish-black. The bandage that was removed had a piece of rotten flesh sticking to it. The odor—impossible to describe—almost made me faint. Uncle held up a large tweezers, and dipped a cotton ball into some salty water to wash the wounds. No matter how strangely this man screamed, Uncle was patient, systematic through it all. Looking at Uncle's enormous back, I thought he was a mountain pressing down on that pathetic, hopeless guy squirming in his hands. Later on, the guy's screams gradually weakened. Uncle was still working energetically. By the time he had finished swathing the man's whole body in fresh bandages, the guy had almost no voice or breath.

"He's finally gone to sleep." Pointing toward the bed at the thing wrapped in bandages, Uncle said, "I'm an old hand at this. At the beginning, they always fight it with all their might, but they fall silent in the end."

Uncle said this with a hint of a smile that gave me goose pimples. I suspected that the man on the bed had already died, and the more time passed, the more strongly I suspected this, because after a long time, he still hadn't moved at all. When Uncle wasn't looking, all at once, I grabbed that person's foot. The foot was so rigid that I was scared to death. I wanted to run outside, but Uncle held me fast, and ordered me to be good and wait. And then he also wanted me to look at this person's eyes. Not until then did I see that his eyes were still open, and a frightening light shot out of them—a gaze just like that time when he gave me the dickens. Even the thick bandages couldn't block the malice he telegraphed from his eyes. Even though I was frightened, I was even more exultant. I thought of Helin who was back at Uncle's. I didn't know how she was doing at this moment. If she could get well at Uncle's, now wouldn't it be unnecessary for her to go back to her scary home? By the looks of things, she no longer had a home. As soon as this old guy died, she would be completely liberated. I asked Uncle why we were staying here so long. Uncle said it was to keep his old friend company. And he also said that he was too lonely. I asked how Helin's father had been injured, and how he had come to this thatched hut. Uncle said it was all because of Helin's meddling. Then he wouldn't let me ask anything else. He called me "mouthy."

I held my temper and stayed in the thatched hut for a long time. The old guy's eyes kept following me, making me quite uneasy. I thought, if his wounds heal, it would be odd if he didn't rip me to shreds. But what had Helin had to do with all of this? Had her father already been sick for a time before she came here with me? Could it be that she had brought her father to this condition and then asked someone to carry him to this thatched hut? Could it be that she had come here last night?

When we left for home, Uncle took a new lock out of his bag, and locked the door of the hut. Just then, the cooper let out another scream, just like a pig being butchered. From the sound, I could tell that for the moment he couldn't die. Uncle said he had locked Helin's father inside to keep Helin out. If she came here again, she would be able to talk with her father only through the door. This would be better for both of them, because the two of them were both crazy in the same way.

Until Uncle and I reached the forest of fir trees, I could still hear the plaintive cries of Helin's father. All of Uncle's energy was gone. He knitted his brows, walked for a while, then rested. I didn't know what he was thinking. Because I was worrying about Helin, I urged Uncle to step on it. I said if we dillydallied this way, we wouldn't even get home by dark. Angry at my constant urging, Uncle said:

"What's wrong with taking it slow? I've let you have both biscuits. You can't be hungry again. What's the hurry? After dark, we might run into Helin on this mountain!"

"Helin? How do you know she'll take this path?"

"To get to her father, this is the only path."

The appalling thing was that Uncle suddenly said he was sleepy again. As he talked, he leaned against a slippery cobblestone, fell asleep, and began snoring. I was angry and scared. I wanted to leave him behind and go back by myself, but I'd forgotten the way. It was gradually growing dark. Three woodcutters had already loaded their firewood and were on their way home. They stopped next to Uncle, and—full of suspicion—they watched this fatso for a long time, asking me all kinds of questions. I wished that I could turn into a stone. Finally—irresolute—they looked at me, looked again, and, picking up their firewood, they left us. They hadn't gone far before they put their loads down again and retraced their steps. A hand dug into my shoulder. Weaving back and forth, the man asked, "What are you up to?" The three of them made a tight circle around me, as though they meant to eat me. Their hullabaloo didn't have the slightest effect on Uncle. He was still snoring on the rock. When these people saw that they weren't getting any answers out of me, they shoved me roughly. I hit my head on the trunk of a big pine tree, and saw stars as I fell to the ground. Afraid of getting into trouble, the men immediately fled. I got up slowly and simply went crazy. I kicked Uncle several times, but no matter how much I kicked, he didn't wake up. Luckily, just then I heard Auntie shouting in the woods. I answered right away. Stamping her feet, Auntie—flustered and exasperated—gave the sleeping worm several resounding slaps. Uncle finally woke up: rubbing his stinging face, he asked what had happened.

"Helin went back. You good-for-nothing. You don't get anything right!"

"Posh! That's inconceivable. She'd leave just like that? She doesn't even want her father?"

"Of course she's left! Who told you to meddle in her business? I told you a long time ago that she had very big ideas! You were foolish to get mixed up in all of this. My God! This afternoon, your sister also came over. She said she'd thought it through, and doesn't want her son Alin and would give him to us. But I don't want her son. No matter how I look at him, I think he's like a little hooligan. Just think about it: He had the guts to swindle the girl into coming to our house!"

Suddenly, the two of them focused their anger on me. Auntie said that my mother was actually "passing the millstone" to them, and that would ruin their sunset years. Uncle sighed in despair. He sat on a rock and cursed my mother. He wanted me to promise that I'd leave first thing in the morning. With the situation changed, naturally I didn't want to stay another day, I assured Uncle immediately. As soon as I agreed to go home, the two of them gave sighs of relief in unison. Supported by Auntie, Uncle got up from the rock with great difficulty. Then, leaning on her, he limped toward the path that would take him home. The moon had already come out. The backs of the two fatsos ahead of me were blurry now—like big wounded black bears. I remembered that when we had left the house this morning, Uncle had been full of energy and that later, he had worked hard changing the bandages for Helin's father. I didn't understand what had happened today. How could he have changed like this? And then there was my mother. She actually didn't want me—her own son—just because I had run away. Our relationship had turned out, after all, to be a fragile one. As they walked on, they moaned and gasped for breath. Then, at last, they began crying. As he wept, Uncle poured the words out. He talked about Helin's

father's tragic life, about his little fantasies, his capacity for enduring
hardship, his determination not to change. I certainly didn't understand Uncle's intense emotion. But under the moonlight—surrounded by the shadows of swaying trees, with the withered leaves crunch-
ing under my feet—I began to think about the future, and I wanted
to cry, too. I made a few tentative wails. At this, the two of them
stopped crying, turned around, and looked at me curiously. And so I
shut my mouth right away. Uncle looked very disappointed.

"Go ahead and cry. Cry!" He urged me.

It was a pity that I couldn't. I didn't know, either, what Uncle
expected from me. And because of this, I began worrying again.

The path home was a long one. When we got there, it was very
late. The roosters crowed crazily when they heard us. Not until I sat
in front of the kerosene lamp to eat rice porridge did I remember
that I had chucked the basket of mushrooms away on the mountain.
No wonder Uncle laughed at me for being "a collector for petty
profit." After I had finished a second bowl of rice porridge, I heard
something in the kitchen.

"Is that a wildcat?" I asked.

"It's Helin coming back," Auntie said, as if nothing had happened. "She wants to backtrack. She thinks of everything!"

I went into the kitchen. Helin was peeling asparagus—getting it
ready for tomorrow's breakfast. Her hair was combed neatly, her
clothes clean. She was absolutely different from the way she looked
early this morning. I walked over, sat next to her, and helped her peel
the asparagus.

"Helin, I saw your father!"

"Don't mention him. I don't like it when other people talk idly
about him. You don't understand the situation at all," Helin said gently but decisively.

"Are you going to stay?"

Helin didn't answer. With deft movements, she soon finished
peeling the asparagus. Carrying it in a basket, she went off to wash it.
She looked like a village woman familiar with housework, and that
amazed me. Helin turned around and smiled at me, revealing her
decayed teeth. Then, with a pout in the direction of the bedroom,
she said, "It's getting late. You still haven't gone to sleep. Uncle will
be angry."

This was the second night at Uncle's home, and it was already after midnight. The roosters made one report after another. I was exhausted, but not the least bit sleepy. I heard Helin running water in the kitchen. How could she have so many things to wash? As I listened to the noise Helin was making, I started hatching some weird and flaky plots. There were always two actors in these plots: she and I. We ran and ran, set aside her father, and threw off my mother. We didn't even want Uncle and Auntie. After a while, Helin couldn't run anymore, and I ran with her on my back. I had become a Hercules, running over one mountain after another. If she whined, I would leave her behind and run off by myself. And this way, she would plead with me to take her with me . . . Or we wouldn't in fact run off. We would just stay in whoever's home we wanted to. Her father couldn't interfere with her, nor could my mother interfere with me. Uncle didn't have any way to hang on to us, either. The children certainly wouldn't dare glower at us, nor would the adults dare point at the one as a way of cursing the other. If Helin still wanted to sleep in the glass cabinet, that was fine, too: I would move her glass cabinet to the courtyard, and let her take in the sun. By the time I came up with a fifth scenario, it was daylight, and Uncle's thunder-like snoring quieted down. As soon as he turned over, he sat up and asked if I'd seen Helin. I said she was in the kitchen washing vegetables.

"You've taken the bait!" Uncle roared. "You imbecile, she's gone to see her father!"

I put on my shoes right away and went out to the kitchen. Sure enough, Helin wasn't there. Who had been running the water during the night?

"So I wasn't wrong?" Uncle said smugly. "That little girl's schemes are deep. Luckily, we locked the door. Otherwise, she would rip the bandages off him and everything would be a mess. We've all experienced her hysteria. It's because she loves her father too much."

As I was eating breakfast that morning, I almost choked to death on a cornmeal biscuit. I was woolgathering, and eating too fast. With great difficulty, I recovered. Looking up, I saw two boys standing at the door. They were from the old house over the mountain, and they had actually run over here. When I glared at them, they immediately hid. Uncle saw them, too, and said:

"Your actions certainly do attract people!"

Curious, Auntie went outside to take a look. I heard her talking with the two boys. It was a long time before she came back in.

"They weren't looking for you. They're looking for Helin. Go talk with them," Auntie said without looking at me.

I went outside. The tall, thin one approached and told me, "Helin can't go back. Angry parents have already torn down her house. The glass cabinet has been smashed to pieces. As they smashed it, the parents said, 'Let her go off and be a homeless soul.'" His gaze was unsteady, as if he was reluctant to say these things, and his companion continued to stand some distance away. He was looking at me coldly. Finally, he wanted me to pass the word on to Helin: "She should not by any means go back. The parents are looking all over for her."

I wanted to tell him that Helin and I weren't afraid of the grown-ups. We really wanted to go back and see what they dared do to us. But I didn't say anything. This boy's attitude was cold, as though I had nothing to do with Helin's trouble and he just wanted my help in passing on the message, that's all. I invited them in, but they turned me down flat. The other boy had climbed a tree and was gazing into the distance keeping a lookout. This was getting complicated. I didn't know how long these two kids meant to stay, and if by any chance Helin came back, how they would describe the situation at home to her.

When Uncle saw my woebegone expression, he began laughing.

"Are those two monkeys in the tree threatening you? How about if I help you get rid of them?"

With that, he walked over to the tree, and clapped his hands for the two boys to come down. He told them that Helin had gone to see her father, and pointed out the path. The way Uncle handled this stirred me up. Off to one side, I shouted that this wasn't true. Helin certainly had not gone there. She was lying in bed inside. She was sick. When the two boys heard this, they slid down immediately, and shouted impatiently, "Helin! Helin!" And they charged toward the house.

"Helin is with her father." Barring their way, Uncle said to them sternly, "If you take that path, you'll find her."

At that moment, I really hated Uncle, and I yanked at his clothing and tore his overalls. I saw those two guys—harboring evil intentions—streak away, cross a small hill, and quickly disappear from my field of vision. I angrily picked up a handful of mud and threw it at Uncle. Uncle brushed at his clothes, and asked why I had to get so angry. Shouldn't Helin be told of the situation at home as soon as possible?

I wearily went for a walk, and hunkered next to a ditch to wait and see what would happen. In the ditch, an old crab lived under a large rock. Last year, when I'd come to Uncle's home, I had become acquainted with it. Now, I saw it climb out and look around for a while, and then slowly shrink back in. I moved the rock, and it didn't climb out again, but just stayed in its dark nest without making a move. I couldn't imagine how long it had been there. For sure, lying in its hole, the old crab was completely self-confident. It not only heard the sound of something stirring on the surface of the ground, but also heard things going on underground. The strange pattern on its back probably recorded momentous events. What could they have been? His old family must live in the gully on the mountain across from me. What had made it move to this populated place?

As I was mulling over the riddle of the crab, Uncle and Auntie were sitting side by side in the kitchen, each smoking a very long bamboo pipe. I walked into the kitchen and choked on the smoke. They both ignored me, as if they wanted me to realize my own mistakes. I stood in the kitchen for a while, then quickly went into Auntie's bedroom. I saw one of Helin's hairpieces on their bed. It was an eyeball made of ox horn—something Helin wore every day. On the windowsill was a small iron box. I removed the tight lid and saw to my surprise that it was a box of dirt. In the center of the dirt was a seed that had just sprouted. This gave me a really weird feeling. I opened it wide, so that the seed could get some air. There were also two fresh, muddy footprints on the windowsill—probably Helin's. I imagined that at night she jumped in and out from here. I was about to leave when a disturbing sound stopped me in my tracks. Bending over, I saw Helin under the bed. Her hands were tied behind her back, and her face was covered with dust. She was rolling around under the bed. "Helin! Helin!" I cried out sadly, and made my way under the bed to liberate her. But Helin didn't need my help. She kicked me hard—so hard that there was no way I could get close to her. All I could do was creep away despondently.

"Helin, let's leave," I hunkered there, pleading with her.

"Bug off!!" she shouted. She was beside herself with anguish.

I was scared, so I left the bedroom for the moment. With my heart in my mouth, I pressed my ear close to the door and listened.

Helin was kicking at the bed boards irritably—*deng-deng*. You could hear this from a long way away. Yet, Uncle and Auntie were calmly smoking in the kitchen. Why had they wanted to tie her up, and why hadn't she let me free her? I thought even if I racked my brains over this, I wouldn't be able to figure it out.

I always used to think that the hardest person to understand was Helin. Now, it seemed it was probably Uncle. Last night, I had nicknamed Uncle "Daddy Bear." A bear was both clumsy and docile, but in fact, it could eat people up any time it wanted. Uncle had thought of each detail in a calculated, measured way—very likely so that he could enjoy this final, sanguine moment. When I reached this conclusion, I charged into the kitchen hopping mad.

"What on earth are you so worked up about, sonny?" Uncle said coldly.

"Let Helin go, or else something's going to happen here." I squeezed one word after another out from the cracks between my teeth.

"That's what I was going to do. Okay, okay. I'll let her go. Who do you think you are, eh?"

He and Auntie traded obscene smiles. Putting their pipes down simultaneously, they headed toward the bedroom.

When Helin heard them, she came out from under the bed. Uncle bent over, and lifted her up with one hand. Auntie cut the ropes—*kacha*—with scissors. Helin threw herself into Uncle's arms and made a great sorrowful sound. She was like an aggrieved child acting coquettish with her parents. Uncle stroked Helin's hair with his big hand, not minding that all the dust on her face was being wiped onto his body. In a changed voice, he humored her: "Okay, okay. There isn't any river Helin can't cross."

Auntie chimed in, "Helin is ruthless. She can do anything."

After Helin stopped crying, she washed her face, and then she looked a lot more relaxed. A little while later, she was really happy. As she helped Auntie pickle radishes, she began humming some songs. I really couldn't figure out what she was thinking.

Uncle sat in the shadows behind the cupboard. I walked over and asked him quietly why he had tied Helin up.

"We were afraid she would hurt herself. Those two young hooligans: what can't they do? They must have already kicked the door open, and thrown my old friend's body into the field. I saw the determination in their eyes, though I suppose it's better for this sort of thing to occur sooner rather than later."

"Didn't Helin take care of her father?"

"Didn't we tie her up? She rolled around under the bed the whole day, grieving so much she wished she were dead." Then she said, "Just now, your mother came by."

"What did she want?" I asked warily.

"She brought your clothes. She's a woman whose whole life has been filled with bitterness. Everyone is hostile to her. She's always tried hard to make up to them. I guess finally she'll achieve her goal."

Uncle sank into faraway memories, narrowing his eyes to slits. He yawned twice. He complained that he was really sleepy, and he went to bed. Suddenly, I also felt very sleepy. I hadn't slept well since coming here. I made my way groggily to Uncle's bedroom, but in the hallway, Helin held me back. I asked her what was up, and she said her heart was beating very fast. She reckoned her father had already met with trouble. Those two "sad sacks" (that's the way she said it) must have taken her father's life. I said drowsily, "Weren't you really happy just now—even humming songs?" Her expression immediately turned serious: she said I was too childish and would never grow up. At the beginning, she had thought she could rely on me for some things. It was only now that she realized she had misread me. She also said I was just like a pig—just sleeping and eating, without being at all aware of major events going on right next to me. But her scolding didn't banish my drowsiness. I couldn't keep my eyes open, and I dropped straightaway down on a wooden trunk in the hallway and fell asleep. This made her even angrier. She grabbed a chicken-feather whisk broom and lashed my legs with it. It didn't hurt much. As I snored, I listened to her rebukes. I heard everything she said. In my dreams I saw Auntie driving her out. Auntie's last words were, "Don't expect an idiot to straighten out his ideas."

As soon as I woke up, I felt bad: I shouldn't have made Helin angry. I had betrayed her trust in me. Outside, a lot of dogs were barking like crazy. It was their barks that had awakened me. I hurried to look for Helin. She wasn't in the house. Behind me, Auntie said coldly, "You come to see people whenever you need help. What a despicable person!" When I saw that it was growing dark, I felt terrible. I shouldn't have fallen asleep just now. Couldn't I have tolerated even a moment of drowsiness? If I had tried hard to put up with it, Helin wouldn't have felt I had let her down so much. I really had no willpower. I wanted to go outside to look for Helin, but Auntie wouldn't let me. As soon as dinner was over, she tossed two sieves at me, and told me to winnow the rice.

By the light of the kerosene lamp, I was half-heartedly winnowing rice. I stopped several times to listen to the sounds outside. The dogs were still barking, and the mountain wind was blowing—*hu——hu——*.

Auntie came over and grabbed a handful of the rice, looked at it, and shouted, "You call this winnowing? The rice is full of chaff! You're cheating us! You parasite!"

This was more than I could put up with. Flinging the sieve to the ground, I shouted at Auntie, "I'm not doing this anymore! I'm leaving! This is really a prison. You and Uncle—you are demons!"

Auntie was distracted for a moment by my outburst, and all of a sudden she wasn't the least bit angry. She led me over to the kerosene lamp, and began taking stock of me. Just then, Uncle also showed up. The two of them were exchanging glances and sighing. They sat down and smoked, and I repeated that I was leaving. Uncle shook his head slowly. He asked me what my plans were. I said I was going to look for Helin. "And then?" "Go home with Helin." "Don't even think about it!" the two of them said in unison. Not wanting to pay any more attention to them, I turned around and went into the kitchen to get my clothes.

"Hold on!" Uncle blocked my way with his big hand. I saw that Auntie looked hostile, too. She was gripping a club, as though about to charge over and whip me. Instinctively, I held my head and hunkered beneath the hearth. They strode heavily out of the kitchen. And then they locked the kitchen door—*kacha*. And then I couldn't hear any sound in the house. I just heard the gradually diminishing sound of dogs barking in the distance.

In this odd, hopeless moment, I suddenly thought of Mother. I remembered that Uncle had told me that Mother had come by today. If she hadn't come out of worry for me, then what had she come for? This was the first time in my life that I had been suspicious of Mother. Could she have any connection with what was going on now? Since I didn't understand Uncle at all, maybe I didn't understand her, either? What kind of people were this brother and his sister? I'd grown up under Mother's worried gaze and sorrowful sighs. Without words, she'd conveyed to me that my birth was really not a good thing.

As long as I could remember, I'd struggled against this verdict of hers. At first, I'd been scrupulously careful to avoid making mistakes. But even so, I never noticed Mother's eyebrows relax at all. Rather, the way she talked conveyed the idea that she thought I was frail, and that it was for fear of death that I was so cautious. I wasn't like a child at all. Back then, her sobs often woke me up with a start in the middle of the night. She sat at the head of my bed, and stared at me like a ghost—making me tremble all over. Finally one day, I made up my mind to free myself. I wouldn't be scrupulous any longer. I'd do whatever I wanted. I even ignored what Mother said, and sometimes purposely did things she told me not to do. For example, I'd jump into the muddy pond and get dirty all over. I'd lie down outside, pretend to be dead, and scare the wits out of passers-by.

The more I indulged myself, the sadder Mother became. Once she said to some visiting relatives, "This child was born with a premonition of doom." As it happened, just then I came back from playing outside and heard this. My face turned white. My breath felt ragged. That night, I thought the whole night long. In the morning, I couldn't stand it anymore and told her I had to know if I was really born with some kind of fatal illness? If so, she should tell me and not hide it. Then I could take care of myself and keep from getting sick. This was her duty as a mother. Mother calmly turned around from her dressing table, and flatly denied this. She also reproached me and said I shouldn't indulge in exaggeration and woolgathering. She said if I always spent the whole day imagining things like this, how could I go on living? She was speaking sincerely, but why, then, did she still look worried? Then I started suspecting that disaster would befall her. I observed her closely for a long time without noticing any symptoms. The days passed quietly, yet it was clear that Mother was worried about me. Having this baseless anxiety really annoyed me, and later on, I grew even wilder.

What Helin and I did had come about because of this impulse. I thought Mother would catch up with me at Uncle's home and scold me, or forbid me to be around Helin. But the outcome was much more severe. She was thoroughly hurt, and because of this incident, she didn't want me—her own son. Had she always meant to shake me off, and now—as it happened—she had an excuse? She had complained to herself for thirteen years, and now that I had finally left, she had breathed a sigh of relief. Was this possible? Or perhaps—with her expression of displeasure—she had all along been silently urging me to go away, and Uncle had come to an agreement with her earlier? Just because her child had run off for a short time, she had broken off her relationship with him. It wasn't like her to act like this. Could it be that Uncle and Auntie had fooled me? Mother, who had been anxious about me day and night—she must have had another reason for what she did. She couldn't have been as steely as Uncle said. Of course, Uncle must have had his own secret reason to lie about it.

Assuming that she had really hurried over here and told Uncle and Auntie that she didn't want me, and then rushed home again, this off-the-wall behavior must have been the consequence of a succession of events. Now, thinking back carefully, I supposed maybe it was when I first came into contact with Helin that she came up with the idea to get rid of me as soon as possible. Is it possible that I was like a cancer on her body? Is it possible that Helin's appearance was the fatal blow for her?

The oil lamp had been extinguished. Two hens were clucking—one voice high, the other low, echoing each other. Lying on a heap of firewood at a corner of the stove, I could hear faint snoring coming from Uncle's room. After a while longer, I stood up and pushed at the window. I hadn't imagined that the window was immovable. I couldn't open the wooden lattice. I pushed many times, and it still wouldn't budge. Then I kicked the door—kicked it for a long time. My feet hurt, and still there was no activity inside the house.

In my despair, I began shouting, "Mama." I shouted and shouted. I didn't stop until I was hoarse. By then, it seemed unusually quiet all around. Even the two hens were quiet. After exhausting my strength, I fell back upon the heap of firewood and went to sleep. In a haze, I heard the sound of the door opening. A black shadow moved slowly toward me. I smelled Helin's scent. She sat down lightly on the heap of firewood, and then started crying.

"Helin! Helin!" I called out, holding her by the shoulders.

"Do you know who I really am?"

"Who?" My hair stood on end.

"I'm your older sister! My father is also your father. He died today!"

"Helin! Helin!" I shook her suddenly, as though shaking a small tree.

Then I heard her moaning. Through her moans, she murmured despairingly, "He died. He died . . . And yet I'm still alive. What's this all about? Of course, I already know what I should do."

Suddenly, an oil lamp lit the doorway. Dressed neatly, Uncle and Auntie appeared. Clapping his hands, Uncle said, "Good, good, brother and sister are finally reunited! When did this great reunion occur? Isn't this a miracle? My God!!"

"The next step is to go to Mama's home," I said uneasily.

I had no sooner said this than Helin furiously broke free of my arms. She kept saying "Posh" over and over. From her expression, it looked as though she was itching to slap my face.

"You offended her," Auntie said. "Alin is really not very bright."

"In truth, Alin is quite stupid," Uncle said.

"What on earth are you doing?" I flung caution to the winds and shouted, "Why do you have to torture me? Do you want to teach me something profound? Then why don't you just tell me? Why do you have to set up one trap after another? I can neither move away nor flee. What's driving you? Even if that man really was my father, I certainly never thought of him as a father. All along, he wanted to kill me. He . . . "

Before I'd finished talking, Helin sprang to her feet, and slapped me hard twice. Her strength was astonishing, her skinny hand like a steel whip. I almost fainted from the slaps, and with my head in my hands, I rolled around and around on the floor. Both sides of my face were numb.

Helin's slaps made me think of her father. Back then, he hadn't shown any mercy at all, but had similarly used all of his strength in beating me. The way these two people beat up on others was too much alike. In my pain, I heard Uncle and Auntie talking. They praised Helin, and said she was just like her father used to be long ago. In the future she would probably be "a woman hero." I was still moaning on the floor when all of them went out together.

They locked the door again, and it was pitch-dark all around. There wasn't even any moonlight. I would have to sleep as best I could on the firewood. I thought, *If I sleep, maybe all of this will turn out to have been a dream.* Unfortunately, I couldn't sleep. One side of my face was swollen, one tooth was loose, and blood was still coming out of my mouth. I considered the most suspicious point: how could a girl who had been sick for a long time and slept in a glass cabinet be so unusually strong? Was she faking her illness? Or perhaps the illness was one of her weird ideas. And it comes and goes whenever she wants it to? Hadn't I seen her get sick and faint at the door of her home? Even harder to understand was her using all her strength to hit me, on behalf of her father (or my father). What the hell kind of relationship had she and her father had? And how was this connected with my mother? The conclusion I reached about what had happened these two days was: these people certainly wouldn't tell me anything about any of this. They just wanted me to be blind and rush around. They enjoyed being ruthless.

All right then, tomorrow as soon as it was light, I'd go home and ask Mama. Even though it seemed that Mother was in this with them, I still believed that she couldn't have faked her concern for me for more than ten years. All I had to do was wrap her around my little finger, and wheedle, and she would finally tell me what I wanted to know. I also remembered that Helin lived not far from me: How could it be that in more than ten years I had never seen her once? And yet when we were skipping rope, as soon as I saw her, she changed my whole life. At the time, some magical enthusiasm controlled my behavior. Perhaps it was simply the blood relationship at work? In fact, I had often seen this father. He was a cooper, and everyone sought him out to fix their wooden buckets. I didn't have the impression that he was a fierce person. When he fixed buckets, we children all loved to crowd around and watch. He didn't get angry with us, but—eyes downcast—he went on with his work. But I hadn't seen his daughter, nor had I heard others mention her—not until that day when she came to skip rope and fainted. The other children certainly knew her. I was the only one who didn't, and so I was curious and couldn't wait to find out about her. If it's said that this was a conspiracy, then the plot had begun at my birth. Otherwise, why hadn't I seen Helin before? As soon as I saw her, I was attracted to her; then that father beat me to death and Mother acted as though she was submitting to the will of heaven; and then Helin acted as though she and I were in the same boat, and tempted me into running away. Usually, boys aren't interested in jumping rope, but that day I was drawn to it. Looking back on it now, it was really strange.

I wanted to leave Helin because of everything that had happened in the last two days. I had learned that Helin wasn't a puny girl at all;

sometimes she was super fierce and cruel. I had heard Uncle say that she had done away with her father. And after all, this was really frightening. Father must have seen through her fierce, cruel nature, and finally taken her away to stay with him. Yet in his eyes, the true cripples were Mother and me.

The more I thought of these things, the more I felt chilled to the bone. I pushed at the window's wooden lattice again. Several times. The left side actually gave way. I lifted it energetically, and pulled out the two tenons. I pounded some more, and pushed it out further, and then stood on a stool, dropped down, and took off running. I ran to the hilltop, then slowed my footsteps. By then, it was already growing light.

I entered our town in fear and trembling. At a glance, I saw the children crowded around something on the other side of the street. Not until I walked over did I see what it was: it was the glass cabinet Helin slept in. A little boy was sleeping in it. And the cabinet was shut very tight. The tube on the side had been taken out. The boy's eyes were closed, and it looked as if he were dead. Everyone was holding their breath, watching this boy. No one paid any attention to me.

Just as I was about to leave, I suddenly discovered that Mother was also in the crowd of children. I had never seen her look like that before: she was slovenly, her hair as messy as straw in a chicken coop. She was holding a little girl in her arms, so that the child could look at the glass cabinet over the other children's heads. A little boy was tugging at her clothes and begging her to let him get an eyeful, too. I pushed through the crowd to Mother's side, and called out softly, "Mama! Mama!"

"You?" She turned and looked at me, put her free hand to her lips, and said, "Shhh—don't make a sound."

I waited until I was fed up, and then went home alone.

The house was the same as always. I fell into bed and went to sleep. Before long, shouts woke me up. It was Mama bringing the crowd of children in. These children got into everything, threw everything into chaos. They flung the teacups—one by one—to the floor and shattered them. One boy even piddled on the floor in my room. When I pushed him out the door, he wailed and threw himself into Mother's arms. Everything was in an uproar before they scattered.

"Mama, how did you get mixed up with these children?" I asked with an annoyed frown.

Mother was excited, and looked all around; she turned, locked the door, and then said in a low voice:

"This is a ploy that I figured out. See? If I get along well with the children, the adults won't be able to do anything to me. This has been very effective. But now you've come back, when I had thought you wouldn't. And so there's another obstacle to my work. We have to work hard on this together and we'll find a way out."

The plaintiveness that I had seen on her face for more than ten years had completely disappeared. She had become another person— animated and purposeful. I felt consoled. After all, she hadn't yet forsaken me. I wasn't interested in her tactics, because I certainly wasn't interested in establishing any relationship with those devilish grownups. For me, the most pressing matter now was to find out all about Helin—the facts about everything. Without preamble, I asked Mother if Helin was my older sister.

Mother blinked her eyes several times in confusion, and then went to the kitchen to rinse the bowls. I guessed that she wouldn't answer my question, and I felt really depressed. But after a while she came out again, and said that it was very difficult for her to give me an authoritative answer, because she had amnesia and what she had forgotten could never be recalled again.

"You, for example. You're my son, because I see you every day before my eyes. If you'd been gone a little longer, I would have quickly forgotten you. It would have been as though I'd never had a son. After three years, or five, if someone asked me, I wouldn't remember anything about a son. I'm not exaggerating. This is really how it is. So, when you ran off to your Uncle's home for two days, in my eyes, you didn't exist anymore. And I was rather happy about this. Later, your Uncle mentioned you again, and I thought you should live in their home. Uncle is a pundit and could be a good influence on you. This Helin you mention—as far as this girl and her father are concerned, I really don't have any inkling about them. Didn't we also hire that cooper to fix buckets? If it is said that in the past he and we were one family, that's certainly possible. Just now in the kitchen, I was thinking and thinking. It's as though there's a bit of truth to this. Did she tell you herself that she's your older sister?"

"Mama!"

"Did she say her father is already dead?"

"Yes."

"What a strange world this is."

"The more you say, the more bizarre it seems. I want to go out and roam around."

"Go ahead, go ahead, my good boy." She put out her hand, stroking the air as though it was my head. "Go a long way away, a long way. Maybe you'll run into your sister. That would be extremely meaningful."

Three days later, as soon as it was light, I set out. My destination was a big city in the east. I had heard that there were more people in the city than there were bees in a beehive. In a place like that, no one would pay attention to me.

# THE LURE OF THE SEA

## PART 1

**H**ONG LEFT HIS MESSY COURTYARD, AND TOOK THE PATH LEADING to the seaside, where there were lots of reefs. He seemed to be acting rashly because of feeling wronged: he walked fast without looking back. His wife Yishu stayed at the window staring at his receding figure. Still holding the bowl from which she had just fed the chickens, she was looking thoughtful.

The night before, Hong and Yishu had talked about their plan all night long. They wanted to make some changes to their house. But for a variety of technical reasons, they couldn't settle on a plan. They also discussed the possibility of moving away from this spot; for instance, they talked of settling down on the plains to the east, but they realized that, if they actually did that, there would be no end to their difficulties. On the eastern plains you couldn't hear the roar of the ocean waves, but this wasn't the most vital thing. The main issue was: what was it like over there? Aside from some hearsay, they'd rarely learned anything concrete about it. Sure, Hong had been there a few times, but he'd just seen some taciturn people going about their work in the large paddy fields. Hong wasn't used to talking with strangers. One time, though, he'd screwed up his courage to go up to a home next to the road, and asked the owner if there were any rentals available.

Staring at him, the owner said not too happily, "Plenty. If you want to move here, just go ahead. But don't nose around."

What he said scared Hong. Houses in the east probably didn't cost much. But if they rushed in so rashly, would these people be hostile to them? If they didn't do it right, wouldn't it be even worse than staying where they were? Hong and Yishu analyzed their present situation again, and once more they concluded that it was so bad it couldn't get any worse. Hong relied on a tiny legacy from his ancestors. He'd never worked at a steady job. When he met Yishu, he was an assistant in a dye workshop. Yishu was a girl from a family that had once been well off, and had a higher education. Back then, she wasn't interested in Hong. As the story goes, later on, it was the expression on Hong's face that attracted her; something about it made it seem that he didn't belong to this world. Later on, this girl, who despised old-fashioned and unreasonable customs, threw herself resolutely into Hong's embrace. The two of them trudged along together and came to this village by the sea. They bought a small house and settled down.

The farmers in this village raised vegetables for a living. Although Hong didn't have to worry about making ends meet, he bought two small plots of land and grew some vegetables in order to pass the time. The first two years, before their daughter Juju was born, he was even rather interested in raising vegetables. Especially when he went barefoot into the garden to pick beans and chilies, he felt the novelty was irresistible. Naturally, they didn't sell their vegetables, but just ate them themselves. This was a lot different from the farmers who for generations had sold vegetables for a living, and it was also the origin of their conflict with them.

When they first arrived, neighbors often came over to chat. On the surface, they seemed amiable and guileless, but on the inside they were deeply prejudiced. They were there to pry into Hong's background. They always asked nosy questions. At first, Hong got along with them rather well. It was his wife's conduct that caused problems. Ever since giving birth, she'd grown more womanish, fussy. Her bearing revealed that she was from a family that had once been well off, but had now declined.

When the neighbors came over, sometimes she was bursting to show off her background. Sometimes she even seemed to want to appear to be a cut above everyone else, as though her coming to this kind of place to settle down was simply expedient—just something she had to get used to. "What kind of ungodly place is this?" She always talked like this. After a while, the neighbors' expressions changed: they no longer looked friendly. Instead, they seemed standoffish, displaying a tacit scorn. They didn't come by very often anymore. Many—without further ado—stopped calling at all. Naturally, Yishu saw the change in the neighbors, but—not a woman easily bested—she had no intention of changing. Furthermore, she had so much housework that, even if she wanted to change, she didn't have the energy to do so. Hong thought to himself, actually the way she is

now, you can't see one bit of her former breeding. She dressed sloppily, and, in doing the housework and raising the child, she was just
so-so. Whenever anything required a decision, she shoved it onto
Hong. What was it that she insisted on in front of other people?

Hong also thought, perhaps he was the one who had made her
like this. Back then, when the two of them had headed for the seaside, they'd had only some vague yearnings. They hadn't given any
thought to a real life in the future—they wouldn't have even known
where to start. Hong had felt just one impulse: to bring order to his
life. He had subconsciously chosen this place at the seaside, because
he longed to think about things while listening to the surf. The surf,
breaking time after time, would shatter barriers in his thoughts, and
in this way he would enter a misty terrain where his soul could linger
for a long time.

There finally a day came when none of the neighbors came by:
that was when Juju was almost two years old and could walk over to
the bamboo fence to play. Hong took stock of Yishu, noticing that
the stubborn wrinkles on her forehead had deepened. She was like
Hong—constantly busy in and out of the house, doing the endless
household chores.

Their house was a four-room bungalow. The window was small
and narrow, the front door very strong. It was said that this house had
been built by a rich man, who had later moved south and sold it to
the village. The village then sold it to Hong. When he was buying
the house, Hong had wondered if the narrow window could have
something to do with everyone's hostility toward them. Since the
window was narrow, it was dark inside. Yet, this precisely met Hong's
wishes: in the dark, he could break through his own logic and think
of the gray area between black and white. But in this hazy environment, Yishu's temper became worse by the day. One day, when Juju
was four years old, she went to the neighbor's yard and dug up
worms. She was chased and beaten up by the little neighbor boy, and
fell on her face. When Yishu found out about this, she was shaking
with anger. She took Juju to the neighbors' house to try to reason
with them.

"What's so wonderful about you? Isn't it just that you have a little more filthy lucre? Who knows where that money came from?"
the neighbor woman said enigmatically as she cast a sidelong glance
at her.

Yishu was so furious that she kicked the neighbor's crock of pickled vegetables over, and then left with Juju in tow.

After Yishu told Hong what had happened, he began waiting. At first, he thought about reinforcing the front door, but after thinking it over, in the end he didn't do it. He just told Juju that "if the bad guys came," she should hide under the stove. He rehearsed it with her several times.

In the wee hours of the morning, a gang of guys charged in. They rammed the door open handily with something or other. Anything in the house that could be smashed was smashed. They even took the bedding outside, doused it with gasoline, and burned it. Among the men were several neighbors whom they often saw, and also some of their neighbors' relatives from other villages. Hong knew them all. When they'd finished all of this, they left swearing a blue streak. The strange thing was that after the attack, Hong seemed to feel relieved. It was as though all that was left to do was straighten up the mess.

He remembered that Juju climbed out from under the stove and asked him when the bad guys would come back.

Afterwards, a serious illness left Yishu much less haughty. She began talking less and less, yet Hong knew that inside she was the same as ever. As time went on, Hong and Yishu conversed little, and when they did, it was always about moving. Finally, with Juju in primary school, the topic cropped up more and more often. And after several years of silence, Yishu gradually began talking more. She often urged Hong to take a look at other areas in the vicinity, and sometimes went withhim by bus to look at the eastern plains. The places they visited were all sparsely populated villages. They didn't investigate cities. In spite of looking at lots of places, Hong kept hesitating: it always seemed, after all, that the disadvantages of moving outweighed the advantages. He had never been as impetuous as Yishu, but he had become even more muddleheaded in the last few years and had begun to not give a damn about anything. Now and then, sitting and thinking next to the vegetable plot, he was scared witless. He also hung several dark-colored blinds at the windows, making the room just like a darkroom. He was often in this darkroom letting his confused thoughts run wild. He enjoyed this. Of course, sometimes Yishu ran on at the mouth a lot. He gradually came to believe that Juju's problem—at school she was often teased and discriminated against—was indeed a problem. Would it be even worse if they moved? Hong liked to think this way.

But Yishu was singleminded. When she got an idea into her head, it took root there. She hardly ever gave it up. Since Hong was unwilling to move, Yishu had recently come up with a plan to renovate their present house: enlarge the windows, make the door smaller. If they did this, their house would be almost like the neighbors' houses. Hong knew why Yishu wanted to make changes: she must think that it was the unusual style of their house that had made the villagers jealous and resentful. If the house were remodeled so that it was like other people's, their hostility would gradually diminish. Sometimes Yishu was as innocent as a child. Hong didn't have any confidence in her plan. To put it off, he had to carry on endless discussions with her. And because he'd been woolgathering when they discussed it yesterday, Yishu was angry. When Yishu was angry, she took out all of her discontent from the last few years on Hong.

"Now who can possibly recognize the old me?" She said, "In the last few years, this house has turned into a prison cell. At night the seething sound of the surf is like a monster puffing and gasping. It's as if it wants to draw me down into its belly. I don't believe you aren't afraid. One night, I saw you cover your head tightly with the quilt. You were shaking so much that the bed boards rattled."

"Sure, I'm afraid," Hong said calmly. He caught a glimpse of her as she was about to break into tears.

As Hong was mulling over these worries and about to reach the seaside, he heard Jinglan calling him. He stopped in amazement. Jinglan was his old friend whom he'd lost track of a long time ago. He had formerly been in the business of selling raw materials for decorating. Jinglan was walking toward him from the seaside, carrying a large suitcase. Behind him was a sailboat—a very old fishing boat. The boat's owner was taking down the sail. Perhaps Jinglan had disembarked from that very boat. He didn't look a bit older; his manner was just as composed as ever. Walking up the path, he shook hands with Hong, but averted his eyes.

He said, "Why did you come to the seaside? To clean your dirty mind, or to dirty the ocean?"

"Where did you come from? You couldn't have known that I'd moved here, could you?" Hong was astonished.

"Let's not talk about that right now." Jinglan skirted the question

vaguely, and began talking about his business. It seemed his business
hadn't done well. He kept being cheated and losing money. Recently,
he had been pretty much as poor as a church mouse. His wife had
already divorced him, but had also purposely left their ten-year-old
son with him; he had to work hard every day just to earn a pittance.
His health had also pretty much broken down. As he was talking,
Hong kept looking at him. Hong thought his friend was in good spirits. His health didn't seem to have broken down. Yet, he sure did
want to make it seem that his life was such a mess, it couldn't get any
worse. Why? As they talked, they walked right to the seaside. The
sea was so unusually calm that it seemed dead. As Hong considered
this simile, he smiled briefly: he knew this was just a pose. The two
of them climbed onto a rock and sat down. The water was a turbid
green. From a distance came the sound of a sea vessel's whistle.
Jinglan opened his suitcase, and searched inside it, mumbling.

"What are you looking for?"

"Me? As soon as I saw you, I thought I have to show you a picture of my son. Let me tell you something strange. I've taken photos
of my son so many times. Each time they're developed, they're
always blank. This is just inconceivable. There was just one exception: that time he was standing next to a big rooster. Ah, I can't find
it right now. Forget it."

Hong wanted to ask him where he was living now. He was on the
verge of opening his mouth when he realized that he wouldn't get the
truth, so he immediately shut it. He had known Jinglan well for
years. Just look at him—dressed like a professional traveler, and yet
hadn't he just said that he had a ten-year-old son to take care of? As
Hong thought of Juju, a feeling of gratitude welled up in his heart. It
was wonderful to have a daughter growing up quietly beside him.
The water began crashing against the large rocks at their feet,
because a passenger boat had rolled by toward the wharf in front of
them. Hanging all over it were small colorful banners. Some passengers were standing on the deck. Looking excited, Jinglan waved, as if
greeting someone on the craft. Hong knew that the boat was so far
away that no one on it could possibly make him out—he certainly
didn't need to be so vigorous about it. The vessel passed quickly, and
the ocean grew calm again. Hong felt that the ocean was a little different today. Ordinarily, even if it was windless on shore, there was
always a little breeze on the ocean. If you stuck your feet into the

water, you'd feel the ocean's strength as it tried mightily to restrain itself. The force was terrifically violent. Living at the seaside, Hong had heard a lot of frightening legends about that.

"I want to take you to a certain place today," Jinglan said, his head hanging down.

He seemed inwardly tense: his hands betrayed this much.

"Sure thing. I knew that we couldn't have run into each other for no reason," Hong said in a comforting tone.

Smiling absent-mindedly, Jinglan shifted positions a little. Hong thought he was going to stand up. Little did he know that he would sit back down. He seemed to be thinking, yet also dillydallying. His profile reminded Hong of a kind of emptiness. Hong was muttering to himself: why had Jinglan come to the seaside? In the past, when he was in the outback, he'd been busy all the time. He really couldn't see that he had any interest in the ocean. Hong himself, though, had often talked with him of his dreams of the ocean. Back then, Jinglan always just snorted contemptuously, and said that Hong was one who "loved what he actually knew nothing about," and that at best, he'd "only ever go to the beach and collect little shells." For no reason, Hong always felt attached to Jinglan; this began when the two of them met. As soon as Jinglan left, this feeling of attachment vanished. But now, Jinglan sat there without making a sound, and Hong felt that he was like a magnet. He was always drawn to him; he couldn't shake these feelings. Years ago, when they lived in the city, they were on intimate terms with each other. Sure, Jinglan always stood high above him, not wishing to be on an equal footing. But Hong wasn't convinced by this, and so he couldn't avoid arguing with him.

Each time they parted after a bad argument, Hong decided Jinglan was no longer his friend, but as soon as Jinglan showed up the next time, Hong's resolve was broken. Jinglan's spell lay in this: as soon as he met someone, he could lead that person around by the nose. His logic swept everyone along. Hong felt he would never be able to break away as long as he lived. The year before Hong moved to the seaside, Jinglan had disappeared. In those days, Hong felt that—little by little—his own vigor was being sapped from his body. Just then, Yishu rushed into his life, and as a last effort in his struggle, he embarked on the journey to the seaside with her.

The two of them sat there in silence for a long time—until it was almost dark. A lot of vessels went past. And each time, Jinglan stood up and waved and shouted. At last, the sun began to set below the surface of the sea. And in the sun's remaining splendor, the ocean seemed a little lonely. Hong felt a series of chills. Finally, Jinglan stood up, and with his suitcase on his back, he said, "Let's go. You must be hungry. I'll take you out for some beer."

As Jinglan swung his thin legs down from the rock, Hong felt once more that the suitcase on his back was so large as to be a little strange. Walking along the path next to the ocean, they swerved when they came to the rocky mountain, and then climbed it. Even though Hong had occasionally come to this mountain, he hadn't been to all the spots there. This was a large mountain, partly submerged in the ocean. The huge rocks were rugged, the path filled with twists and turns. The ground was heaped with bird droppings, and nearby the seabirds were rustling. It was absolutely dark. Hong wasn't familiar with this way. Jinglan was leading him ahead. For a long time, Hong knew only that he was walking on this path that rose and fell and where water dripped from the rocks on both sides. It appeared that Jinglan was familiar with this place. When they left that small winding path, a large bird circled overhead. Jinglan howled fiercely, and Hong felt hot, watery bird droppings streaming down his face. Panicky, he wiped them off with his handkerchief, then gnashed his teeth and began cursing. "This place might as well be the kingdom of the birds," Jinglan said. "They make trouble for anyone passing by. . . . My home is just ahead. Look, the candles are burning. That's Mimei. She's waiting for us." Hong was surprised, because Jinglan hadn't said a word about a woman in his life.

Jinglan pulled him down from a steep slope, and they went into the house. To be precise, it was just a tent. Inside were a simple, crude table and several rectangular stools. In the center of the table stood a large red candle, its flame leaping constantly. Because the woman was sitting in the shadows behind it, Hong couldn't see what she looked like. His gaze darted all around.

"Are you looking for my son? Don't waste your energy. No one can see him, including Mimei and me." As he sat down at the table, Jinglan said, "He never comes in before midnight. He plays with you for a while and then leaves. He isn't one bit patient."

Hong shivered.

Mimei placed a large plate on the table. On it were chicken, fish from the ocean, and some other dishes to go with the wine. They were all mixed together. You could tell that the food wasn't very fresh. Mimei, a tiny, dark-skinned woman with astonishingly big eyes, was wearing overalls. She kept staring at him blankly. This made Hong uneasy. As Jinglan opened the bottles of beer, he told Hong, "Mimei is a cook at a restaurant in the area. She brought this food home with her." The three of them drank and ate in silence. Meanwhile, outside, the night birds were making a fierce uproar. Hong began worrying a little. He didn't think he could spend the night in this kind of place, so would Jinglan see him home? He wouldn't be able to find his way himself. Taking stock of the dark places in the tent, he suddenly stopped short. Two people were in the shadows. They weren't moving. Hong was so startled that he almost spit the meat out of his mouth.

"Don't pay any attention to them," Mimei said to him gently, though her voice was rough. "They keep hanging around here. They're as curious as children. I don't have the strength to drive them out. Anyhow, we all have to leave before flood tide tomorrow."

"Flood tide?" Hong was even more startled.

"Right. Didn't Jinglan tell you? This is just a temporary home. We move once a day. The ocean is right under your feet. Half of this mountain stretches into the sea."

Hong pricked up his ears. Sure enough, he heard the sound of billowing waves. Listening to the sound of the ocean waves here was completely different from listening to them at home. At home, the ocean—roaring from a distance—gradually drowned out his recollections, muddling and stupefying him. But here the ocean wasn't benevolent. It seemed to be watching him sternly. Imagining how this place looked when it was flooded, all at once Hong understood Jinglan's innermost gloom. Just now, Jinglan was concentrating on eating a chicken foot. He was spitting out the tiny bones a few at a time. Every now and then, a merciless expression crossed his face.

After dinner, Hong rose to take his leave, but it was as if Jinglan hadn't heard him. He was fiddling with the pile of chicken bones in front of him. Mimei pushed Hong back onto the stool, and said, "There's no way you can go now!" Hong asked why not. She said that the path they'd taken was already blocked by a flock of birds. It would be difficult to take a single step. He'd have to wait until morning. Hong was outraged. He felt he'd been duped. Knowing how worried Yishu would be, he was filled with anxiety.

"You can't leave, so there's no point in thinking about it. You can sleep with those two people on the mat in the back, okay? The mat is wide enough."

Jinglan set up a simple bed there, and then took blankets out of that humongous suitcase. It also held sheets and pillows. He made up the bed quickly. Mimei had already cleared the table. Taking Hong's hand, she led him to the dark spot at the back of the tent, and Hong took in the heavy smell of soot in the woman's hair. Abruptly, she pushed him hard, and he fell onto the mat. The man next to him was smoking a pipe, the glow flickering. The other man was lying on the mat, his face in his hands, assessing the situation and not making a sound. Mimei was rattling on and on about something as she took a large piece of cloth from the suitcase, shook it out and hung it in the center of the tent, thus dividing the tent into two parts. The three people on the mat were in darkness. Hong heard Jinglan begin to sigh, as if he was uneasy. After a while, he left the tent. Hong wanted to go along, but the pipe smoker beside him stopped him, saying, "Hurry up and go to sleep, because before dawn they have to dismantle the tent and run off. A catastrophe might strike during the night. It's said there'll be a landslide. But we can sleep peacefully through the first stage of the danger." Hong heard Mimei chattering to herself as she got into bed. She blew out the candle and—in the dark— began grinding her teeth. The man in back also stretched out and went to sleep. Hong and the pipe smoker were still sitting on the mat. A long time passed, and Jinglan still hadn't come back. The pipe smoker lay down, and so did Hong.

He heard the water surge up from the crevices in the rocks. He began unfolding his body and swimming to a deep spot in the ocean. Just then, the water began pulling at him. Different currents were pulling at his limbs. He struggled hard and felt his neck was about to be twisted off. Now and then, he woke up and discovered that actually it was those two men who were tangled up with him and tearing at him, pressing him down. When he threw them off at last, he entered the ocean once again. He didn't struggle any longer, intending to drift with the tide. Naturally, his four limbs were still taut, and he felt as if he would be torn apart. He was in great pain. Just then, a large shadow shaped a little like an octopus appeared above him.

Hong was too scared to move. The feeling of impending death was undeniable. He bit his lip unconsciously, bringing the taste of blood to his mouth. When the octopus turned its head and attacked him, he awoke with a start. Like a carp, he broke loose from those two men, stood up, and fumbled to put on his shoes. Then he went outside. As he left the tent, he stumbled over someone. Mimei.

"I couldn't sleep, and just got up. It's always like this. After a while, I have to go to the restaurant. Jinglan really worries me. I often look and look, walking all over the mountain." Because she'd caught a cold, Mimei's voice was even hoarser.

Hong went in and out of the dark paths with her. Sometimes, they ran into night birds that attacked them. They not only shit on them, but also drew blood when they pecked at Hong's face. Mimei's face was covered with a straw hat, so the birds couldn't peck at it. After they had walked on the slope for a long time, they finally emerged from the pitch-dark path. Ahead was a flat hill. Mimei sat down on a large protruding rock, and Hong stood beside her. In the moonlight, little waves were rising in the ocean. They looked benign, not at all fierce like the ones Hong had seen in his dream. Mimei took a sausage out of her handbag and gave it to Hong.

"He always hides around here." She said worriedly, "Usually, it's a little boy's voice that is calling outside, and then he goes out. He says it's his son, but I've only ever heard the sound. I've never seen anyone."

When she gazed out at the sea, Hong noticed that a green fluorescence shot cat-like from her eyes. Her small, thin body was filled with energy, and it threw off the scent of balsam. Beside the sea, Hong felt powerfully attracted to this woman—but it wasn't a sexual attraction. The sea began to be turbulent, sensual. Hong was mesmerized. A steamship was going past. Mimei sprang to her feet, and standing on tiptoe, she raised her straw hat high. She kept shouting nonsense until that ship disappeared.

"Jinglan does the same thing when he sees a ship. Who are you calling?" Hong asked.

"His son was lost on a boat. He's never given up the idea of finding him. We moved to the seaside, because he wanted to get the whole story. You know, he doesn't sleep at night. I'm really concerned about him. Luckily, I found work in the restaurant, and he helps out there in the daytime. That's how we can keep going with this wandering life. You know, we often move, and he always chooses the place nearest the sea. At flood tide, we're in a tight corner. He isn't afraid of trouble. . . ."

"Has he been doing this all along?" Hong asked. He didn't want to say that Jinglan was "keeping up his involvement with the ocean."

"When I first knew him, he wasn't at all like this. Then the steamship carried his son off. I think it must be because of his hatred of the sea. What else could it be? At night, I come out to look for him, but I haven't found him even once." Then Mimei sat up straighter and tapped the large rock with the heel of her shoe.

Hearing the noise, the big bird circling overhead didn't dare attack them.

Hong was imagining Mimei coming out every night to look for Jinglan. He felt as if an immense current of heat were shoving them into the center of a whirlpool. A very long time ago, he had experienced the same kind of feeling.

"I have to go to work," Mimei said, looking at her watch. "It's three o'clock now. You just stay outside and look hard. Maybe you can find him. This way, I won't be so worried."

Abandoning Hong, Mimei made her way onto the path that he'd taken to get here. The bird flew off along with her. The sound of her footsteps quickly disappeared in the darkness. Hong was fretting that he certainly wouldn't be able to find the way back. The best he could do was wait here on this hill for daylight. As soon as it was light, he'd go home. At home, Hong heard the waves every night—not violent, but always loud, sending his thoughts whirling around. What the hell was the inside of this silent sea all about? In order to make sure what he had heard, he frequently questioned Yishu about it at midnight. Yishu also heard it. She hardly ever said exactly what she thought it was like, but her response was the opposite of his: she always grew irritated, got up, and went outside. She walked until it was almost light before coming home. Looking worried, she'd say, "I can't get into the ocean." Hong recalled that in the beginning she, too, was determined to hurry to the seaside. He felt sorry for her.

Hong was looking at the sea, silent in the moonlight. He wondered: was it only in dreams that people could feel the throbbing of the sea? When Mimei was sleeping in that tent, was the sea of a certainty even more violent toward her than toward him? Was it possible that it was because of this that she and Jinglan wanted to live in a place where they could hear the pulsing of the ocean's heart? Was Jinglan so infatuated with the sea because it had carried his son away? Did he perhaps also want revenge? Revenge toward the sea or revenge toward himself? Just then, Hong saw a dark shadow in front of him. Dodging out from the path, the shadow moved toward him slowly. Hong thought at once of pirates, and he was very much on edge. Then he heard a match being struck. The person lit a pipe, and Hong relaxed. It was the pipe smoker.

"Can't sleep?" the man asked, and without waiting for an answer he went on. "It is really hard to sleep in a place like this. Anyone would go crazy if he thought all night long of emergencies like landslides. No one but Jinglan can come up with an idea like this. It's really admirable. It was because I was strongly attracted to him that I came here with him. Everyone wants to experience that kind of state."

"You came outside. Are you thinking of looking for him?"

"Right. But this mountain is crisscrossed with paths. Generally, anyone going in has trouble coming out. It's bad enough in the daytime, but in the middle of the night, it's worse—looking for someone here is like looking for a needle in a haystack. We won't be able to find him."

"What does he do on the mountain?"

"You really think he's on the mountain? Actually, he's underwater! He always comes back completely drenched before flood tide. Once, he told me, he lay on the bottom of the ocean and listened to the steamships rushing by."

The pipe smoker also told Hong, "A family lives on this mountain. They built their house right next to the sea. They're just like Jinglan and his wife: at flood tide, they move their things, and when the tide rolls out, they move back. The only difference is that their house is wooden and fixed in place. When it was a little over a year old, the wood had already almost rotted. There's a child in the family." He asked Hong, "Want to go over and see them? It's really interesting, especially the child." Hong said it wasn't a good idea to call on people in the middle of the night. The pipe smoker said, "It doesn't matter—by now, the whole family must be awake." So Hong stood up and went along with him. When they were walking along the path, once again two birds attacked them. One of them perched on Hong's shoulder and wouldn't leave. Hong couldn't do anything about it. He knew he couldn't win in a struggle with it. Finally, they saw a light, and the bird fluttered away. They looked in a window. Three people were sitting woodenly in front of the candlelight. The little girl—about seven or eight—was wearing red wool clothes. When they went in, the man was just turning around to pack his suitcase. He seemed a little impatient. The woman turned a dreamy expression toward them and smiled absently, then lowered her head again to contemplate her worries.

"Little Yun, did anyone come by here last night?" the pipe smoker asked the girl.

"Are you still looking for that person? We haven't seen him even once. Sometimes he knocks on the door and then leaves. By the time Papa opens the door, he's long gone. Who is this person? Does he intend to settle down here? I guess so." Thinking herself clever, the little girl gazed at Hong.

When the girl looked up, Hong noticed that her forehead was very wrinkled. And the hand she extended wasn't like a child's hand, either. The blood vessels stuck out, and her fingers were withered. Hong swept a glance over the room: the floor was wet. The man was still working hard at stuffing sheets and pillows into the suitcases. At his feet were three bags. Hong was puzzled: why wasn't the woman helping him pack? She sat there, as if his hard work had nothing to do with her. Had the ocean brought her to this state in her dreams?

The little girl rushed over to the window and drew a design in the steam. With her head inclined, she screamed at the top of her lungs: "Ya! Ya! Ya!" In the dark night, her childish voice made everyone's hair stand on end. Outside, a lot of birds seemed to be flying over, and were beating against the glass. The little girl opened her mouth and laughed. Hong noticed that it was all black inside the child's mouth. She didn't have even one tooth. Hong tapped his companion, indicating that he wanted to leave. The man, smoking his pipe, was listening closely to the noise outside. The little girl suddenly turned around, and touching Hong, frowned and said,

"You—how did you come here?"

Everyone was staring at Hong, including the woman. Hong suddenly felt the atmosphere was frightening—his legs were shaking a little. He dashed outside. In the pitch dark, he ran without stopping, slackening his pace only when he realized that no one was chasing him.

He took a path, now and then holding onto the rocks on either side to avoid slipping on the ground. He went with the turns, but he had no idea where he was going. As he walked aimlessly, the birds no longer followed him, but the sound of the onrushing waves reached his ears. The sea was beginning to roar and the sound of the wind was frightening.

Hong squatted down, happy to be hidden on the mountain. He thought again about those other people just now, and didn't understand why he had been so afraid. What the hell was he afraid of? The pipe smoker had told him that a lot of households like this were concealed on the mountain: like seabirds, they all built their nests on the seaside. They were all depressed, or even malicious, people.

In the roar of the waves, Hong was thinking wildly: suppose he and Yishu built a nest here, too? How had Jinglan rushed over here to live among these stragglers? As he was wallowing in this mood, in his mind's eye he saw Juju's image superimposed on that of the little girl he had just seen. He was terrified. Exhausted, Hong sat down on the ground, but he didn't doze off. The heart-quake of the sound of the waves never relaxed. It was as if the ocean were stacking itself up against the mountain. No matter how much willpower a person had, he probably couldn't survive an attack like this. Hong felt himself breaking down.

When the sky grew light, Jinglan appeared and the sound of the wind subsided. At the sight of him, Hong felt fresh hope rise. Jinglan squatted down, and slinging his arm around Hong's shoulder affectionately, said, "Let's go to Mimei's restaurant. They have really good corn porridge."

"Why did you go out alone at night?"

"Aren't you alone, too?" Jinglan said with a smile. "Even that little girl—you must have seen her."

Mimei's restaurant—lit up brilliantly by candles—was in a col of the mountain. Lots of people—even several children alone—had come here for breakfast. After a while, Hong saw that little girl sitting at a table with her parents. Her round eyes were darting around. Hong walked past her. She looked as though she wanted to jump up and bite him. Her mother still looked dreamy, and didn't even turn her eyes.

Mimei was in the kitchen frying dough sticks. The smoke from the oil surged up as she deftly maneuvered two long wooden chopsticks. She made a face at Jinglan, indicating that they should sit at the table next to a cupboard. After serving them corn porridge and fried dough sticks, she sat down with them. Gazing at Hong's eyes, she said, "You surely couldn't get used to this kind of life. Jinglan was right. You're the kind who pretends to love what you really fear."

Eating his porridge, Hong felt confused. Looking at the customers going in and out of the restaurant, he already saw what they were like, and understood, too, how this out-of-the-way col could have such a restaurant. What a strange world it was. At first, when Jinglan ran off to do business away from home, Hong didn't understand why he wanted to be so busy, did he? Jinglan's determination in his work left Hong in the dust. This was also what attracted him to Jinglan—in general, Hong was happy that he hadn't seen much of the world, but his happiness was not without regrets.

"True. I probably couldn't get used to it," Hong answered with an absentminded smile.

Jinglan didn't eat much, and quickly put his chopsticks down. Picking his teeth, he said, "That little girl you see—a few years ago, her parents wanted to get rid of her. They ran off before flood tide, and left her alone on the seaside. She never knew what was going on. Later on, someone saved her. Afterwards, it was on that spot that her parents built their house. She became very canny, and stayed close to her parents. Everybody here knows her story. You also see that couple. Relations among the three of them are extremely tricky. You've never seen anything like it. I've been observing them all along. Look: they're leaving. After breakfast, they go to the railroad tracks and unload goods. That's tough work. The child stays by herself next to the tracks."

Mimei went back to the stove. Gazing at her, Jinglan whispered to Hong, "I'm planning to leave her. She's been with me too long."

"Just like the little girl's parents left her?" Hong blurted out.

Jinglan slumped into contemplation, his hands propping up his chin, his gaze flickering. Hong thought Jinglan's heart was a bottomless abyss.

Everyone else had already left the restaurant—it seemed these silent people ate really fast. Mimei was deftly cleaning up in the kitchen without making a sound. Jinglan stood up and said, "Hong, you gotta go home. Otherwise, Yishu will be worried." He walked outside with Hong, and Hong instantly knew the way home. After walking on the path for a while, Hong ran into the two men who had stayed with him in the tent the night before. They were carrying the huge mat, with the tent on top of it. It seemed the pipe smoker had no use for Hong. He looked down, not meeting his eyes. The other one was a shorty, about fifty years old. With Shorty's curious gaze glued to him, Hong was uncomfortable.

"Need any help?" Hong said, his face flushed.

"Nah, nah. Why would I need help from you? That wouldn't do. No way could you help. Just mind your own business." Seeming afraid of Hong's help, Shorty quickened his steps.

## PART 2

When Hong got home, his heart was heavy as he sat down on a rock in the courtyard. Recalling Yishu's mood swings of the last few days, he felt that he couldn't ignore the hard knot that had long lodged in his heart. When Yishu came out, he saw that her hair was all in place, and that she didn't look angry anymore. Rather, she looked a lot happier.

"Is Juju at school?"

"Yes. I've been meaning to talk with you about Juju. I still think she should stay here; we can't go. I just heard that the rural area in the east is worse than here. It doesn't even have a school. It's simply rough, barren land. After all, we've lived here a long time. What would anyone dare do to us? I won't renovate the house, either. We shouldn't have brought that up."

She still looked arrogant and proud. Hong took stock of her curiously.

"Has someone been here?"

"Yes. Jinglan came over during the night. He talked with me about his son. I thought it over and over, and concluded that neither of us has Jinglan's nerve. Why should we make things difficult for ourselves? Don't you think Jinglan is terribly ill? Yesterday, I looked at his face in the lamplight. Truly, I didn't have the heart to look at him long. How could he have changed so much? He's almost bald, and he doesn't have many teeth left, either. The corner of his mouth was twitching all the time, and he was drooling."

"Are you sure it was Jinglan?"

"Who else could it have been? I'd know him anywhere! When he left, I gave him a cane."

After what his wife said, the hard knot in Hong's heart gradually came undone and became like a large lump of wet fog. The sun gradually rose higher, and the vegetables in the garden glistened in its light. In the breeze, the old camphor tree's leaves were alive with rustling. Hong recalled that twilight years ago, when he and his wife had put up with the hardships of traveling to come here. Wasn't it exactly this bright view of the present that appeared in their murky brains back then? What was blocking their imagination now? Was it because they couldn't get along with the sea? But the sea was everywhere. Even if one wanted to break away from it, it wouldn't be possible. Wasn't it because of the sea that they had both rushed over here in the beginning? Looking at his wife's silhouette shuttle back and forth in the shed of kidney beans, Hong sighed with deep emotion. She wasn't old yet , but she was exhausted body and soul. He really couldn't bear to look back on these last few years. Especially at night, one time, Yishu had walked outside barefoot, and in the end, she had walked more than three miles, not returning until morning. Her feet were covered with blisters. That was just when their relationship with the neighbors was strained. People stole more than half of their vegetables. Hong knew that in the past few years, Yishu had been considering escaping all along. She was the kind of person who had to act on her ideas at once. At this point in his thinking, Hong couldn't help starting to respect Jinglan a lot. Who else would have been able to persuade someone like his wife? Hong looked up and saw a shadow moving evasively next to the bamboo fence. After a while, the bamboo fence began burning. Hong rushed over with a roar, and the person took to his heels.

He and Yishu had to work hard to put the fire out. They looked at one another's dirty faces, and burst out laughing. If the fence had burned, it could have set fire to the firewood stacked up next to it. A lot of combustible things were also strewn on the ground. If they hadn't put the fire out, even the house could have caught fire. Hong was on guard: he raked the hay and wood into a large pile. He was sweating a lot from working so long.

After a bath, Hong sat at the table, and as he drank tea, he told Yishu of his night's adventures. Yishu was chopping vegetables. She seemed to be listening but she really wasn't. Still preoccupied with the terror of the fire, she was thinking she had to buy a fire extinguisher. Hong knew that she'd already heard about last night from

Jinglan. How had Jinglan described him? Hong couldn't guess. He had never guessed right about Jinglan. He was rather discouraged, for it seemed he had no way to convey his impression of last night to Yishu. But this wasn't very important: hadn't Jinglan already persuaded her to change her mind? Hong's mind suddenly went black: a new thought made him weak all over.

"How was he?" he asked Yishu, at the same time turning his gaze toward the wall.

"So-so." Yishu went on chopping vegetables. "Now it's hard to remember what he was like. But at the time—ah, what's a good comparison? It's as if I were possessed by the devil. Everything was involuntary. Maybe he possesses a certain kind of sorcery."

Yes, Jinglan truly knew witchcraft. Hong felt despondent, but he also felt that Yishu's impression of Jinglan matched his own. A new relationship was beginning between Yishu and him. As Hong recalled the people at the seaside, he couldn't help forcing a bitter smile. It appeared that he and Yishu were longing for the same thing, yet expressing it differently—just like sleeping in the same bed, but dreaming different dreams. The nature of the dreams was the same. With things at this turning point, Hong faltered a little, not knowing how best to treat Yishu. She, however, was unperturbed: just as if nothing had happened, she sprinkled the kidney beans with salt, and stirred them in a wooden basin.

Watching her, Hong recalled that she used to find Jinglan annoying. Whenever Jinglan came over, she'd never been able to conceal her disgust. She threw things all over the place, and sometimes was bitingly sarcastic, too. No sooner had Jinglan left than she called him a "hoodlum." Back then, Jinglan didn't pay any attention to her; it was as if she wasn't there. What a strange world it had turned out to be! When had it begun—that the guy had built his own little kingdom on the rocks by the sea? He lived so close to them, and yet they hadn't run into him even once! Or, perhaps he was the only one who hadn't, and Yishu had run into him lots of times? Didn't she always wander around in the middle of the night?

It was too late to be thinking of these things now. The issue was whether or not to change the status quo. After experiencing the events of last night, Hong didn't want to alter it one bit. He couldn't understand how he could have ever had any thought of changing it. Probably he wasn't the one who'd thought this; it was just Yishu who had. And now Yishu had changed: Jinglan had changed her. Life's complex relationships made Hong start to long again for the sea. Perhaps now the sea would no longer be as it was in the past—shattering the barriers to his thoughts, letting him enter the painless land of mist. Perhaps it had to be another kind of space—one where the imagination ran free.

In the afternoon, when he was working in the vegetable garden, he saw Yishu standing motionless at the window. She had never behaved like this before. Hong was so hard at work that it was late before he went inside. He thought of how carefully he tended the vegetables and with the unremitting feeling of dejection produced by his "fruitless effort," everything went black before his eyes.

That night, Yishu suddenly exploded with enthusiasm and nuttiness. Hong, who had been silent for a long time, was infected by this, too. Afterwards, he recalled that this feeling was unexpectedly much the same as the dream he'd had the night before in the tent. After they made love, Yishu sat nude on the quilt, and gazing at Hong, said, "I know who set the fire. He came again in the afternoon, and threatened to burn us to death."

Hong thought that, with her hair down, she was a little like an imposing lion. He hadn't guessed that she had this much energy stored up in her body. He had really underestimated her.

As soon as it was light the next day, the neighbor came over. It was the woman who had argued with Yishu before. Shouting, she sat at the table with her legs apart. She announced that she'd come to make up with Yishu, but she didn't look at all as if she wanted to make up. Her words were acrimonious, and she kept kicking the legs of the table—until the teapot overturned and the tea streamed onto the table. Struggling with Hong for the dishcloth, she made as if to wipe the table. In the scuffle, she cut Hong's finger with her fingernail. Hong just stood there without moving, watching the act she was putting on.

"Neighbors should live in harmony," she lectured. "In this place, no one can get away from anyone else, and nobody can be elevated above anyone else. If you want to boost yourself over others all the time, you have to hide such thoughts in your heart. We've lived here for a generation, and we've seen all kinds of people. In the past, some other folks wanted to set themselves up against us, too. They couldn't live here, and all they could do was leave. Your former landlord was one of them. He regarded the villagers as enemies. Guess what happened to him? One night, he dreamt that he was being chased by a vicious dog. He jumped out of bed and ran outside—ran into the mountains. A poisonous thorn plunged into his foot, and he couldn't get out of bed for six months. I was the one who advised them to leave. This wasn't a place where they could stay a long time. After you came here, I often wondered: could you be the same as that family? At first, I thought so. These last few days, though, I've slowly begun wavering. Why? You're bringing up a child here, and the child is starting to grow up. That other family didn't have a child. This is a huge difference. Some people describe this place of ours as a barren desert. Have you heard this?"

"You've really had a lot of experience," Yishu said insincerely. "We ought to drop our haughtiness around you."

At this, the woman abruptly turned bashful. To begin with, she laid it on thick about Yishu's skill in pickling vegetables. Yishu said this skill wasn't worth anything. Unable to go on watching, Hong retreated to the bedroom. He sat there a long time, listening to the two women's spirited whispers. Hong couldn't get used to the sudden change in Yishu's character. It seemed suspicious to him. What kind of scene could there have been between Jinglan and Yishu? Hong couldn't imagine it. In the past, he'd thought that Jinglan was a little like a blast of air. That's why Mimei's story about looking for Jinglan at night touched him so deeply. No one could feel sure of his real feelings about such a person. Hong didn't feel any intense jealousy, because Jinglan lacked substance. Now, Hong began imagining what Jinglan was doing at this moment.

He was probably helping out at the restaurant. If Hong wanted to go back to that restaurant, he wouldn't be able to find his way. At the time, when he left that place, he'd been confused. He hadn't paid attention to the route; even if he had, he'd only seen it. Probably he couldn't remember it. Those small paths were too intricate, filled with twists and turns. Now he couldn't figure out how he had emerged just by relying on instinct. That was a little like "clutching at straws in desperation"; he had seen a path and had known right away that it was the way home. On the way, there must have been numerous forks in the road that he had just walked by. He hadn't stopped to choose. He had just walked along as if he knew the road by heart.

Now, remembering, he couldn't get a handle on it. Jinglan now was working in that col, whose location was a mystery. How could all this be? That strange rocky mountain that was half submerged in seawater, where so many spooky people were living—there was actually a restaurant to serve these spooks! Wasn't it peculiar for a person like Jinglan to live in such a place? In the past, when he'd lived in the city, Hong had noticed Jinglan's mercurial nature. He'd seen that he couldn't be pigeonholed. The neighbor woman finally left. Yishu came into the back room and sat down on the davenport with Hong.

"She came over to sound us out. I had to go through the motions. Just think, something is going to happen sooner or later anyway; even if you resist with all your might, it's useless. In any case, we don't have many belongings anymore. It seems as if something is constantly invading our home. I think, if worse comes to worst, we can always take Juju and live by the sea, just like those others."

"You've been leaning toward that kind of life all along."

"Don't twist my words, okay? I'm terrified out of my wits by it. And especially after listening to Jinglan, I became completely reconciled to the status quo. But to think of such a thing as settling down in the crevices of the rocks by the sea is like taking a tranquilizer. It calms my nerves. That woman couldn't break me down. There's something I haven't told you: Jinglan came to say good-bye. We won't see him again. He went away on the boat. Actually there wasn't any need for him to say good-bye to me. When he isn't around, I don't even remember what he looks like. He said I should hide the fact of his leaving from you, because it would hurt you. Do you really care about him?"

"I don't know. Sometimes, I can't recall him either. Why is it that we have roughly the same impression of him? He's become too deeply wrapped up in our lives. Even if he doesn't show up again, it isn't any different."

Yishu fell silent. She turned around slowly and went into the kitchen to attend to Juju's breakfast. Then she took her to school, because recently a wild little kid was always waiting next to the road to tease Juju. Even her book bag had been torn.

One day, after hoeing the garden and watering the vegetables, Hong went into the house and discovered a lot of neighbors sitting in the hall. They were all holding tobacco pouches and blowing clouds of smoke—so much that Hong couldn't keep his eyes open.

Yishu was shuttling among them serving tea. She appeared very live-ly. As soon as she saw Hong, she asked him to buy some wine for the guests. Hong silently went to the store and bought two bottles of wine.

When he came back, all the neighbors ignored him. This was fine with Hong. In the past few years, they'd never paid any attention to him anyhow. He stood in the center of the room, stupefied for a while, and then went into the bedroom. Yishu was pouring wine for these people. When Juju stretched out her hand and grabbed some peanuts from the table, Yishu slapped her. She shrank unhappily back under the table. From the bedroom, Hong heard the village head spouting off. His voice was so loud that it was impossible not to hear it. First, the village head talked of the friction between Hong's fami-ly and the villagers. This had eroded the village harmony. Next, he said that, on the other hand, this sort of rancor was also a good thing, because it enhanced mutual understanding and clarified interrela-tionships. What the village head said wasn't at all like what the neigh-bor woman had said about coming by to "smooth things over." Hong thought that what he said was really insidious, concealing brutal intentions: exactly how would he "clarify" their interrelationships?

He continually accused Hong and his family, as though they were such evil scum that they couldn't be pardoned. Yet, he said, the villagers were kind and charitable people who—under genuinely unbearable conditions—had still put up with them, no matter how much the Hong family had hurt village interests. How could the vil-lage take this position? At this point, the village head employed a spine-chilling proverb to describe what everyone was thinking, "You have to lure the wolf with the baby."

Hong's heart was beating fast. The changes in his home over the last two days were dizzying. He couldn't understand how their fami-ly could have suddenly become the target of the crowd again. Did they really need to consider moving into the crevices of those rocks by the sea? Along with that thought, he saw the little old face of the girl by the sea superimposed on Juju's face. He also heard Yishu deliberately put on an innocent act and ask the village head, if this state of affairs continued, what would happen to their family? Could he give her a few details? This infuriated the village head. He said she'd "gone crazy."

Pounding the table, the bystanders also denounced her every

which way. Hong imagined that right now Yishu was absolutely on her own, so he went into the room and stood next to her, intending to boost her courage. He didn't expect that Yishu would stare at him unhappily—as if to stare him back into the bedroom. As soon as Hong came out, those people had all grown quiet. One by one, they lit their pipes and smoked. Not one person glanced at him. The village head, sitting off to one side, turned his back on him.

"Who told you to come out?" Yishu said in a small, furious voice, her face reddening. "This doesn't concern you. Why do you have to butt into other people's business? Look, no one is interested in you. You've ruined my plan."

Hunh. So Yishu hadn't needed his protection at all. Astounded that he'd been so far off base, Hong vowed not to get involved in her business again. Dragging cobbler's equipment over to a corner of the hall, he started plaiting straw sandals. He was doing this deliberately to make them uncomfortable. He noticed that these people were all gathered at the table, talking in low voices. Each one held a pipe above his head, pointing it backwards. What a ridiculous posture! Yishu was with them. It appeared that she'd become one of them. For the first time, Hong realized vaguely that Yishu's innermost being had become unfathomable. Hong could hear everything they said. It was the same old story—nothing new. They just kept repeating the same accusations, censure, and threats, with great hatred, their fists balled up tightly, swaying back and forth with their pipes raised up, as if they wanted to beat people up. As for Yishu, she kept asking nit-picking questions that enraged these guys. After polishing off the two bottles of wine, they finally stood up lazily and took off.

When the village head walked into the courtyard, the alcohol suddenly took effect: he grabbed a hen, twisted her neck until it broke, and threw it into the air. Feathers flew everywhere. The hen—its neck broken—fell to the ground and ran around desperately. The others all laughed their heads off and kicked the bamboo coop into pieces. Picking up a shoulder pole, Hong was going to chase them, but Yishu dragged him back.

"Haven't you changed a little too fast?" Hong sneered.

"I wish I could chop these guys into minced meat!" Yishu stamped her feet fiercely.

It took Hong the whole afternoon to repair the chicken coop. Yishu was a little distracted—from time to time running over to where the bamboo fence had been destroyed by the fire. She forgot to cook dinner. Hong asked her what she was looking at. She said he knew exactly what, so why bother asking? Hong guessed that she must be waiting for Jinglan, and he felt a little jealous. But he was wrong again.

At dusk, Yishu saw the person she'd been waiting for—the midget who lived at the end of the village. The midget stood and talked with her for a long time. Hong noticed that she bent down to listen intently, and patted the midget's head. Then she ran home and got a package of top grade tobacco to give to him. Even when the midget had walked a long way away, she still stood there deep in thought.

"For the moment, the village head and the others won't do any-thing to us. Just now, that midget gave me that information. Still, aren't we just waiting for disaster—always waiting around like this? I think we should do something. Just now I was thinking: could we grow vegetables on the rocky mountain? Of course, this was just a flash in the pan—nothing more. Even Jinglan had to abandon that spot. Living there must be really impossible. Especially at night, when I might be scared to death. You've noticed that I often have to run out at night—and run so far, too: this is because I really can't bear the howling of the ocean storms. One night when I got up, I saw Juju standing next to the front door. When I asked her why she'd gotten up, she said it was fun to play at night. I never told you that, but it couldn't have been a good omen."

"Maybe it was," Hong said, his thoughts drifting again to the seaside. "Isn't it better for her to get used to things that will happen sooner or later? I met a little girl at the seaside . . . "

Hong thought, wasn't this just repeating what Yishu had said? Recently, this sort of thing was happening more frequently. The night before last, he'd said to Yishu, he wanted to rebuild the house like a blockhouse. Yishu had said his ideas were getting old. For a long time, the two of them had discussed what direction his thoughts would take. In the past, Hong always thought that it was he who had guided Yishu to a life connected with the sea. Now, gradually taking stock of it, he thought it had been Yishu who had guided him. In the past few days, after her entanglements with the villagers, she had completely changed. Her long-held desire to escape had begun to fade away. Hong thought that when she interacted with other people she even appeared to be intoxicated. He found this repulsive. She was now able to accurately assess these people. She had a firm handle on them, it seemed she could always manipulate these people's feelings. Hong admired this. He didn't know how she had managed to become so untroubled. Perhaps it was Jinglan's influence on her.

That day, Juju wasn't going to school. Hong was taking her to the seaside. He sat down on the same rock that he and Jinglan had sat on, and let Juju pick up shells on the beach by herself. This time, the ocean wasn't very calm; there were small waves. A battleship was just passing by. Hong sighed with emotion at this scene. Yishu hadn't accompanied him to the seaside even once. She always said, "I don't like that face-to-face torment," adding, "Listening to its sound at night is more than enough." Actually, Hong thought the sea affected her much more than it did him.

When Hong looked up, he suddenly realized that his daughter had walked farther and farther away. Her little silhouette had disappeared behind a large rock. Hong flew over there right away, shouting and running as fast as he could. Because of the wind, he couldn't run fast, and unluckily, he was also wearing dress shoes. It was terrifying. With great difficulty, he finally reached that rock, and saw Juju squatting below it organizing shells, placing them in a small basket one by one.

"Why didn't you answer me?" Hong was furious.

"I thought, oh, you'd come in any case." His daughter gave him a disdainful look, pouted, then stood up. Carrying the little basket, she walked along with Hong.

Her answer alarmed him: this plump little girl, the darling apple of his eye—how had she changed so unrecognizably? Could it be a case of "like mother, like daughter"?

After walking in silence for a while, Hong—pointing at the rock ahead of them—said to Juju, "In the col over there, there's a little girl about your age living in a strange house."

"I know. There's nothing fun over there. Shall we go back?"

"How do you know?!"

"I went there once. Auntie Caixiu took me. That mountain is filled with birds that want to eat people. They pestered me until I ran for my life."

Caixiu was the neighbor woman who had quarreled with them. And yet she had actually done this under his very eyes! Cold sweat poured down his back. He held Juju's little hand tight, as if afraid of losing her. After shouting that it hurt, Juju broke loose. She walked over to one side. Hong realized that he'd been acting strangely, and made an effort to compose himself.

"Did you go with her just because she wanted you to?" His voice was shaking a little. "She's our enemy."

"I don't have anyone to play with. She said she would take me to look at the seals. Actually, she tricked me. There aren't any seals over there. Just huge birds. And when we got there, she threatened to throw me into the cave. I cried then." Juju's train of thought seemed very clear.

As soon as Hong got home, in exasperation, he called Yishu into the kitchen for a talk.

"I've known about that for a long time," she smiled disapprovingly.

"Weren't you afraid? Would you sacrifice even your own daughter?" Hong roared in a low tone.

"Do you have a better idea? Have you thought it all through? Juju is your daughter. She was born and grew up here. She isn't like us—coming from another place to find shelter here. What do you think we should do? Yesterday, you yourself said we should let her start getting used to it here. Besides, that woman didn't want to kill her. Don't you understand? Let me tell you: we don't have any way out. You visited that mountaintop, didn't you? Good for you. How can you still be in the dark?"

Now, no matter what they argued about, Yishu was always right. Hong had thought his thinking was weak; now he felt pretty much like an infant. He noticed that it seemed he was in the midst of molting. Maybe the whole family was molting, reduced to soft, translucent protozoans—they were blending into the environment all around, as if melting into the ocean. How had those people in the crevices of the rocks gone on living? No matter how he looked at it, he felt that life could only be a dream, like algae's dreams, because that sort of dreariness couldn't last long. Hadn't Yishu said that Jinglan also left that place? Of course, it was possible that he'd gone somewhere even more dangerous. Jinglan probably was like a true protozoan.

It appeared that Hong had to let Yishu manage things at home. Now she was sitting in the hall shelling soybeans. Her expression was one of exuberant vitality. Her eyebrows were black and glossy. Hong looked in the mirror on the wall: on his face, he saw evidence of decline. All of a sudden, he had a bizarre feeling—as if his life were floating away from his body and pouring into his wife's.

When Yishu woke up in the middle of the night, she woke Hong up. She was trembling all over from terror. She was a different person from her daytime self. It was a moonless night. Hong had no sooner turned on the light than Yishu told him to turn it off. She whispered, "That makes us too big a target. It's dangerous." They sat in the dark for a long time, painfully shifting around on the bed. Then, all of a sudden, Yishu suggested that Hong take her to look at the rocky mountain by the sea. Scared out of his wits, Hong kept saying that it was pitch dark and they would surely get lost. It would be better to wait until dawn. Yishu seemed angry, and jumped out of bed without a word. Hong could only follow her outside. She walked fast, like a large fish swimming—calmly and smoothly. Hong stumbled along behind her, ashamed of his showing.

"You were so terrified at home. As soon as you left the house, you were free," Hong complained.

Dumbfounded, Yishu stopped, went over to Hong, and pulled at his arm. They were walking together, but Hong couldn't be as free as she was. It seemed it was always bumpy underfoot. He stumbled so much that he kept leaning on his wife. She was dragging him ahead. "You aren't used to walking at night," she consoled him. The difficulties underfoot tormented Hong. He had no time to pay attention to anything else. All unaware, they had reached the mountain. A cold wind howled eerily. Familiar with the area, Yishu led Hong into a cave where they finally sat down. Listening to the thunderous sound of waves, Hong realized that the answer to life's riddle had unfolded before his very eyes.

"Yishu, Yishu. Why are you always scheming like this? So many years have passed. You've got me in your grasp. I used to think I was the one who had a firm grasp on you! What a strange world it is."

Yishu grabbed Hong's hand, held it tight, and whispered to him, "How come you're being sentimental? It's silly. You've also taken hold of me. What's wrong with this? We've finally come together again. We've come to this misty black mountain for one thing. But, even with it in front of us, you can't see it. I can. I can tell you what I see. Isn't this great? Listen—a boat is coming into the harbor."

They stayed in the cave until daylight, and then walked all over the paths on the rocky mountain. They couldn't find that restaurant or those people. Hong knew that he was the only one looking; Yishu was just along for the ride. True, several birds were on the mountain, but not the strange birds Hong had encountered that night. They didn't chase them; instead, they flew off when they saw anyone. The sea was quiet, as though asleep. All of a sudden, right under his feet, he saw the path going directly to the sea, to the large rock where he and Jinglan had sat that gloomy afternoon. Now they saw Jinglan was on that rock smoking, the large suitcase resting next to his foot. Hong began hesitating a little, but Yishu dragged him firmly ahead. When they reached the rock, Jinglan turned around. It hadn't been Jinglan after all: it was an old man with a wrinkled face.

"Good morning. Are the two of you going to board the morning boat? Let's go together." He jumped up from the rock.

"No, we aren't boarding the boat," Hong said.

"Oh, too bad. Good-bye." After putting his large suitcase on his back, he waved at them and walked toward the wharf. After a few steps, he stopped, turned around, and shouted, "Don't make the mistake of missing this opportunity!"

Yishu was stunned as she watched the old man walk away. For a moment, her expression was hard to read. Only after a long time did she recover. She said, "I know you mistook him for Jinglan. You never believe me. Jinglan is for sure an insubstantial sort of person whose whereabouts are always unpredictable. Why didn't you think this through? Are there any traces of him on this mountain?"

When they got home, they saw someone sitting drowsily on the stone stool in the courtyard. Juju was sitting on the ground next to him. When that person looked up, it turned out to be the village head. His face was solemn, and he said in a low voice, "The village didn't have a good harvest this year, and the budget is tight, so the village council has arranged for a lonely old woman to stay with you. It's up to you to take care of her. She's already here—sitting in your hall."

In the hall was Old Woman Ji, who lived at the other end of the village. She was so old that she couldn't remember her age. An unidentifiable odor wafted from her body. She was half-blind. Her chicken-claw-like hands were waving in front of her eyes as if to ward off mosquitoes. Her bearing was overconfident, as if she thought she was superior to others. Hong noticed that the village head had already taken off. He and Yishu stood in the hall looking at each other in speechless despair.

"In all things, one has to think about the way out. I've already reached my conclusion." Wiggling her toothless mouth, Old Woman Ji went on, "In any case, you won't be able to put up with me. People like you must be coldhearted, but you don't have any way to get out of it, since the village council has already made this arrangement. I've taken a look around your home, and scoped things out. As I see it, the only place suitable for me is the little storeroom next to the kitchen. This is also precisely your plan. I'm not wrong, am I?"

In fact, Hong and Yishu truly hadn't thought of asking her to live in that small, dark building. That was where they put their farm implements and fertilizer buckets. To be blunt about it, they found Old Woman Ji really annoying. They saw her as a great burden. Her suggestion that she live next to the kitchen coincided exactly with their view. Yet, as soon as they realized that the old woman had seen through them and had scoped everything out, they both felt uneasy. They felt vaguely that this was no simple matter.

It took Yishu and Hong a long time to empty out the small room, set up an old bed, make it up, and also put in a stool and a small wardrobe. During this time, Old Woman Ji stayed in the hall smoking a pipe. The whole room was smoky.

"I'll just sit in the hall in the daytime, and not go into that small room until evening. You won't begrudge me this little bit of freedom, will you?" As she was talking, Old Woman Ji bent over and tapped her pipe on the ground.

At last, Hong and Yishu finished scurrying around and went back to their bedroom. They both felt that a great catastrophe was about to befall them. But Hong realized that Yishu was in a more tranquil frame of mind than he was: she was even a little curious about the old woman. As Hong saw it, Old Woman Ji was exactly like an irritant newly grown in his mind. He couldn't get comfortable, and just wanted to forget this whole thing. He would never have imagined that everything could change like this. This was bizarre. Recalling the string of recent events, Hong grew suspicious again: could this Old Woman Ji have some strange connection with the sea? Her earlier attitude of not giving them the time of day made Hong think of those serene animals that never moved at the bottom of the deep sea. Now that she intended to sit in the hall all day, Hong and

Yishu felt they had become prisoners in their own home.

Old Woman Ji didn't eat much. She was picky. She ate just a few hearts of vegetables, and then put her chopsticks down, saying that she still wasn't used to such "coarse food."

Yishu chuckled at the serious way she talked. Then without another word, Old Woman Ji shuttered her face. Hong saw that Yishu looked ashamed. As she cleared the table, she stole a look at Old Woman Ji, who continued to sit there earnestly smoking her pipe.

That night was the first time in years that Hong hadn't dreamed of the sea. No matter how worried he was, the sound of the waves had always come rapping lightly from that distant spot. But now, there were obstacles between him and the sea. He was a little dispirited when he woke up. He saw that for the first time Yishu was sleeping soundly beside him. Hong put on his shoes and walked out to the hall. Old Woman Ji was still sitting in the same place smoking her pipe. In the moonlight, smoke curled all around.

"Mama Ji, why aren't you sleeping?"

"I'm old. It doesn't make any difference if I sleep or not. I'm thinking about Juju's future."

"Hunh?"

"This child is very smart. She's sleeping in my room right now. No one has instructed her. She stuck right to me the moment I walked into your house. Her nose is sharper than a dog's. She deserves to be your daughter."

"Juju? Why?"

"Do you have to ask? It's because this little scamp has her own ideas. From the sidelines, she's seen that neither of you is reliable. That's why she threw herself into my arms. Of course, I wouldn't spoil her. I would be strict with her."

The room was dim. In the light blue smoke, Old Woman Ji's creased face—a black form in darkness—was wobbling strangely. Hong felt a twinge of anguish.

"She's already figured out that no matter how she acts, the two of you will cast her off. I'm the only one you won't abandon. She is really unimaginably bright. You weren't dreaming just now, were you? Your daughter has taken possession of your dreams. She is the heir to them. From now on, you're probably the one who will wander all over. It used to be Yishu. I ran into her lots of times."

Hong walked into the small room. Sure enough, his daughter was there. She wasn't sleeping. She was sitting in bed in the dark playing noisily with a box of shells. Even though someone was now living in the room, there was still a strong musty odor—probably because the room was windowless. Hong sat down on the bed. Still, his daughter didn't utter a word. After a while, Juju pushed him away because she wanted to go to sleep. With a sigh, Hong went back to his own room. Yishu was still sound asleep. After he nudged her awake, she said unhappily, "What's going on?" Hong told her that their daughter had already seen through them.

"Good." Yawning, she said, "No sooner did Old Woman Ji show up than everything changed a lot. The way she sat so boldly in our hall showed that she already considered this her permanent home. We're doomed to take on this burden to the very end. Really think about it: if Juju goes with Old Woman Ji, we won't have to worry about her. In the end, she'll have a better life than the little girl by the sea. Juju is a survivor. She'll be okay."

Turning over, Yishu kept saying she was sleepy. She began snoring lightly. Hong had never seen her so sleepy.

As Hong was in the vegetable garden pollinating the pumpkins, the village head arrived. Weighed down by worries, the village head stood next to him stroking his long black beard. He didn't say anything for a long time. Hong found him irritating, and so he purposely didn't say anything, either. Then without further ado, the village head sat down on a tree stump next to the vegetable plot, and began smoking. Hong cast indignant sidelong glances at him. He couldn't figure out why he had come here to watch him. Didn't he have anything better to do? After a while, Hong went to clean out the latrine. It stank to high heaven, yet the village head still sat there. Hong finished composting, ready to knock off for the day. Only then did the village head speak. He actually didn't have anything important to say; looking up at the sun, he just talked of the weather. When Hong headed toward the house, words suddenly leapt from the village head's mouth, "I hear that you think the miserable old woman is a burden?"

His manner was serious.

Hong didn't know how to answer him, so he didn't. They both paused.

"Without a harmonious family life, the old woman might get

depressed and die." The village head made an intimidating gesture.

"Then what?" Hong blurted out.

"If she dies, you'll be in trouble."

After making his threat, the village head went into the house, and sat down next to Old Woman Ji. The two of them lit up their pipes. Hong thought to himself, since he had long ago quit smoking, the villagers looked down on him. Just then the village head called Juju; Yishu walked up and told him that Juju had gone to school. The village head said that it was good to go to school. She would have a good future.

Narrowing her half-blind eyes, Old Woman Ji told the village head, "I want to do a good job of bringing this child up. I've been making plans these last few days."

When Hong heard this, he thought he'd explode from irritation. Old Woman Ji merely went on talking of her plan. As she talked on and on, she puffed smoke at Hong—almost choking him. Looking on, the village head burst out laughing. For whatever reason, Yishu felt that Hong was acting disgracefully. She pushed him hard, wanting him to leave.

"I'm not leaving!" Stiffening his neck, Hong said, "What the hell are you plotting in my home? Spit it out!"

Suddenly, Yishu became violent: she picked up a stool and hit Hong in the back with it. He fell to the floor. Before he blacked out from the pain, he heard Yishu say to the village head, "Don't pay any attention to him. He's a fool."

When he came to, the three of them were standing over him talking about him. This was even harder to take than being hurt. He bent over on the ground, unable to move. Old Woman Ji walked over, and looked at his hand for a moment. She said, "It doesn't matter. It's good for this kind of person to be hurt sometimes. You've helped him. He's never known before that he should be grateful." The village head kept saying, "It serves him right. Serves him right."

After they left, it took a lot of effort for Yishu to get Hong into bed. She rubbed some ointment on his back.

"How could you be so cruel to me?" Hong said brokenheartedly.

"Because you're going to destroy this family."

"How come?"

"Do you really not understand, or are you faking it? Just think, if Old Woman Ji hadn't come, we would have gone on dreaming.

What would we have done? Wouldn't we have ended up going to the rocks by the sea and pitching a tent there? Wasn't that our goal for years? One day, I realized that sort of place wasn't the answer for us. It's only in our dreams that we can come up with impetuous ideas."

When she said this, Yishu was calm. The sunshine coming in from the narrow window fell on her face. Hong suddenly thought that her face had become youthful again.

"Just give up. That's another way to free yourself," she said gently.

That night, Hong once more entered into the ocean. He bored his way in through a cave beneath the rocks. The edge of the cave was filled with sharp burrs. When he squeezed through, they cut his skin, and his blood colored the water around him a pale pink. He was twisting for all he was worth, and the pain was excruciating. His twisting, though, also gave him pleasure that was difficult to express in words. He was writhing in the pink water, imagining that he was a dying fish. Now, as he heard the whistle of the steamship departing from the wharf, he felt the ocean waves stirred up by the ship. Still writhing, he screamed inaudibly. He screamed and screamed. How strange, he thought, that the water wasn't choking him.

When he woke up, he heard Old Woman Ji coughing hard in the hall. It was only three o'clock—long before daylight. When Old Woman Ji finished coughing, much to his surprise he heard Juju start talking. Hopping mad, Hong was thinking of getting up when he discovered that it was hard to move his injured back. Yishu pushed him down gently, and whispered, "Shh! Don't move! I've been listening for a long time." Just then, a sound came from the two in the hall; it was obvious that they were going outside. "They're going to Old Woman Ji's home," Yishu said, exhaling slowly, as though letting go of a burden. "You have to get well."

## Epilogue

The day that Hong recovered, he went out for a walk. The sun was warm, and no one else was out. Without being conscious of it, he walked once more to the rock where he and Jinglan had sat. He sat there in a daze. Five or six boats went by. He thought and thought, but he couldn't figure out how Jinglan had suddenly appeared at such a place. Maybe Jinglan had been pursuing him his whole life. At first, it was as if he and Yishu were possessed when they rushed to the sea-side: had they been fleeing from Jinglan? And why would they have wanted to avoid him? These several decades, all along, Hong had been engrossed in pursuing the sea at night. He hadn't noticed before that their neighbors were also pursuing him. It appeared that Yishu had noticed; most recently, she was always working on bonding with them. Yishu doubtless understood the essence of the sea better than he did. In contrast, he was a little like a beached fish.

It was possible that this woman had been keeping up her relationship with Jinglan all along, just as he was keeping up his sentimental attachment to the sea. In the end, what was she all about? Hong couldn't help but think this was a question as deep as the sea—one that he would never fully understand, even if he tried hard. Perhaps she'd come to him when they were young in order to purposely exhibit her enigma in front of him. The night before, when he'd gone into the hall, Old Woman Ji wasn't sitting there. Then when he checked her room, neither she nor Juju was there. Annoyed, he'd gone out to the courtyard. There, he'd seen two figures—one large, one small—rushing off toward the seaside. The sound of their footsteps seemed to be mocking his obtuseness. "All streams lead to the ocean," Yishu whispered to him. She'd followed him outside. Standing side by side, they looked up at the sky. Suddenly, the stars turned into a shower of meteors. Half the sky was alight. "Ah!" Hong said fearfully.

The sun was brilliant today. The sky was still the sky. The sea was still disguising itself as before. Hong thought he would swim into the heart of the sea. What would it be like inside?

# SNAKE ISLAND

**Y**OU COULD SAY THAT UNCLE SAN IS THE ONLY RELATIVE I HAVE left. Whenever I think of my small, remote, depressing home village, a shiver runs down my spine. Called "Snake Island," it's situated on hilly land. When I was a child, I always wanted to learn the derivation of its name, because we didn't have any more snakes there than any other place. An older youth had told me there used to be snakes here. Sometimes several of them hung from a tree. Uncle San's family lived at the end of the village. As if their house had ostracized itself, it was located next to paddy fields, about a hundred paces from other people's homes. Back then, Uncle San was always carrying radishes to sell in a distant town. He generally set out in the morning, and didn't return until almost midnight. The poverty there was appalling. It was said that because of the poor quality of the land, the harvests were always poor. For the most part, beginning in the winter, all of the villagers ate only red potato gruel; they did that right up until the new rice was ready to harvest.

I hadn't gone home for more than thirty years. Even Father's death couldn't call me back. My mother had died earlier, and I was the only child. It was Uncle San who buried Father. At the time, he sent me a scrawled letter: the gist of it was that the funeral had been taken care of and I didn't have to go back. One line in the letter was engraved on my heart: "The sooner you forget this hopeless village, the better off you'll be." Even though Uncle San was a farmer, he'd been rather well educated. People called him "scholar." For years, I'd wondered: I'd been gone for more than thirty years. Why hadn't any of my fellow villagers (including my old father) come to see me even once? It was a long way away—that was one reason—but it certainly wasn't so far away that one couldn't make the trip. I was living just a little more than a day's journey by train. We were all part of the blood lineage of Snake Island.

The letters my father wrote me always emphasized that the villagers now lived well: no one was starving; the young people were leaving and going all over the world. He never suggested that I come back for a look; instead, he told me that one room in our house had been destroyed by mountain floods. Now our house had only one room left, so if I went back, there'd be no place for me. I'd just be able to stay with Uncle San. It was as if he was offering me an excuse for not going home, and yet that wasn't all of what he was implying. Perhaps he and Uncle San were standing their ground about something? What could it be? After Father died, no one wrote me letters about what was going on in the village. My contact was completely broken. I knew that Uncle San was still living; twenty years younger than my father, he was in good health.

Destiny likes to play tricks on people. Just as I had almost forgotten my home village, one day (I still remember it was my birthday), my boss called me into his office.

"Recently, you haven't been very enthusiastic about your work," he said, motioning to a hard chair—indicating that I should take a seat.

"I'm sorry. I wish you'd tell me if I did something wrong."

"Actually, it's no big deal. It's just that I heard someone say that you haven't gone home for thirty years. As soon as I heard that, I felt ashamed of myself. I haven't shown enough concern for my employees. No wonder you've begun to lose enthusiasm for your work. So now I've made a big decision (it wasn't easy to make this decision, because this is a busy time for the company): I'm giving you two weeks off, so that you can go home and see your father."

"My father passed away a long time ago."

"Really? You didn't even tell me such an important thing. I say you—ah, you're really too tolerant and quiet. I can imagine how much you suffered at that time. Then there's even more reason for you to go home for a visit. Go back and take care of your poor father's grave to comfort the old man. You'll go tomorrow."

Even though I didn't much want to go, one had better do as one's superior orders. And so I—an uninvited guest—went home.

But my hometown looked completely wrong. The strange thing was that no matter how I combed through my memory, no matter how I stared at the scenery, I couldn't call back that old village. As soon as I got off the bus, I thought I'd recognize the mountain road that went through our village—that twisting cobblestone road that I'd taken countless times from childhood to young adulthood. But—where was the road? Even the mountain had disappeared. In the open country stretching to the horizon was a walled community of bungalows in garish colors. There weren't even many trees near the houses. Wondering if I'd come to the wrong place, I went to ask a farmer's wife.

"Snake Island?" She squinted, responding in the village dialect that I hadn't heard in ages, "This is it."

"Where?"

"All around. Who are you looking for?"

"My third uncle."

"Oh, you're from Xu Liang's family. Aren't you already dead?"

"Me? Dead?!"

"Your grave is at one end of the village. It never crossed my mind that you would come back."

She drew closer, and pinched my back with two of her fingers, as if to make sure there was really a person underneath the clothes. She was still exclaiming, "I'm not dreaming, I'm not dreaming." Suddenly letting go of me, she darted away. Her figure flashed through the paddy field, but she didn't rush toward the bungalows: she disappeared behind them.

Taking the only road, I went into the village. The first home was an ugly two-room grass hut. I was doubtful that anyone actually lived there, so I just walked past. I stopped at the door of the third home, where I saw two little girls, roughly seven or eight years old, plaiting straw sandals. I supposed they were about the same age as my grandchildren. They both ignored me. All I could do was brazenly ask, "Is anyone home? I'm looking for someone." Finally, the one who was a little thinner looked up and said, "Go away."

My only option was to knock at the fourth home, but this door wasn't actually locked. As soon as I knocked, the wind blew the door open. I took in the furnishings at a glance. An old man was asleep on the bed in the inner room. In the gloomy interior, his long snow-white hair was striking. I was surprised at how elegant this gaffer was—actually wearing his hair long.

"Grandpa, I'm looking for Xu Sanbao."

The old man twisted around on his bed, indicating that I should approach him.

I realized he was ill. His chest was heaving. The sound of his coughing was muffled, and he was in tears.

"Looking for Sanbao?" He said huskily, "Good. In the end, someone has come looking for him. He hasn't waited all these years for nothing. Good."

"I'm from Xu Liang's family. I've just come home."

"Xu Liang's family. Good. Before long, I'm going to go over to the other side—where you guys are. You—you're looking for Sanbao? That's really difficult."

I thought this old man was already gaga. To continue here would just be a waste of time, so I left him and went on looking. I walked past several homes. I saw a middle-aged man in one of them. He was sun-drying mung beans on the ground. I didn't recognize him at all.

"Could you please tell me where Sanbao's home is?"

"You're from Xu Liang's family? Ha! It's really so!"

"Did someone tell you I'd come?"

"Naturally, naturally. Welcome. The news of your return has circulated all through the village." With some exaggeration, he sketched a big circle with his hand.

But he didn't invite me into his home. He just stood outside talking with me. I saw a woman shake her head inside: it was the same woman I had just run into in the field. I asked again where Sanbao lived. The middle-aged man looked embarrassed. He hemmed and hawed, and finally told me, "Sanbao doesn't have a home anymore. Ever since that tragedy, lots of people have been homeless. Now everyone has grown used to it. You're the only one who doesn't know. In fact, this happened years ago." As he said this, his wrinkled face showed the changes he had seen.

"So where is he?" I asked.

"You have to change your mental concept of the village. To give you a simple example, when you came to the village today, did you run into dogs? No. Do you see any dogs anywhere? Hey. You ask where he is. This question is asked only by people unfamiliar with our situation. Aside from the village, where else can he go?"

"Then, where is he now?" I asked patiently.

"You'll run into him!!" he said indignantly. Abandoning me, he went inside.

I asked at several homes. If those people weren't extremely impatient, then they gave irrelevant answers. I was exhausted from carrying my suitcase. Just then, I recalled that my grave was at the end of the village. Gritting my teeth, I walked once more toward the

other end of the village, where I put my suitcase down under an emaciated camphor tree and sat down on a rock to rest. I gazed ahead:
linked together with the paddy fields were a lot of grave mounds, but
not one of them had a tombstone. How would I know which one was
mine? Probably I wouldn't even be able to locate my father's grave.
In spite of this, I dragged myself over there. The graves were almost
all alike. It seemed there was no way to distinguish them. Some of
them were actually open, with the people's dry bones flung around
next to them. Lingering too long here, I felt the gloomy air rising
and so I left in a hurry. By this time, I'd concluded: *That farm woman
completely fabricated the story that my grave was at the end of the village.
So, is this really Snake Island? If it isn't really Snake Island, then how could
those two people just now have known who I was? I can't leave this unfinished. I have to wait in the village—wait right up until Uncle San shows
up.* I opened my bag, took out bottled water and sausages, and started eating my lunch. My thoughts were all mixed up.

Once more, I took careful stock of the village. I recalled what the
middle-aged man had said about a disaster. Truly, not one little thing
about my surroundings reminded me of my hometown. I had evidently come to a different village, yet the people in this village somehow all knew me. Had there really been a disaster here? If so, was the
history of Snake Island buried in these unkempt graves?

I intended to go back to the village and make inquiries at one
home after another. I had to get everything straight. On this trip
home, I had planned to spruce up my parents' graves. If I couldn't
finish even this task, what would I be able to tell my boss? After
catching a second wind, I approached a home whose outer wall was
golden yellow. I put my suitcase down at the door and craned my
neck to look inside. Suddenly someone clapped me on the shoulder
from behind.

"Haha! It's really you! What a strange world! Interesting, interesting. I'm one who doesn't believe in evil. What's the proverb?
Right: 'Continue undeterred by the dangers ahead.' Now you've
finally come to the right person!"

This was an old man with a gray goatee. He was another person
I definitely didn't recognize. Yet I wasn't prepared to ask him probing questions. The old man sat down on a stone stool in the courtyard, and motioned to me to sit beside him. After a while, a young
woman came out—probably his daughter or daughter-in-law. The

woman asked the old man if the guest would be eating with them. Glaring at her, the old man answered fiercely, "Do you have to ask? We'll have a good meal. Tonight, we still have something to do."

Without arguing, the woman went back inside.

I began examining this face across from me. I looked and looked, and still couldn't call up any memory of him. When the man saw me staring at him, he began laughing, revealing his yellow teeth. I didn't know what he was laughing about. Then, my neck began itching strangely. I slapped it hard, and killed two mosquitoes. In the ditch in front of the house were swarms of mosquitoes. I couldn't sit still. I took a towel out of my bag and wound it around my neck. I put my hands in my pockets. Even so, the noxious mosquitoes attacked them through the cloth of my pockets. I looked at the old man again. He was sitting there without moving. He wasn't aware of these mosquitoes at all. The woman came out again just then and gave the old man a pipe. The old man started smoking. I was bitten two more times on the face. I really couldn't stand this. All I could do was stand up impolitely and walk around. At the same time, I warned myself: under no circumstances should I ask improper questions, in order to avoid angering the old man. I didn't ask anything and he didn't say anything. It was awkward. After he finished smoking, he finally opened his mouth, "I'm telling you, only at night can you meet up with him."

"Is it Uncle San you're talking of?"

"Who else?"

"Can you take me?"

"Sure thing. I'll take you there, but then you'll be on your own. I cannot go in. I've tried all kinds of times, and each time, I've been driven out. Once, a guy was hewing in my direction with a two-pronged hoe. He hit a tree trunk. Now, that tree still bears a scar the size of the rim of a bowl. It's that camphor tree that you saw over there."

"Who are those people?"

"I think they are people like you. They have marks on their faces. When I saw you just now, I thought of that incident right away. How many people now still remember to go back to their home-towns? Only people like you."

His words made my hair stand on end. I was vaguely aware that the place he wanted to take me to was that stretch of unkempt graves.

Did Uncle San live in the midst of the unkempt graves? Why did everyone here consider me a dead man? As I was mulling this over, he clapped me on the shoulder and invited me in for dinner. He looked quite affable, and I relaxed a little.

Their son came for dinner, too. Nodding, he gloomily sat down next to me. The women came in and out carrying bowls. Besides the daughter-in-law (not, after all, a daughter), there were two middle-aged women whose positions in the family I couldn't figure out. They seemed to be relatives. The food was bubbling and abundant; it filled the large platters. There was wine, too. It was hard to imagine that in such a barren place one could eat such a sumptuous spread. Head down, the son was concentrating on eating. The two middle-aged women seemed on edge. They kept staring at me, not eating much. The old guy was shouting at me to drink some wine— this was a homemade wine that tasted rather bitter. After two cups of it, I was quite dizzy, but the old guy didn't let me off: as he kept plying me with wine, he served me some delicious wild duck. All styles of dishes were heaped up on my plate. I kept murmuring, "This is too much. It's really too much. . ." After another cup of wine, I thought the sky was spinning around. I was dazed. The old guy's voice seemed to be coming from far away as he recited a line from a poem, "When the hero leaves, he doesn't look back."

When I woke up, I discovered that I was still hunched over the table strewn with cups and dishes, but the others had all disappeared. I looked outside: it was already dark. I thought I'd better spend the night in the village. I stood up and, walking around the interior, I looked inside each room, and didn't see even one person. Just then, I noticed that my suitcase had been brought in and set on a chair. Crickets were singing incessantly in the kitchen. I thought, I shouldn't question this family's intentions and hospitality, even though they are a little odd. It seemed I should stay in their home tonight. After reaching this decision, I walked out to the courtyard. In the moonlight, there was nothing but paddy fields as far as the eye could see. All the villagers were sound asleep. In the courtyard, someone was sitting on that rock that I'd sat on during the day. I walked over: it was that old man.

"You'd better go on your own. I can't help you. Just now, the wine gave me enough enthusiasm to go over there, but I was thrown out again. I hurt both legs when I fell. Aiya! Aiya!"

He bent over and began groaning with pain.

I didn't know what to do: I didn't know if he had broken his legs. I asked where his son and daughter-in-law had gone. Did he want me to go and tell them to come back? The old guy gestured dismissively, and said, "Absolutely not." He moaned again for a while, then seemed a little calmer.

"My son is young and aggressive. He's still over there fighting with them. All of those guys are wielding hoes. We didn't take anything with us, though. We went empty-handed. Your Uncle San's weapon is a large sickle. Just seeing that sickle was enough to make me run for my life. How would I—a handful of old bones—be able to resist him? Listen, my son has come back. It really upsets me that this guy is so useless."

I heard hurried footsteps outside circling around to the back of the house.

"He's embarrassed to come in the front door. He's ashamed of himself."

"Did you say Uncle San was wielding a large sickle?"

"Yes! He's over there—where you went in the daytime. I don't think he would hurt you. Why not go and try your luck now?"

When I reached the graveyard, all was quiet. I couldn't find the camphor tree that was my landmark. I thought, *If I just stay here and don't move, Uncle San will probably find me.* I looked up: in the moonlight, the undulating grave mounds were like a herd of cattle. As I thought of the old man's description of the fighting that had just occurred, I was afraid to go any farther.

I sat at the edge of the graveyard for a long time. Nothing happened. Had that old man perhaps just been talking rubbish? I thought and thought, but it didn't seem so. I forced myself to go on waiting. It was probably almost midnight. I sat awhile on the rock, and then stood up and walked. In my eyes, the village became completely unreal. The tile roofs pitched at random heights and the mottled outer walls had seemed awfully vulgar in the daylight; now, by starlight, they revealed their incomparable timelessness. I suddenly felt, perhaps the person I was meant to find wasn't Uncle San (he'd probably been dead for a long time), but this strange old man and his son that one couldn't get close to. And even the old man's daughter-in-law and the two middle-aged women, and the crazy old guy that I'd encountered at the fourth home. And the farmwoman, the first one I'd seen, and her husband whom I'd run into later. Even the two little girls I'd bumped into at the third home. Were they from a different world? Or was I the one who was difficult for the people to understand? In the eyes of so many people, wasn't I already dead? How should people interact with a ghost? Did they tacitly believe that the only way to deal with a ghost like me was to reject him? Somewhere, far away from here, a dog began barking. It seemed that lots of dogs were barking in unison. That sound was familiar: it was the barking I remembered from childhood. So, I'd come to the wrong place. This wasn't my hometown: this village was a trap set next to my hometown. First, I had to suffer through the night, and then look for that village of mine. After coming to this decision, I walked toward the old man's home.

When I got back there, I noticed that the door was already closed. Probably everyone inside was already sound asleep. I rapped on the bedroom window. I rapped twice. But there wasn't any movement inside. "They closed the door on me," I said sorrowfully to myself. I sat down on the stone stool in the courtyard. Distressed, I rested my head against the trunk of the dead tree next to me. "How does it happen that even trees can't grow here?" I asked myself drowsily. Although my eyes were closed, I could still see the big stars in the sky. I could also hear the crazed barking of dogs in the distance. I couldn't get to sleep in this odd position. I felt terribly uncomfortable. Probably it was well after midnight when the door clanged wide open. I saw the father and son run out. After they left, the door still stood open. I slipped inside the house, fell onto the wooden sofa in the hall, and went to sleep. The wooden sofa was short. I curled up, hoping for a good sleep before the two of them came back. I was awfully tired. In a fog, I noticed that the whole room was brilliantly lit. I also noticed that the women were already in full swing in the kitchen sharpening knives and boiling water. Several times, I struggled to wake up without succeeding. But finally the women noticed me. The three of them stood next to the sofa watching me wordlessly. I sat up, but they didn't say anything. They were still watching me as they wept sorrowfully.

"Haven't they come back yet?" I asked.

"Why are you here?" The three of them said in a tone of prolonged weeping.

I supposed that for some reason they were greatly disappointed in me, and that because of this, they were being hateful toward me. Probably I shouldn't have stayed in their home. Probably just now they'd been hoping I'd gone with the old man and his son to fight in the graveyard. Now, if I hurried, I should still get there in time. Really, how could I have forgotten my responsibility in coming here? If I didn't find Uncle San and my boss asked about him, I'd have no answer. In the eyes of my superior, I'd be done for. As I stood up and walked to the door, the three women let out sighs of relief. They commented quietly, "He has a sense of responsibility, after all."

It wasn't actually very dark outside; it was probably almost dawn. I looked back at the little house: the inside really *was* illuminated by lamplight. I didn't know what the women were so busy with. When I reached the graveyard, the old man and his son were lying on the ground moaning. When the old man saw me leaning over him, he waved and said, "Over there. Go over there. You're one of them. I can't ward those guys off, and neither can my son."

"There isn't anything over there. Leave them alone. Why ask for trouble?"

At this, the old man stopped moaning and sneered, "We aren't convinced. Who can be sure that they can win every time? Open your eyes and look carefully. Isn't your uncle over there? Look: he's slipped over next to the vegetable plot. Hey: old fellow, your nephew is here! Ha! This trick is really effective: he's getting out of the way."

While the old man was talking, his son got up and walked home without a word. Just then, the old man suggested that he go with me into the graveyard, so he could show me my grave. I cheerfully agreed. Supporting him with my hand, I walked toward the undulating grave mounds. The old man said feverishly, "Since we're together, those devils are all getting out of the way." As he walked, he asked me if I saw my uncle, and I said I didn't. Disappointed, he rebuked me for not looking hard enough. The old man told me to stop in front of a grave mound that had been excavated, so I faced that large, pitch-dark hole.

"Is this my grave?"

"Yup. Everyone knows this. The one next to it is your uncle's. Your father's is behind them. Look, everyone is together in death. This is wonderful."

He sat down on the muddy ground and started smoking. It was as though all his injuries had healed. I wanted to tell him that I certainly hadn't died. I was a living person, not a ghost. But I couldn't open my mouth: what use would it be to explain? He believed only his own experience. Now he and I were walking among the graves, and nothing was happening; but before, he and his son had been knocked to the ground so they couldn't move. What could be more convincing than this? But then, why were the ghosts afraid of me?

"I live and work in the city. I certainly didn't know that I had a grave in my hometown." I was trying to engage him in conversation.

"That's because you didn't come back and look around. As soon as you came back, everything was clear." He said calmly, "Your uncle is a tenacious old guy. Each time, he has to knock me down. Did you notice the difference between our village and the outside world?"

"What difference?"

"It's like this: stand up and look around. Do you see? The quick and the dead each occupy one half. That old camphor tree is the boundary. We each have our own territory. For several decades, we've always had to struggle fiercely against each other. During the day, you also saw that not even trees could grow in this village. The harvests aren't good, either. The dead struggle for the territory with the living. Just now, we were fighting fiercely. As soon as you got here, they all turned meek. They aren't used to your scent yet. If you stay here long enough, they'll get used to it. It's really difficult. This time, you didn't come back until we had sent you numerous telegrams."

"You sent me telegrams?"

"Didn't you know that? Your boss received all of them. He's my younger son."

He began laughing hollowly. The village was floating before my eyes. Concealed in these farmhouses were so many secrets. They converged in an ocean of nothingness, and sailed toward me like boats, as though to crush me. Probably nothing could ever really be forgotten. Nothing. I thought of my bespectacled boss: he did resemble the old man's gloomy older son. I was a son of this "Snake Island." My hometown, after all, hadn't forgotten me. After all, I'd lived all along in its primordial memories. Who was this old man before my eyes? In such a large village, he was the only one who had welcomed me, but I hadn't even asked his name. As I sat next to my grave, I pondered these things. In this strange night without end, I lost my grip on myself. But who the hell knew what tomorrow would bring? Thinking these thoughts, I didn't have any more misgivings. The night wind carried the sound of the old man's son shouting through his tears: "Papa. . ." His voice was hoarse and indignant. I couldn't see the old man's expression, but I knew he was indifferent.

"Add it up. How many years have you been away from home?"

"Thirty-one years. I never thought I'd come back. It's really quiet in this graveyard!"

"They've all gone into hiding, probably because they aren't used to you. Just now, it was as lively as a marketplace. I come here every night to while away the time. It's commonplace for me to scrap with them. Anyhow, the old don't sleep much. No fooling: beginning this year, I haven't slept yet. Look, your uncle is coming again. He looks humiliated. Generally, they blow hot and cold when they see strangers, but you're certainly not an outsider. You're one of them. This is a little strange. Hey, where are you going? Don't run around aimlessly!"

I was running in circles among the grave mounds. I wanted to shake off the old man, and go and see Uncle San. I thought to myself, it was the old man blocking my field of vision that kept me from seeing Uncle San. I ran without stopping, but in fact there wasn't anything going on in this graveyard. A thin mist was in the air. Probably some of the graves were newly excavated, for I could smell the mud. At this moment, the graveyard didn't give me an eerie feeling at all. Rather, it made me feel at home. What's more, no matter where I looked, I couldn't see any ghosts. The old man stood there all alone. It seemed he was listening attentively to some sound. I ran in a large circle and returned to his side. All at once, I figured something out. I said to him brusquely, "You're my uncle, aren't you?"

"This doesn't make much difference to you now, does it?"

I thought about it, then answered, "That's right."

The night was endless. As I smelled the fresh earth, a profound weariness spread from my bones all through my body. When we were young, we had thrown ourselves into fleeing from this place. We'd run far away—into the midst of strangers. Simultaneously, here at this place—my hometown as tenuous and wispy as smoke—a process that couldn't be reversed was taking place. My hometown that had experienced such misfortune had long ago changed beyond recognition. Even more likely, none of its former appearance had ever existed, and what did exist were merely illusions transmuted by the River Lethe. In the grip of illusions, naturally I couldn't recognize Uncle San. To be blunt about it, who could recognize those people and events that he had downright forgotten? As I was mulling this over, I saw from Uncle San's profile that he was sort of in a trance: he was beginning to wobble.

That night, in Uncle San's small, narrow bedroom, while enduring the mosquitoes' attacks, he and I began a rambling talk. Outside, it was dark. Uncle San's son was snarling angrily in the courtyard. I don't remember exactly what we talked about. It was that kind of heart-to-heart exchange, yet most of what we said was rather incoherent. Even though we confided in each other for a long time, Uncle San's former appearance wasn't restored at all. Slowly, the stubborn feeling I had of wanting to match my recollections with the present grew hazy. This old man before me had become a mottled portrait, a call from the ancient past difficult to discern. . . .

# NIGHT IN THE MOUNTAIN VILLAGE

OUR HOME IS IN LAKE DISTRICT, WHICH WAS ONCE COVERED BY A lake. Later, people stopped up the lake with dikes. All around, paddy fields stretch to the horizon. The land is fertile, and the rice and rape grow well. We should have had an affluent, peaceful life. Unfortunately, the enclosures built of earth were always giving way. Whenever this happened, our homestead was swallowed up by flood-water in an instant. As I recall, this terrifying thing occurred every two or three years. Generally, the cresting lasted more than ten days, and Mama grew agitated. She made pancakes from morning to night, the salty sweat dripping from her forehead onto those pancakes.

Finally, when all the flour had been made into pancakes, Mama put them into bamboo baskets, shouldered the load, and told my four sisters and me to each pack a suitcase and follow her out. We walked along the dangerous, high embankment. The sun beat down on our heads like a ring of fire, and the vapor from the boundless lake waters braised our heads until we were dizzy. Carrying a roll of cotton wadding, I followed Mama. Behind me were my four unkempt sisters. As I walked, I hallucinated. I felt the bank begin swaying under my feet, and so I screamed, "*Help!*" The people struggling on the embankment were confused for a moment, but they quickly calmed down and shouted obscenities at me. I blushed and tears ran down my face. When Mama saw this, she didn't stop and console me, but just pressed me to walk faster. Usually, we had to walk a whole day before getting out of the flood water and coming to the mountain called "Seven Monkey Immortals." With the pancakes for suste-nance, our whole family had to stay on the mountain for about a week. It was like this every time. When we came to the last of the pancakes, they'd gone completely bad.

Life inside the cave was unbearable. Each day, we had to go out and dig up weeds for food and collect firewood. Several hundred people lived in this cave. As soon as it was light, we spread out over the mountain like monkeys. When we'd dug up all the edible weeds, we picked leaves. When we'd collected all the dry firewood, we cut down small trees. Every once in a while, we went to the summit to gaze out on the cresting floodwaters. In these dizzying days, I encountered some mountain people. These scary-looking people lived in a col of the mountain. Sometimes they came up the mountain to cut firewood. From their point of view, we plains people were invaders, so when they saw us, they always looked angry. It's very difficult to describe the appearance of the mountain folk. They're a little like the savages you read about in legends. But they had unusually keen vision: it seemed they could look right through you. In general, they refused to be distracted. After expertly chopping the firewood, they tied it up beautifully with rattan into two bundles, and then sat down for a smoke. It was when they were smoking that I got up my nerve to edge closer to them. Altogether, there were six of those longhaired, long-bearded men sitting in a row on the ground.

"Hullo," I said.

As if they'd heard a signal, they turned toward me in unison. Anger quickly appeared on their faces, and their mustaches quivered.

"I, I want to ask directions. . . ." I explained, withdrawing.

No one answered me. Their eyelids all drooped. It seemed they wanted to obliterate me from their minds. I heard one of the old ones say, "The water will begin receding tonight." As I walked away, I looked back and saw that they were still sitting there smoking. Soon, I saw people from Lake District—from my hometown. They said I was really gutsy. They'd seen the scene just now while they were hidden in a clump of trees. They'd all thought that I'd purposely tried to get a rise out of the mountain men, and that I was a goner for sure, because a few days ago, someone had died and been thrown into a heap of leaves, his head severed from his body. Later on, Mama came up, too. When she heard what the villagers had to say, she began beating me with a cane. I couldn't stand it, and yelled, "Mama, why not just let me die at the hands of the mountain men? Let me die at the hands of the mountain men!"

As she beat me, Mama said, "No way! No way!"

Later, I saw a chance to escape.

Strolling on the mountain, I was thinking resentfully about what had just happened. I thought, *Violence can't get rid of my curiosity; it can just nurture it*. After a few days here, I already knew where the mountain people's village was. Tomorrow, while cutting firewood, I'd go there. From the summit where I was now standing, I saw that everything was a boundless expanse of floodwaters. I couldn't even see the long embankment we had walked along. Floating on the water were some dark specks. I didn't know if they were animals or furniture. They could also have been trees or corpses. Even though Mama had spared no effort to deceive me, I still knew that we were running out of pancakes. Yesterday, when my little sister was crying for another one, Mama slapped her face. If the water didn't recede, what other wonderful way did she have to get us through this difficulty? This mountain was the only refuge for miles around.

It was said there was a faraway city, where people came and went, and which didn't flood, either, but to get to that place, we'd have to have a boat and float on the water for seven days and seven nights before we'd be able to glimpse the high-rises of the city. Those buildings were as high as the mountain. For a seventeen-year-old boy to think of going there was nothing more than a daydream. I don't know why I thought that the mountain people had gone to that place; maybe I'd seen it in their eyes.

When I went back to the cave, Mama had already lit a small fire and was simmering some beans. My eyes brightened, and my stomach began growling with hunger. My oldest little sister told me they'd gleaned the beans from the mountain people's land. They'd already finished harvesting, but they were slipshod about it, and they were also all nearsighted. And so they hadn't picked them clean, thus giving us an unexpected bounty.

"How do you know they're nearsighted?" I asked.

"Everyone says so. Otherwise, why would they live in this mountain col generation after generation? It's just because they can't see well. They really don't know of Lake District, nor do they know of the city. Everything is a blur to them. They even think this mountain is the only place in the world!"

"You've looked into them really thoroughly," I sneered.

With beans to eat, everyone was in high spirits. All of us sat around the fire. We even ate the pods. Mama told us confidently that she'd also seen some wild vegetables near that place. As soon as it was light the next morning, we'd all go and dig them up.

It was cold in the cave at night. Our worn-out cotton wadding was placed on top of the piled-up twigs and grasses. Everyone slept together. I heard Mama sigh in the dark. Worried by the sound of her voice, I sat up.

"Are you thinking of breaking away from this family?" Mama asked me.

"I want to have a look around and find a way out. Anything wrong with that?"

My voice was filled with complaints and disgust. I knew that my sisters weren't asleep. They were all listening intently. To avoid arguments, I went outside.

The mountain wind was blowing so hard that I got goose pimples. The wind held the smell of lake water. I hadn't walked far when I ran into people from my hometown. They couldn't sleep, either, and had come out for a walk. We'd grown up in the Lake District that stretched to the horizon, and we all had good eyesight. As long as there was hazy moonlight, we could easily distinguish the paths. Now for example, I saw a girl about my age standing in front of me. She was eating something. I couldn't be sure if she was a mountain person or someone from our village, so I walked up closer. When I'd almost reached her, she began tittering and turned to look at me. Actually, she was a lot older than I. Her face was pockmarked.

"How about some melon seeds?" She squeezed toward me with her hands full of them.

"No! No!" I dodged away.

Melon seeds were what girls ate. I didn't. Now I knew she was a mountain person, but she was different from the mountain men I'd seen. She drew her hand back, and snorted arrogantly.

"Coward! Your ma is too strict with you. I've been to your Lake District. It's really a barren land. In a place like that, probably no one loses any sleep."

"It's this wasteland of a mountain that's a barren land!" I flung her words back at her. "Over there, all we have to do is plant seeds and food will grow. We have plenty of food and clothing."

"Let's introduce ourselves. My name is Little Rose."

Looking at her rough, pockmarked face, I could hardly keep from laughing at this name, but I contained myself.

"My name is Long Water."

"That name is really drab. I noticed you a long time ago. You're my Prince Charming. It's a pity you don't have a good name. Let me choose one for you. From now on, I'll call you Black Bear. How's that? I bet you'll grow up to fit that name."

"Whatever," I said. In fact, I was really pissed at being called this. And I couldn't call her "Little Rose." Privately, I called her "Pocky."

Pointing to a turnoff, she said, "Let's take this path. Your mother is looking for you now."

"How do you know I wanna go with you?"

She pushed me hard from behind—pushed me onto the turnoff, and then said, "Because—because I'm the only one in your heart."

I was really pissed off now: she had actually projected her desire onto me, but said it was my desire. Although this is what I was thinking to myself, I couldn't find any reason to brush her off. It seemed as if my feet weren't my own but were being led ahead by her. As we walked into the jungle, the light dimmed. It took a strenuous effort on my part to distinguish the path. I asked Pocky how she could see the path. She said she didn't actually see it: she knew this mountain as well as she knew her own body. She went on to say that, in fact, we Lake District people didn't train our vision. We flattered ourselves in thinking we could see things; in fact, it was merely a false impression. As she talked, she walked faster, but I stumbled and fell behind. If she'd abandoned me then, I'd have been a little concerned, because lots of wild animals roamed this mountain.

We walked quite a ways on the mountainous path, and kept ascending, but when we reached level ground, I realized that we'd actually come down the mountain. This level space was the village's threshing ground. Pocky wanted me to go to her home. I asked if that would cause trouble, and she said as long as I said I was her fiancé, there'd be no trouble. She also said that it was so dark outside that there was no way I could go back: if I entered the mountain, I might run into wild boars, so I'd better just stay at her home.

"How could you turn back at this stage?" she said in an overbearing tone, her breath gushing against my face.

This was a medium-sized village. All the houses were low: if you stretched your hand out, you'd touch the eaves. The whole village was silent now. Not even the dogs were barking. Only the pigs in their pens were snorting.

While I was still standing between the houses and looking around, a low door suddenly opened, and a hand pulled me in. Before I knew what was happening, I tumbled onto a bed.

"This is my mama. Black Bear, you mustn't make her angry," Pocky said in the dark. "Mama, what do you think of my fiancé?"

"He's too skinny," the old woman said without a trace of politeness. She was sitting to my right. "And where are you going to put him? There's only one bed in this house; it can't hold three people. If I had anything to say about it, he'd drown in the floodwater, too."

Her last words scared the shit out of me. I almost started running away. I heard the old woman groping for firewood; it seemed she'd also knocked something off the windowsill. She was swearing under her breath.

"Rosy, oh Rosy, couldn't you give me a break? How much are you going to mess up our lives?"

"Mama, how could I hold back when Prince Charming was right in front of me?"

Pocky's voice had turned into that of a spoiled child. I couldn't help feeling jealous when I recalled my own mama. I also felt a little puzzled: Pocky actually didn't like me at all. Why did she have to talk like this to her mama? It appeared that these mountain people were all really strange; they didn't seem at all like my fellow villagers. Just then, I heard a door creak near the bed: mother and daughter had quietly gone out and left me alone in the room. In their pen, the pigs were squealing as if being butchered. Maybe a thief had come to steal them.

I sat there alone for a while, then tried to go outside and take a look. I'd just reached the passageway when mother and daughter both shouted at me to stop, and asked me, "Where are you going?" They also blamed me for not doing a good job of guarding their house. "What if a thief had slipped in?" I said I'd been sitting in the dark room and couldn't see anything. Even if there'd been a thief, I couldn't have done anything about it. At this, they said in unison that I "had no conscience." As they were talking, a tall man appeared behind them. He was holding a lighter. After striking it several times, it finally caught, and I saw a large mustache. He was stuffing his pipe into his mustache.

"This boy complains that he can't see anything," Pocky said to the man.

"People from over there are all like this," the man stated conclusively as he smoked his pipe.

I wanted to engage Big Mustache in small talk, but before I'd opened my mouth, Pocky dragged me over to one side, and admonished me under no circumstances to talk nonsense. She also said that her mama had just now agreed that she could take me around to get acquainted with the village.

"That man killed an old guy from Lake District." Pocky told me this only after we'd turned out of the passageway.

"Some people say that the old guy was his father. I don't put much stock in this kind of thing. You, for example: it's impossible for you to become one of us. You grumble that our house is too dark."

"If that's so, why did you still say I was your fiancé?" I interrupted.

"You've been looking down on me after all!" She raised her voice sharply, "If you're so dissatisfied, you do have feet on your body: you can just leave! But you won't go. You're afraid of the wild boars in the forest. No. It isn't just this, either. You still intend to thoroughly check us out, so you can go back and brag. You flunky! I'll root the evil out of you."

Pocky said she'd take me to an old guy's home. He was the village head. He usually didn't sleep at night. Whenever villagers felt depressed, they sought him out. Everyone called him "Uncle Yuan."

We got there in no time. Uncle Yuan's house was slightly higher than the others, the windows slightly larger, but—like the others—there was no light in the house. It was so dark outside that if you put your hand out you couldn't see your fingers. After I went in, I heard lots of voices discussing something. When I walked over to them, they stopped talking. I felt people staring at me.

A youthful voice told us to go upstairs. Pocky said it was Uncle Yuan. Uncle Yuan pushed me onto a very narrow staircase, and the three of us filed upstairs, to a very low loft. I had to bend to keep my head from bumping into the ceiling. Some chickens were being raised in this loft and let out squeals of surprise. I guessed they were shut up in a basket. Uncle Yuan pulled me down to sit on a mat. Pocky sat in another corner. I got the impression that Uncle Yuan was a young guy. I didn't know why he was thought of as an old geezer.

After sitting there a while, I heard sobbing downstairs. At first it was one person, and then it was a chorus. The sobbing was larded with the sound of sniveling. It seemed these people wanted to unburden themselves of an untold number of sorrows. Neither Pocky nor Uncle Yuan said anything. They probably were concentrating on listening. As I continued listening, the sound of sobbing stayed the same. It remained grief-stricken and hopeless, but lacked any explosiveness. All along, it was oppressive. Had Uncle Yuan sent me upstairs so that the people below could cry their hearts out? It hadn't occurred to me that these mountain people were so emotional. This probably had something to do with their nearsightedness. My impression of these people was much different from that I'd had of the other people in the daytime.

After sitting there for a long time I felt bored, and so I started imagining Pocky's worries. I thought, *This ugly girl brought me here to impress me with something novel. The reason she's being so quiet now must be that she was wondering about me, waiting for my questions. If I really ask questions, she can show off with her condescending attitude and lecture me.*

Just then, a commotion downstairs interrupted my thoughts. It was as if those people were fighting with clubs. One person yelling "Save me" was about to run up to the loft. When Uncle Yuan heard this, he shouted something I didn't understand at the head of the stairs; the guy who was halfway up the stairs went back down. I figured they'd leave then. It didn't occur to me that they'd stop fighting and once more sob in unison. This time, it was even more grief-stricken and hopeless. They were also stamping their feet, as if each one was just asking to die sooner. Their voices made the caged chickens jump constantly. My nerves were on edge. I finally asked some questions, because if I went on keeping quiet, I knew I'd start crying. I asked Uncle Yuan why the people downstairs were sobbing. He said, "Nights on the mountain are filled with intense emotions. They're summoning the souls of the dead. This is the most active time deep down in the rock formations."

"Can you people see those things?"

"That's a snap for us."

I wanted to ask more, but from her corner Pocky rebuked me unhappily, and said to Uncle Yuan, "Ignore him." Uncle Yuan was quiet for a while, and then crawled over to the chicken basket. When he turned around, he gave me two eggs, and told me to crack them open and drink the insides. I did as he said. The eggs tasted great. It had been a long time since I'd eaten anything so good.

Just then, another guy charged upstairs. Uncle Yuan pushed me over there, and told me to ward him off. I stood holding onto the railing tightly with both hands. In a moment, I felt that it wasn't just one person charging up the stairs, but a powerful army. It was as though my legs had been broken. I started falling down the stairs involuntarily, but not all the way down: I was blocked crosswise on the stairs. Downstairs, it grew silent all of a sudden. It took a lot of effort before I could extricate myself and shout for Uncle Yuan. I shouted and shouted, but no one answered. Pricking up my ears, I listened intently: I couldn't even hear the chickens clucking. Holding onto the railing, I gingerly made my way down. When I got to the room downstairs, I groped my way along the wall until I came to the benches where the keening people had just been sitting.

The front door was wide open. There was a little light outside, but you still couldn't see anything well. I didn't know if Uncle Yuan and Pocky were still upstairs or not. I guessed they had probably left from the other side of the attic. I couldn't stand this deathly silence. I wanted to smash something. I felt around, touched a kimchee vat, and threw it to the floor as hard as I could, but it didn't break. On the mud floor it just made a muffled sound, and the salt water flowed everywhere. After throwing the kimchee vat, I was even more terri-fied; in desperation, I dashed outside.

I groped my way forward between the houses, sometimes touching the low eaves on both sides to keep my balance. The ground was very uneven, as though the bumps were man-made. All the doors were tightly closed; no one came out. After a while, it seemed to me that I'd walked through almost the whole village, and still hadn't run into anyone. I thought I'd go back to the village head's home, but I couldn't find it. And I didn't dare barge into these people's homes. I was afraid they'd think I was a thief. So I just stood like this on the narrow path, one hand touching a thatched rooftop on one side. I took in the night sky, as well as the monster-like mountain below it.

At this unseemly moment, I recalled Mama. If the water never receded, Mama and my four sisters would be trapped. Second Sister had gotten a stomachache from eating too many fruits and wild veg-etables yesterday: she'd rolled around on the ground from the pain.

If the water did recede, we'd have to rebuild our house—plait the wall from thin bamboo strips, paste fresh cow dung onto it, and transport straw from far away to place on the roof. If the house had collapsed, it would be even more trouble. I don't know why when I thought of these things it was as if I was thinking of someone else's problems: I was neither pissed off nor self-pitying. I thought these things were related only to that me of the past. I didn't know what this me of the present was all about. I was seventeen, and I'd never been to such a strange place before. The people here spoke the same language as I did, but it was almost impossible to understand them. Their innermost anguish also scared me and made me think that a disaster would soon befall the world. Still, I was inexplicably fascinated. I'd come here with the thought of finding a way out: now, though, I'd already flung the issue of a "way out" from my mind. After listening to the keening just now, I knew that the mountain people didn't embrace any hope for the future. Just think: would any Lake District family raise chickens in the loft?

Just as I was woolgathering, a little kid tugged at my clothes. A boy.

"Black Bear, Uncle Yuan wants you to go home with me to help my grandpa take a bath." He said loud and clear, "But don't lean on our roof with your hands. The house could collapse. You're too tall for your own good."

The little kid said his name was "Mother Hen." His family lived close to the main road. He walked fast, leaping along, leaving me in the dust. Whenever I shouted, "Mother Hen! Mother Hen!" he turned around and said my "stalling for time" was really annoying. We finally arrived.

Bending over, I followed him into the low house. I heard him splitting firewood. Then he lit a small kerosene lamp. He said that the village head had told him he had to light a lamp as a favor to me. Holding the lamp high, he approached a bed. I saw the old guy lying on the tattered wadding. He was groaning and struggling, like an injured mantis. His grandson patiently held the lamp up high. Several times, it seemed as though he wanted to sit up, but each time he fell back on the bed with a thump, and then renewed his struggle. I said to Mother Hen, "Let me hold the lamp while you heat water for your grandpa's bath." Mother Hen sniffed at my idea. "Heat the water? You moron. We all take baths in cold water."

His grandpa slumped back again and began weeping hopelessly. Without saying a word, Mother Hen held the lamp up. I was about to go over and support the old man, but Mother Hen fiercely held me fast and said I would "scare his grandpa to death." I had to retreat and wait obediently beside the bed.

"Who's here?" the old man wheezed.

"A young man. He's come to help you take a bath," his grandson answered.

"Tell him to leave. I can take a bath by myself."

Mother Hen indicated that I should go over to the door. He and I both retreated there, and he said softly, "Grandpa has a strong sense of self-respect. We need to be rather patient."

After struggling for a while, the old man actually moved his legs down from the bed. Holding the bedposts for support, he stood up, wobbling. Mother Hen joyfully cheered his grandpa, but he didn't do anything. He just let the old man stand there pitifully. I couldn't go on watching. I asked Mother Hen where the basin was. He answered impatiently that it was outside the door. Then he continued cheering his grandpa, shouting, "One, two, three, four . . . "

Outside the door was a well. Groping in the dark, I drew two buckets of water and poured them into the basin. I shouted for Mother Hen to help me carry it into the house. He came out, rudely grumbling that I was useless: I couldn't even carry a basin of water. We put the basin of water in the middle of the room. Mother Hen undressed his grandpa. With arms like a marionette's, the old man tried to break loose from his grandson, and howled like a wolf. But when all is said and done, he was decrepit: he wasn't the least bit strong. His grandson quickly undressed him. In the faint lamplight, his body looked strange: it wasn't at all like a human body. He didn't have any muscles, and his body was creased with wrinkles. His old, dark skin adhered to his frame. If I hadn't heard him talk, I'd have been freaked out by now. Mother Hen swiftly hauled him into the basin, where he sat down. He ordered me to start giving him a bath.

The water was cold, and the old man was crying sorrowfully. When I washed his neck with a washcloth, he cussed me out bitterly. He said I was too heavy-handed; it would be better if he washed himself. I noticed that he wasn't at all bothered by the cold—maybe he'd been numb for a long time. He was terribly dirty. It was impossible to think that this one basin of water could get him completely clean. I suggested to Mother Hen, standing there holding the lamp, that we change the water. He said that wouldn't work, because "Grandpa has a strong sense of self-respect." All I could do was help the old man stand up and hurriedly dry him off. I wanted to get him dressed, but he held me off with his arms. He said I hadn't gotten him clean—I'd just tricked him. As he was talking, he sat down in the basin again, and I washed him again with that filthy water. This time, he seemed more or less satisfied. He didn't cuss me out again, nor did he cry. He sat in the water with his eyes closed. Because he'd been sitting in the cold water too long, he started sneezing. I urged him to stand up and let me help dry him off. He refused, saying the towel was filthy and it would make his washed-clean body dirty.

Just then, Mother Hen said that his grandpa was hallucinating. I waited a long time, but the old man was still stubbornly sitting in the water. It took all my strength to prop him up. He was crying sorrowfully and loudly. All of a sudden, he broke loose from me with a strength I didn't know he had and threw himself onto the pile of tattered wadding on the bed. His body was dripping wet, but he fell into the cotton wadding. I sighed with relief; Mother Hen and I emptied the dirty water from the wooden basin. When we came back inside, I suggested that we help his grandpa get dressed, but Mother Hen said coldly, "Mind your own business."

It was as if Mother Hen had changed into another person. Without paying any more attention to me, he marched over and extinguished the kerosene lamp.

Once more, I couldn't see a thing. The old man was still crying on the pile of tattered wadding. As he cried, he poured out the miseries of his life: he was so old and yet he had to endure such suffering. Over and over, he said, "Why can't I die?" I was standing bent over against the door frame, my eyes fighting to stay open. I thought to myself that it must be almost daylight.

Just then, I smelled the aroma of smoke. It was Mother Hen lighting a fire in the stove. I couldn't help respecting this little boy. He was probably only about ten years old, but he was shouldering the heavy burden of caring for his sick grandpa alone. How could he bear it? He was also composed in all of his movements. Following the smell of the smoke, I felt my way to the kitchen, and saw that Mother Hen was conquering the damp firewood with a thick blow tube. He sat on the floor, absorbed in the task. He was skillful at lighting the fire, and when the fire was blazing, he stood up and added water to a large iron pot. He was cooking something.

"You, Black Bear, you can't do anything. When the village head handed you over to me to take charge of, I knew my work wouldn't be light."

Manipulating the cooking paddle in his hand, he talked arrogantly. I was jealous of him. Such a little child—yet he held a dominant position. He could look down from on high and tell me what to do.

He told me to sit down on the floor with him, and began probing into the details of my arrival in the village. When I mentioned Pocky, he interrupted and said her name was Rosy. He went on to say that he really wasn't interested in listening to me talk of her. I shouldn't have sought her out in the beginning. If he'd known earlier that I'd looked for her, he wouldn't have agreed with Uncle Yuan's request to take me under his wing. His face looked very serious in the firelight. He even looked a little indignant. I sort of regretted mentioning Pocky.

"Her family doesn't even cook at home. At mealtime, they go to other people's homes and cheat them out of food. They also took advantage of me, and took my food by force."

I apologized to him repeatedly. He wanted me to guarantee that I wouldn't pay any attention to Pocky's family anymore. If I ran into them on the street, I had to look down and pretend I hadn't seen them. As we were talking, the food finished cooking. Mother Hen ran over and bolted the door. He said we had to eat fast; otherwise, someone would break in and steal our food. We stood beside the pot, each of us holding a large bowl and drinking this stew. There seemed to be rice bran, kidney beans, and something like taro in it. It was hot and scalded our tongues. I hadn't eaten a real meal like this for a long time.

I asked Mother Hen if his grandpa was going to eat with us. He muttered that his grandpa had a strong sense of self-respect: he didn't want other people to see what he looked like while eating. With that, he filled a bowl and took it to his grandpa's room. The fire had already gone out, and the kitchen turned dark again. It must still be the middle of the night: why were we eating breakfast? In the room over there, Mother Hen coaxed his grandpa to eat. He kept talking tenderly. It was hard to understand his attitude toward his grandpa. It seemed that I couldn't understand even this one mountain child, much less the other mountain people.

After feeding his grandpa, Mother Hen came back to the kitchen. I considered helping him wash the dishes, but I couldn't, because I couldn't see anything. I heard him sigh like an adult and say, "Grandpa—you know, he is exuviating."

"What on earth is that?"

"Molting. When he's in bed, he's always thinking about shedding his skin. Every morning, he tells me that he's a different person. In the evening, he sobs again and says he's going to shed another layer of skin. Listen: Rosy and her mama are beating on our door. Those two bad eggs don't raise any food. They're specialists in eating other people's. My parents live on the summit. Right after I was born, they gave me to Grandpa. It was lucky they did; how else could I have gotten such good training? Now you've come, and I have even more to do. I was born to a life of hard work."

His adult tone made me chuckle. I asked why it wasn't light since it was already morning. He replied that the mountain blocked the rays of light: it wouldn't be light until afternoon. After deftly putting the bowls away, he swept the kitchen. Then he sat down next to me again, and rested his head on my leg. Whispering that he was exhausted, he soon dozed off. Just then, a dark figure appeared at the kitchen door, shouting miserably:

"Ah, Mother Hen!"

It was his grandpa. The old man had actually gotten out of bed. Mother Hen was dead to the world. The old man shouted again. The sound was like a saw slicing through my nerves: it made me think he was about to die. Then I heard him fall with a thump. I pushed Mother Hen hard, but he still didn't wake up. All I could do was put him on the floor, and get up to help the old man.

The old man had collapsed at the kitchen door, but he wasn't dead. He was naked, and his chest was rising and falling heavily. I lifted his upper body, intending to put him back to bed, but he was resisting feebly. A wave of nausea came over me. Finally, I managed to carry him back to bed. When I covered him with the tattered wadding, he suddenly whispered to me, "I was a worker at an oil-press factory in Lake District." Then he was quiet again. I thought, *Perhaps he's finished molting.* After settling him in, I was wiped out and decided to fall into this bed and sleep for a while. As best I could, I lay down on the edge of the bed, but the old man detected me. He was very displeased and kept kicking me in the back. I put up with his kicks, sometimes sleeping and sometimes waking. In my dreams, I had just walked to a well when Mother Hen woke me up with his bellowing.

"This is my grandpa's bed. How can you lie in it? Oh no. My

grandpa will start crying again. When he cries, I won't be able to get anything done! You beggar from Lake District: I really shouldn't have let you stay!"

I explained that I wasn't a beggar. In Lake District, I had my mama and my family: we had ample food and clothing. If it weren't for the flood, I'd never have come to this place. As I talked, I wasn't sure of what I said. After just one day, I already felt my previous life wasn't real. I was imagining a boundless flood, and I became deeply suspicious of everything under the water. Could everything still go back to the way it was? Even if it could, could I still go on like that? I didn't know why: I was growing more and more certain that Mama and my sisters would die in that cave.

Mother Hen was still lighting into me, but the door was pushed open from the outside. It wasn't Pocky who came in, but the village head Uncle Yuan and a young person.

"Did you have your bath? Are you clean?" Uncle Yuan shouted.

At that, Mother Hen's grandpa groaned grievously in the tattered wadding.

"The old man is worried," Uncle Yuan said, bowing in his direction. "What did you say? His hand is heavy. . . . and he doesn't treat you with respect! Haha. These people from Lake District are all like this! You mustn't mind. . . . He's also struggling with you for the bed. Let him sleep in one corner. This bed is very wide! Mother Hen! Mother Hen!"

Mother Hen walked up.

"Be a good mentor to Black Bear. This poor guy can't go home anymore."

"I'll train him until he's as industrious as I am," Mother Hen said seriously.

Uncle Yuan couldn't keep from laughing and praising Mother Hen. I quietly asked the lad with Uncle Yuan why Uncle Yuan had said I "couldn't go home." The lad taunted me, "That's because your wonderful villagers headed west yesterday. They decided very quickly to abandon their homesteads."

When Uncle Yuan heard the young lad say this, he turned around and admonished me "not to lose heart." He went on: "Men can survive anywhere in the world. Does it have to be your old home village?" Then he praised me for adapting and being a quick learner.

For the moment, I couldn't make any response to this news. I just stood there dumbfounded. Maybe encouraged by the presence of so many people, Mother Hen's grandpa told Uncle Yuan about me: he said that just now I'd carried him as if I was carrying a load of firewood—carried him to the bed and thrown him down there. The rough treatment had almost broken his ribs. He was stuttering, and actually wanted Uncle Yuan to help him up so that he could demonstrate what had happened. Bending down, Uncle Yuan softly and gently urged him to be patient, because "everything is difficult in the beginning." While the two of them were talking, Mother Hen and the young person were quiet, though I felt that they were rebuking me with their stares. Their looks made me really feel guilty.

I was like a stupid clod. I didn't do anything right, and couldn't learn, either. I was just a heavy burden for all of them. My sixteen years of life at Lake District had been for naught. At the same time I was feeling guilty, I also felt rather indignant: I really just wanted to get out of there, but where would I go? It was obvious that no one in this village would have a different opinion of me. I knew that already from my experiences here. I didn't quite believe that Mama and the others would have left me and gone to the west. I was her eldest son—the family's main worker. Even though they might still survive if they moved far away without me, that wasn't the way she usually operated. I thought she must be waiting in that cave: even if all the others left, she'd still be there. But this would be dangerous. If they stayed in that cave, they might all starve to death. At this point in my thinking, I acted impulsively and slipped quietly toward the door. Mother Hen hopped to in a panic, and said loudly, "Look: he's running off!"

At that, the young person shot to the door like an arrow and stopped me. He said, "So you still don't believe me. How muddle-headed you are! See here, this is your teapot. Before she left, your mother asked me to bring it to you. I brought a message from her, too—'If you can't go on living, you should die away from home.'"

Touching the little clay teapot, I didn't understand Mother anymore. Did everyone who came to this demonic mountain go crazy? If she'd had this idea of abandoning me from the beginning, then why did she have to beat me that one time? Mother was neither muscular nor strapping, but she had hit me vigorously with the club.

The old man in bed said something again. He seemed to be criticizing me for being flighty. He also cried and said, "He always disappoints me. He didn't satisfy me even once." As soon as he cried, all three of them leaned over the bed and consoled and massaged him. The scene made me want to crawl into a hole. Mother's attitude made me realize that my sixteen years had truly been lived in vain. That must be so—even if I wasn't fully convinced. This instant was like torture, and I suddenly thought of Mother Hen's grandpa shedding his skin. I couldn't help saying, "I want to shed my skin, too! I want to shed my skin . . ."

At first, they were dumbfounded; then they began laughing in unison. Uncle Yuan stopped laughing right away, and said, "Don't dash cold water on this commendable enthusiasm." He turned around and hugged me, saying affectionately, "You need to keep your temper in check. After a while, Rosy will come to take you away. She's a beautiful young girl with lofty aspirations. If you're with her, you'll make progress day by day."

After coaxing Mother Hen's grandpa into going to sleep, they all surrounded me. They wanted me to take out the clay teapot for them to admire. They passed it around from one to the other, but they didn't give their opinion. Even Mother Hen didn't utter a word. He just brought the pot to his ear and listened. Then Uncle Yuan asked me if I'd already made up my mind to stay in the village. When I said yes, he sighed and gave the clay teapot back to me. The three of them decided to leave, and Uncle Yuan told me to wait in the house.

There was a foul smell in the house. Mother Hen's grandpa kept talking fiercely in his sleep. After feeling my way to the kitchen, I sat down. I put the clay teapot in the cupboard, and groped around in the kitchen. I discovered a large pile of grasses—used for kindling—next to the stove. It was fluffy and soft. I fell onto the grasses thinking I'd have a good sleep, but my plan quickly went by the board. The old man began shouting himself hoarse and crying. The sound was so loud that probably everyone for several miles around could hear him. Halfheartedly, I felt my way back to the side of his bed. As soon as he saw me, he stopped crying. Sniffling, he asked me why I sometimes struggled with him for the bedding and sometimes left him all alone. Did I want to trick him? Then he said something vague, and through his sobs, he repeated what he'd said. Since I couldn't hear him clearly, I took my shoes off, felt my way into the middle of the large bed, and drew close to him to listen. Then I could finally hear him: What he said was, "You have to stay with me."

Since I was lying down on this filthy bed, he seemed discontented. He complained angrily that I hogged too much of it, and that what he'd meant before wasn't that I should get into the bed, but just that I should keep an eye on him. A person who was dying, as he was, certainly didn't want someone else in bed with him. I ignored him, and lay there sleepily. Then he kicked me, propped himself up, and swatted me in the face with his withered hand. He kept stuttering, "Are you going to get down or not? Are you going to get down or not?" I didn't resist or withdraw, either, but dozed off on the bed. He was tired out from his struggle, and slumped back with a thump. He was still cussing. I slept a long time this time.

When I woke up, it was already light. I slowly swept my eyes over the room. I was filled with amazement at the crude, run-down nature of this place: the walls were exposed adobe—jet-black from the soot of the firewood, and caved in in lots of spots. The grasses on the roof were all waterlogged. In several places, the light came through. Except for this wood-plank bed, there was no furniture in the house. Behind the door were several kinds of farm implements. The so-called bedding was simply a heap of smelly garbage—pieces of dirty tattered wadding held together by some yarn. Burrowed in this pile of garbage, Mother Hen's grandpa was still sleeping, with one leg outside the covers. On that leg were several large infected sores. I jumped out of bed, because if I'd stayed there any longer, I'd have puked. As I was bending over to tie my shoelaces, Pocky came in. Only then did I remember that I hadn't locked the door before going to sleep. I asked her warily what was up. Squinting at me, she said in a contemptuous tone, "So Uncle Yuan arranged for you to stay in this sort of home."

"What's wrong with it? Don't you come here often to scrounge a meal?" I said sarcastically.

"That twerp has given me a bad name everywhere. I'll break his legs."

In a single movement, Pocky sat down on the bed and patted Mother Hen's grandpa's leg. She made quite an uproar: "Look, just look at how thin he's become—all because that evil kid kept back some of his food and starved Grandpa! He's a bloody little hoodlum!"

I was puzzled: how come none of them thought this house was dirty? Not only didn't Pocky think it was dirty, she even knelt on the bed and tidied the tattered wadding and bits of cloth. She stirred things up so much that soot covered everything. I coughed several times. After she finished putting things in order, she brought a small whisk broom from the kitchen and swatted the bed with it. She said she was "whisking the soot." With that, my best option was to escape and stand outside. She didn't think anything of the thick dust. And Mother Hen's grandpa was still asleep. Thinking back on the attitude the village head and the others had toward the old man, I was certain that all the villagers respected him. Finally, Pocky finished cleaning the house. She came outside, brushing the dust off her clothes with a colorful cloth. She said she wanted to take me to see some great fun on the summit, and urged me to get a move on; otherwise, it would soon be dark. As soon as it was dark, I—this guy from Lake District—would be blind.

She pushed me out of the small house, and as we threaded our way between the eaves, I saw some people in small groups talking about something in an alley. Their appearances all fit the stereotype of wild men. By comparison, Pocky actually was the best-looking person among these mountain people. What did Uncle Yuan look like? I couldn't remember. As soon as those people standing in the alley saw us, they retreated into their houses. They didn't forget to close their doors, either. Pocky lifted her head arrogantly and said to me, "These people are jealous of me. This began yesterday. They don't like Lake District people, but when they heard that I'd found a young guy from Lake District to be my fiancé, they were rather jealous and wished they could take your place." I didn't quite buy this. I thought she was bragging, but I didn't care. I wished she would be a little quicker about taking me to the summit. When we reached it, maybe I could figure out a lot of things. But she began dillydallying. She said she wanted to go back and say good-bye to her mama. "Good-bye" is the word she used. It was really funny. I thought she wanted to go home, but she didn't go. She stood where she was, deep in thought, so I couldn't help but urge her on. She criticized me: "What's the big hurry?" So we just walked in fits and starts. It was a long time before we finally reached the mountaintop.

Looking down from the summit, I saw this scene: the floodwater had already receded, but that long embankment we'd walked on was already gone. The Lake District houses inside the embankment had also disappeared. At a glance, I saw that the flat earth had only low-lying water reflecting light. Looking to the west, I saw a large crowd of people moving like ants. I watched excitedly, but they quickly vanished into the distant mist. On the west side, everything was divided into square paddy fields, just like what one would see in a dream.

"You can't catch up with them—it's too late," Pocky said. She'd no sooner said this than the sky darkened.

Holding my hand, Pocky ran down the mountain. I couldn't see anything in the dark, so I had to follow her. Her sweaty hand was disgusting. Gasping for breath, she said we had to run without stopping. The wild boars on the mountain attacked people frequently. When we were roughly halfway down the mountain, I heard someone talking ahead of us. I thought, *Could there still be some people in the cave who didn't leave?* I flung off her hand, and felt my way toward the voices. After a while, I smelled tobacco: it was exactly the kind the Lake District people smoked. Just ahead, in a small clearing, were three people's figures. They were arguing about something, and then it seemed they reached a consensus. I just saw one who was a little shorter raise a knife and hack ferociously at another person. Because he exerted himself so much, he himself fell onto the ground as well.

Then the skinny, taller one plunged a spear into the short one's back. Not until that person was no longer moving did he pull it out and sit down for a smoke. The skinny one seemed to be waiting for someone. After smoking for a while, he looked in all directions. Pocky said to me, "This person is waiting for you to help him." This scared me so much I wanted to run away then and there. Grabbing my hand, she led me off. At the sound we made, that person spun around and chased us. Several times, I thought he'd quickly overtake us, but each time he stopped and waited for us to run a little farther. Then he'd continue chasing us. He also flung the spear at a large tree trunk ahead of us. I was scared out of my wits.

That person chased us straight to the entrance to the village. I heard him stop and shout, "Long Water! Long Water! You beast! You killed your mama!"

He shouted time after time. The villagers all came out. Even though I couldn't see them well, I knew they could all see me. I wished so much that Pocky would hide me, but she was strutting arrogantly on ahead of me, deliberately striking up conversations with those people, as though she wanted to exhibit my wretched appearance to all of them. These people were all talking about me:

they said I'd "only fled after committing a crime." Pocky told her neighbors that I was now her bodyguard. "I picked him up because of his brutality," she said.

After showing me off, Pocky finally led me into their small house. We went in, and her mother was groaning in bed. Then she propped herself up, and—just like the last time—she went over to the windowsill to look for matches. The match she found was damp. No matter how she struck it, it didn't light. She was so angry that she threw the box of matches on the ground and stomped on it several times. Then she said, "I wanted to get a good look at this guy in the light. It seems I can't. You've brought this sort of person back, but how are we going to deal with him? He isn't a teacup that can be put on the table."

"You can just act as if he isn't here."

"Not here! Do you mean to say that he won't take up any space in this house?"

"Sure, Mama, sure. I'll make him burrow into the heap of kindling in the kitchen. Please don't piss him off. If you do, how will I have the face to look people in the eye?" Pocky was extremely agitated.

The old woman moaned and groaned and complained, and went back to bed again. It seemed she was in pain all over. Pocky quietly told me, "The older villagers are all like this. By comparison, my mother is in good health." She also said, "Your top priority right now is to hide in the pile of kindling in the kitchen. Don't let Mama hear any activity—her nerves can't take it." I asked her where the kitchen was. She said, "Right here; we have just one room—the stove is on one side." I groped my way as I followed her. Sure enough, I felt my way to the stove. I thought uneasily, since I was in the same room, how could I be inaudible? In fact, there wasn't a pile of firewood next to the stove. There was just some rubble. I recalled what Mother Hen had told me: he'd said that this mother and daughter never cooked. Day after day, they cadged food from others.

"This isn't a bad spot. You can have a good sleep in the kindling. You need to think everything through. Don't complain. People can come into this village, but no one leaves. You've come to our village. You can't leave. That guy who lit into you just now was very smart, because he stopped at the entrance to the village and didn't step in." I shifted the rubble, swept out a level spot, and sat down. Pocky seemed to have found some pity for me. She squeezed into this corner and sat down with me. Although she told others that I was her fiancé, I could see that she didn't have the slightest interest in me. It was obvious: I wasn't her type at all, so why did she want to say I was? She sat beside me, her arms hugging her knees. I thought her expression must be serious. Just then, I started feeling hungry: I was dizzy with hunger. When I told her this, she laughed and asked why I hadn't said so earlier. She got something from the stove and gave it to me. A bowl of cold rice. And a pair of chopsticks.

She whispered to me, "Take it slowly. Don't let Mama hear you." Shoveling the rice into my mouth with the chopsticks, I restrained myself with all my might to keep from making a sound. Not until I'd polished off the rice did it occur to me that Pocky had also gone without food tonight. I asked her about this quietly, and she said that was right, she hadn't had anything to eat, because she'd given her own rice to me. But it didn't matter—she wouldn't starve. Sometimes, when she was so hungry she couldn't stand it, she went to Uncle Yuan's second floor and grabbed a couple of eggs to stave off her hunger. Perhaps her mama heard our whispers, for she began fidgeting in bed and threw something like a pillow down to the ground. We stopped talking at once, and I marveled at the old woman's sense of hearing.

After I'd been sitting on the floor for a long time, my rear end was numb and sore. I began shifting restlessly. I looked at her: she was absolutely still and sitting bolt upright. In a flash, I realized how wretched I was. Plagued by this thought, I was looking for an escape hatch. Finally, I stood up and stretched a few times. Heedless of everything, I walked to the door and quietly opened it. Immediately, a storm swept through the house: that mother was pounding the bed boards for all she was worth. She shouted, "Ah! Ah! He's going to murder me! Save me!! Uncle Yuan! Uncle Yuan!!"

Pocky jumped up and held her mother in her arms. The two of them rolled around on the bed. I was panic-stricken by the extent of the old woman's strength as she struggled mightily to break free. She actually broke the bed's headboard with her kicking. The pillow and quilt flew to the floor. As I saw the terrible trouble I'd just caused, I wanted even more to sneak away. Pocky stopped me with a stern shout. She said I shouldn't even think of making a move. After several attempts, she finally brought her mother under control. The two of them lay on the bed gasping for breath.

A long time passed before the old woman finally broke her silence. She said resentfully, "Okay. Let this bad boy stay. If you weren't my daughter, I'd break your neck, just the same as I did away with that wolf cub not long ago."

Pocky got out of bed. Taking my hand, she wanted me to go with her to the pigpen to "avoid upsetting Mama."

Once outside, we turned and climbed several flights of stone steps into the pigpen. The two pigs began creating a hubbub with their snorts. Pocky asked me to sit with her on a pile of straw. Outside, the moon had already come out, its silver rays flashing. Sitting here, unexpectedly, we could see the entire village. I thought this place was wonderful, and thought to myself that I wouldn't think again of leaving. She was uncomfortable, though: she was worrying about her mama. She also said the pig shit was much too stinky. She'd never thought she would be disgraced to the point that she could stay only in this sort of place.

"Before you came, Mama and I were always very close," she said haughtily.

As I sat comfortably on the straw, admiring the beauty of the mountain village, I recalled the days in Lake District and the enigma of my family. And for the first time in a long time, I recalled my father who had drowned in the lake. Father had drowned while fishing. An eyewitness had said the boat had definitely not capsized. It was Father's impatience: he had jumped in to wrestle with the large fish he had speared. He'd jumped into the lake and hadn't come out. Afterwards, his corpse hadn't floated up. I also thought back on those loblollies that I'd seen this afternoon from the summit: that used to be my homestead. In no time, it had ceased to exist.

But now, I didn't feel at all sentimental. I was sinking into a humongous shadow, in which life was brand-new and completely incomprehensible. I thought I would certainly become an industrious mountain man. After several more years, I would have the same piercing, penetrating eyes that they had. I'd be accustomed to distinguishing everything in the dark. As I was thinking these thoughts, I also felt a spark flickering in my heart: it was the first time since I'd come to the village that I'd felt a faint sympathetic response to this homely girl beside me. I didn't know what sort of sympathy this was. I thought I'd eventually figure it out.

# SCENES INSIDE THE DILAPIDATED WALLS

"INSIDE THESE DILAPIDATED WALLS," SKETCHING A CIRCLE WITH HIS hands, he gestured, "you'll see pleasing scenery everywhere, even if your eyes are closed. For example, this wall: we don't know when it collapsed, nor do we care, but from this crack, we can discover algae. Algae."

He plastered his floppy ear against that crack, but this didn't attract the slightest attention from me, because he did it many times a day.

"Bo, bo, bo. . . .," he said, "bubbles. This marsh is a special one, soft and exceptionally springy. People can walk to and fro on top of it without sinking in. Algae grow in the watery depression over there—packed in really close together! I see that you're sneering, so it's clear that you see it, too. Our eyesight is about the same. Listen: bo, bo, bo. . . Can you ever deny that this sound of bubbles is unique? You've stood up. What are you thinking? Do you think she'll come?"

"Of course she will. The sun is growing older by the day, and my clothes are too thin. If there's a frost at night, I really don't know what it will be like. I've never experienced this before."

I turned my eyes toward the distant sun. Since we'd come here, the sun had changed into a frosty, symbolic spheroid. Looking at its surface, it was still brilliantly dazzling, but when we bathed in its light, we didn't feel the slightest warmth. All we could do was wear more clothes to conserve our body heat. At night, we couldn't expose any parts of our bodies to the air, for there was the constant danger of frostbite. To protect ourselves from the nighttime cold, we wore the gloves and face masks that we'd brought from home. I counted the days. We'd endured one summer in this way, and it was said that one could also get through the winter. Who said that? This was of no importance.

He was always excited like that, talking of all kinds of scenery. Even though I could see what he had, he talked too much. Day after day and month after month, he talked of these boring things, sometimes annoying me so that I couldn't help but suddenly ask, "Could you please talk of something else?" I asked twice. He hung his head and pretended he hadn't heard. Then he didn't say anything for a long time, and so I understood.

Now, as I saw it, those bubbles and the marsh were only scenes floating to and fro. They had conquered my heart with their bright and beautiful, fluctuating colors, but this was long before. At present, the chief problem was the cold. I was wearing all the clothes I'd brought with me, and it wasn't even winter yet.

He didn't give any thought to this problem. He'd also heard that it was possible to get through the winter, and it seemed he had no doubt about this. I was rather resentful of his reckless ignoring of this problem. Sometimes I deliberately said that my toes were frostbitten.

"And it isn't even winter yet!" he said in astonishment. With that, it was as if he immediately forgot this. I really don't know where his confidence came from.

Most of the time, I stared at the sun. Here, since the sun shone every day, you needed only to look up and you could see that dazzling ball.

At first, I came here with him because we both were harboring an interest in the dilapidated walls. We used to arrive here in the morning and go home at night. Later on, the two of us felt this was too much trouble, and so we simply stayed here at night, too. This set our minds at rest. All along, he remained the same as he'd been at first: both day and night, he pressed his floppy ear against the cracks in the wall and mumbled. Whenever I heard his voice, I saw the scenes he described. And so I chatted idly with him from time to time. My topics were always the same, and the words were dry as dust—much less interesting than his. I seldom used adjectives.

When we were bored, we talked of "her." Of all the people we knew, she was the laziest old woman. We'd known her since we were children, but we hadn't ever talked with her. In the daytime, she always slept in her room. Sometimes there was no movement in that room for more than ten hours at a time. When occasionally she went out, she didn't look anyone in the eye. It was as if she were walking along with her eyes closed. Maybe she thought it would use up too much energy to prop open her eyelids and look at people. Anyhow, that's what I thought. Once, as an experiment and also out of spite, I walked up to her. I wanted to see whether or not she would bump into me, but she turned away—still without opening her eyelids.

After we decided not to go home at night, we began talking of her. For no reason, both of us felt she would surely pass by this way. Perhaps our goal in life was just to wait for her to pass by. When the conversation turned to her, I raised a question: "Between her and the sun, which one do you think is older?" He said of course the sun was older, but I said firmly that she was the older one. And because of this, we argued again for a long time. My grounds were: the birthday of the sun could be approximately verified, but she—well, I'd already asked numerous people, and not one could confirm when her birthday was. Even the oldest grandfather among us couldn't say.

Later on, he agreed with me: "So she will surely pass through here. Also, these last few days the algae have begun to wither a little. Is winter coming? What will winter be like? Up to now, there's certainly no evident change in the marsh. And the mosses are really strange: they are always densely matted. My illusions are always stuffed full of them. When I think of this now and then, I feel like weeping."

I don't remember how I got mixed up with someone like him. Back at home, the two of us both loved to show off. In the summer he painted his whole body dark green, and moved around as soundlessly as a fish. I loved to paint my whole body black and find an inconspicuous corner where I could stand without moving. Each in his own way, we got through the endless heat. Everyone knew our strange habits, and said we were "showing off." Maybe it was just because this went on for a long time that we came to appreciate each other. More often than not, he floated up to me like a fish, and then said, "There's a kind of mosquito that is very affectionate. They've been nurtured in the fertile water of the marsh for a thousand years." And so we began to talk affectionately with each other.

Ignoring almost everything, we rushed over here. It was a terribly long day, and the distant sun didn't set for a long time. It seemed both fresh and sentimental. The sound of wheels was rolling in the clear, cloudless sky. Coming from the run-down wall in front of us was the sound of boiling water, and steam was constantly rising from it. At that time, he resolved to call them "bubbles," and I didn't have any doubt about this assertion, either. That day, in the radiance of the setting sun, he solemnly vowed that there would be a day when he would "penetrate and go through the wall" like an X-ray. In the pile of broken bricks, he repeatedly stamped his feet and waved his hands, and when he said this, he was like a human puppet.

He and I both realized that the warmth between us was diminishing by the day. Now, we seldom paid attention to each other, but rather, each of us attended to his own business. But we were both waiting for the turning point—that old woman who had never looked us in the eye. For the cold nights, we took shifts, taking turns sleeping. This had one advantage—the long night became a lot shorter. As the weather grew colder, my anxiety gradually deepened. Yet, he wasn't the least bit aware of my anxiety: he lived blindly in the sweltering marsh, and talked zealously. Because I was steeped in worry, I became over-cautious. Sometimes an eagle would sweep past in the sky, and its shadow would drop down to the wall. My heart would jump and I could scarcely keep from screaming. Every day, I said, "What if there's frost tonight? How will we deal with the question of clothing?" And there was another statement that I made every day, "The sun is growing older by the day." Perhaps because I detested its indifference.

Regardless of how much enthusiasm had bubbled up in my heart, now it too was diminishing by the day. The two of us had stayed here for only a very small reason: we hadn't looked before we leaped. We were too hasty in making straight for this spot. Now, although we said we were waiting for the old woman, any normal person could tell without any hesitation what was really going on here. In the past, he and I had always been precipitate in what we did—our minds "obsessed," as people said. For instance, coming here: at that time, I'd grown excited when he had just vaguely said he "was going to roam around in some other place," and I'd hustled along here with him. If it can be said that it was enthusiasm that made me reluctant to leave, that's too exaggerated. I've already said that my enthusiasm was diminishing by the day, because none of the objects that had induced my excitement existed any longer.

Most recently, because of staring at that radiant sphere too long, I felt my eyeballs gradually beginning to harden. For convenience, I simply made myself into a sort of plaster model. All of my movements were now stiff and slow, and for a long time I hadn't bent over or turned my neck or eyeballs. Noticing the change in me, he laughed and continued with his own recreation. He became stranger and stranger. Once, he even stuffed his head into a crack in the wall and couldn't pull it out. All he could do was shrink against the side of the wall like a bent nail. Later, I pulled him out with such sudden force that his face was covered with blood. Grinning and pointing at the traces of blood on his face, he said, "If I couldn't for the moment become an X-ray, still it's not bad to have become a balloon. When my head was stuck in there, beautiful flies were buzzing next to me, and the flies' wings were like a rainbow. Actually, it's been a long time since we've seen a real rainbow. It's always this monotonous burning sun and clear sky. It's rather disappointing. But, believe it or not, in that instant, the wings of the flies were far more dazzling than any rainbow we've ever seen. As for the tiny black mosquitoes, their singing made me weep. For someone like me, who's lived so many years, to be unable to stop putting my head into the wall—you can imagine how alluring this has to be."

One day, because I was cold and afraid, I suggested to him that we join forces in shouting. That way, perhaps our voices would reach the outside world and bring some slight change to our situation here. Not until we were about to shout did we realize that we'd forgotten how: our voices glided, but without volume there was essentially no way they could reach the outside world. As a result, we were even more afraid, even more cold. So we gave up trying. "We don't have to especially exert ourselves in the attempt," he said. "Just look at this wall. The deep, quiet, narrow paths inside it are as dense as spider webs. I've known this for many years. Another thing—We have to pretend we're waiting here for 'her,' and that gives us the reason for being held up. We still have to make all attempts, but doing nothing more than just shouting a few times can't be taken very seriously. Just to remind you, I'll ask you once more: are you still waiting for her?"

"Of course. Otherwise, what would I be doing here? Just staring at this aged, glaring thing all day long? Afterward, probably no one will pass through here again."

"I like to think of it this way: one day, some people are coming, and this wall and these broken bricks are in front of them, but they don't see them. Talking and laughing, they go on. When I think of this, there is quite a touch of conceit to it. I need to think this way."

"When we hustled over here, someone noticed."

"Exactly. That person is constantly watching our every movement, so the three of us will surely meet."

"Do you think we can get through the winter?"

"I've heard that it's not a problem. And also, there certainly isn't a distinct change of seasons here. I don't think there'll be a great change. It'll just be a little colder than when we first arrived, that's all. Judging from the angle of the sun, there's no real change. I'll tell you a secret: In that marsh of mine, the seasons change in accord with my imagination."

I suggested that we set a time for this old woman to pass by here, because "unpredictability" always is associated with the unpropitious in people's feelings. I settled on a date a month away. In a depressed state of mind, he nodded his head. He was no longer the person I remembered who had painted his whole body deep green. His beard had grown long, and his clothes were in rags. When I mentioned the pigment he'd painted himself with, he laughed, so it was perfectly clear that this no longer meant anything to him.

"Before a month has passed, you'll have forgotten your deadline." Sulking, he said, "She's too lazy. Now she'll probably never start out. For her to come here is a very big decision. I bet she won't necessarily come herself, but will send some kid. A kid would likely run really fast and would also be good at suiting his actions to the changing conditions. Nobody can predict his movements."

Although we covered our faces each night, each time we looked at each other's covered face we were terrified. All around, it was too quiet, too cold—to the point that we each hallucinated that the other was harboring murderous intentions. This would go on for ten minutes or more every night. During that time, he and I were both jumpy, and "unpredictable" scenery appeared before our eyes. That scenery was indescribable—blurry and fluctuating, as if a black rabbit were passing through the wall.

The one month was almost over. He had already clean forgotten my deadline, but I kept counting the days. Yet we were both very clear about it. So I suggested setting a new date. I wanted to make it one year.

"Okay." He simply agreed. "I guess that kid will soon be here. Some day when she wakes up, it will suddenly occur to her to send a kid here. This is very possible."

Recently, the scenery we saw had become rather dull. It was always the same tableau of a brown sandy beach extending to the distant setting sun. Sometimes the sandy beach changed into rivers, and occasionally an eagle or some geese skimmed by in the sky, casting moving shadows down on the ground. He still put his head into the wall, but he seldom mentioned words like "bubbles." Now he always complained of dizziness, because he was empty inside. So he flailed around without any firm foothold. He could fall at any time. He said, "I'm like this inside the wall, too. When I'm on those small paths like spider webs, I'm always falling. As soon as I stop, I see a person about to stick a large hypodermic needle into my back, saying that he has to take out all of my bodily fluids. When he sticks the needle in, it doesn't hurt much, but afterwards I'm terribly dizzy."

"Everything will be orderly." I responded with a gesture like a plaster model. "Look at the sun: doesn't it display more and more of an unhurried demeanor? I bet the old lady sleeps for longer and longer periods. Very likely, she can arrange everything while she's sound asleep. Isn't this the way she is? All we need to do is stick to our usual schedule, and it'll be okay. For example, your problem with dizziness: you have to get used to it. There's no other way out. Once you're used to it, the algae will once again grow all over your head, and you won't be able to keep from making the *bo, bo, bo* sound once more. My plaster-like heart will sometimes also be moved by the unhurried demeanor of that decrepit thing on the horizon. I predict that eventually we'll get used to this."

I don't remember when we started giving up the night-watch duty. Like large rocks, we hunkered at the foot of the wall—unmoving, eyes staring in the darkness, forgetting the passage of time and forgetting the pain that the cold had brought to our flesh. The whole night long, we were like this—sober and uncommunicative.

Time passed even more quickly now. We hadn't had a moment to stop and think how it had gone by. In fact, we hadn't paid any attention. He was still frequently dizzy, but he was also evidently much calmer. The topics of the kid and the old woman still appeared in our talk. We both knew what that meant. I started making up some extremely dull "stories" to tell him. I talked of a certain autumn when I had planted a large field of vegetables on a mountain slope. They grew very well. I didn't talk of this for any other reason than that I wanted to spill from my mouth such words as "autumn" and "vegetables." Such words poured life into my withered body. But after talking about this, it was over, and I didn't feel any long-lasting exhilaration. Another time, I talked of a large watery depression that had been formed by accumulated rainwater at the entrance to the house. I had moved large rocks from a distant spot and placed them in the watery depression. Were those rocks still there now? I had almost completely forgotten all the incidents of the past. I could remember only these dull, fabricated "stories." As he listened to me narrate them, his eyeballs kept moving, and from time to time he inserted some irrelevant adjectives into my sentences. He did this with great finesse, as though he were a skilled worker.

"One Sunday evening," I said at random, "there was a downpour outside. I sat at my desk and spontaneously drew a holly bush."

"Was it a torrential rain?" he asked.

I nodded my head.

"On this day three years ago, the days became shorter and shorter. Before we'd even had time to eat lunch, it was dark." I went on, "But back then, I didn't understand. Not until now did I realize that this is connected with the sun."

"This is what is called time flies like an arrow!" He sighed in an artificial tone, "In the past, everyone said I was like a dragonfly, that whenever I felt good, I was forever circling over people's heads! I was so light that even I couldn't believe it. It's as though I'm remembering, but is this an incident from the past? To tell you the truth, this is a metaphor I thought up on the spur of the moment. My life now is like a metaphor covering a metaphor, or you could say a metaphor within another metaphor. This other metaphor is concealed in an even bigger metaphor. As to my adding 'in the past' in front of it, well, that's just habit."

One day at noon, we invented a kind of recreation—running around the dilapidated wall. We ran and ran, our tattered clothing and our disheveled hair flying up. We were like two ghosts. When each of us looked at the ghost-like features of the other, we screamed and ran even faster. Later, he told me it was while we were running that he saw that kid go past. The kid was carrying a small basket. He popped his head into a hole in the wall over there, and then turned and took another small path.

"While we're running, it would be best if we didn't look at each other. It's dangerous." He went on, "If we just run without stopping, it'll be okay. When I looked at you, I felt chilled to the bone and was scared to death. I am well aware that you're a local person. I've emphasized this to myself, but it's useless. I feel that a great disaster is hanging over us. I think you have the same feeling. We mustn't look at each other while we're running."

I agreed, but I still couldn't keep from stealthily sizing him up while we were running. The desire was beyond my control. Once when I was doing this, I noticed a ruthless expression pass over his face. It was like a blood-sucking black bat in hot pursuit of me. I also felt my neck being pecked. I went numb all over, and all at once cold sweat poured out. His words made sense, but I couldn't resist this desire.

After we finished running, we stood panting at the place we had started from, both of our heads hanging down. When I looked up, I suddenly saw again the sun of many years ago. The sun wasn't becoming old; it was still calm and unhurried as usual. I told him my idea, my tone extremely dispirited.

"We're always the first to be done for. It's always this way. Haven't you figured that out yet? But if we don't leave here, we'll gradually turn into rocks—just like the ones you placed in the watery depression. This story of yours really is incomparably exquisite. After you arrived at this place, you fabricated this story, as if this were pre-destined. Your scenery isn't the same—it's another scene. It's like some shadows. But sometimes, they also overlap with my scenes. And sometimes, they peer at me from a distance. As soon as I gaze at them, I grow dizzy."

I was constantly bothered by the question: *do our voices reach the outside world?*

Finally, I shouted loudly, "Is anyone there?"

It was very quiet in the wilds. The indifferent sun besprinkled our bodies. That eternal spheroid was located in the distance. My voice rotated like a propeller never leaving its original place. After a while, it faded away.

I saw that he was going into the wall. His head was both flat and pointed, and he was extremely agile. From inside the deep and quiet small path, I heard indistinct sound waves—one wave after another, rising and falling unpredictably.

Harboring a common interest in the dilapidated wall, he and I had hurriedly hustled over here, and relied on only one old woman to keep up a wisp of a connection with the outside world. Now that connection seemed more and more tenuous and inauthentic. He and I still talked about the old woman, because she was our only thread. We grabbed one end of the thread for all we were worth, and wrapped it around our hands, but it often broke and slipped to the ground. We never figured out what was really at the other end of the thread, yet we both understood this.

# BURIAL

**M**Y SEVENTY-THREE-YEAR-OLD UNCLE LIVES NOT FAR FROM ME. To look at him—thin and tall, with a head of silver hair—he still has a lot of vitality. His eyes are spirited, but his attention wanders. Uncle doesn't like to spend time with people: when he sees me, he evades me, and generally thinks I haven't seen him. He completely gives me the slip. It doesn't matter whether he's home or out on the street, he always acts like this. I always thought it was kind of comical to see someone with white hair act this way, but I didn't want to give him away, either, and over time it no longer seemed so strange.

Surely, Uncle had not been so eccentric all his life. I remember when I was seven or eight years old, he let me sit on his shoulders to "ride the high horse!" It's unclear when he changed, and no one knows why. I'd heard Auntie say that in recent years Uncle had come up with a sort of hobby: he took small things from their home and gave them away. Who did he give them to? No one could guess. Uncle's social life was very limited before, and as he's grown older, it's become even more restricted, but this kind of thing was difficult to be sure about, because maybe he had a secret friend somewhere. Anyone who lives to be seventy-three must have some secrets.

Most of the things he took from the house didn't have any value to speak of—for example, a teacup, a table lamp, a pen, a flashlight, a history book, a pair of sheepskin shoes, and so forth. These things all had one special point in common: they had been around for a long time. Every so often, Uncle indulged this "addiction." When he took things out of the house, he always looked serious and uneasy. He wrapped the things up quickly, put them in a burlap bag, and hurried out the door. He thought no one saw him (my uncle was a little near-sighted). If anyone brought up the subject of his taking things away, he lost his temper and swore, flatly denying it. Because it wasn't any big deal, Auntie didn't feel like bothering with it. It went on like this until one day—when her grandson told her that, carrying the burlap bag, Grandpa strolled among the tombs on the mountain in the countryside—she finally began really worrying. Auntie thought, *Since he is going to the mountain of tombs, and not to a friend's home, is he possessed by evil spirits? Could it be that some ghost wants his things?* She was a somewhat superstitious woman, and she really wanted to get to the bottom of this, but she didn't dare ask Uncle. She knew his temper.

Conflict finally erupted. When I went to Auntie's home, Uncle had gone out. Through her tears, Auntie sobbed out what was going on. Two days before, Uncle had actually absent-mindedly given away his gold watch. This watch had cost more than a thousand yuan, and he hadn't had it for even two years. Auntie questioned him closely, and at first he was vague about it, but then when he couldn't dodge the issue any longer, he shouted, "It's lost!" Like a clap of thunder, these words blasted Auntie to the point of nearly fainting. Only after a long time did she recover, and then she embarked on a long day and night of grumbling. Uncle's face turned ashen, and his white hair— usually neatly combed—was now a mess. A sharp light broke up the clouds in his eyes, and he didn't say a word. Early the next morning, he went out, taking only a few changes of clothes and a little money.

"Where can he go?" Auntie asked, looking at me dull-wittedly.

Exactly. Even though I racked my brains, I couldn't think of any place he could go. Where on earth was that secret friend of his? And if there wasn't a friend, where had he gone? Auntie greatly regretted not having seen how serious this was: she should have followed Uncle earlier, and seen what on earth he was up to. It was because of her inertia that she hadn't done so. Now he'd gone out, an old guy seventy-three years old, not in very good health and without much money on him. Anything could happen if he wandered around away from here with no money to speak of. The more she thought about it, the more frightened Auntie became. She sat down and wept endlessly. Finally, as we thought it over and over, we remembered the little grandson, and thought that his words held the only clue. When the grandson came home from school, we asked him where he had seen his grandfather.

"At Six Road crossing," he said. "Our school was on an outing in that area. Grandpa seemed flustered. As soon as he saw us, he ducked into the woods and disappeared. There are only dead people and tombs in that place. What was he doing there?"

I made up my mind to go to Six Road crossing to take a look. I might be able to find out what he was doing. Even though these past several years, my uncle had drifted away from everyone for no reason at all, I always remembered sitting on his shoulders and "riding the high horse" when I was a child. Back then, since he was nimble and light in his movements, I felt safe around him. So now, even though he didn't give me the time of day, I worried about him—and not simply for Auntie's sake. Of the two of them, in the past, I had always liked Uncle better. Anyhow, as to his strange attitude of ignoring people, I thought he must have his own reasons.

On my day off, I rode the bus to Six Road crossing. The cemetery lay in the back of the woods, and hardly any path went through the dense grove of trees. It took a long time for me to work myself out of the tangle of branches and exit from the woods. When I emerged, as far as the eye could see, countless tombstones stood on the flat land—all kinds of tombs, one next to the other, silent under this overcast sky. What had I come to do? I didn't know. As I walked around in the cemetery, I found a newly dug muddy pit—but with nothing in it. In this place there was nowhere to take cover from the wind and rain. Naturally, my uncle wouldn't be able to stay here long.

I don't know why, but on the way back I had a premonition: I thought Uncle had gone back home. The cemetery, those tombstones, the newly dug muddy pit, the smell of the soil: my thoughts were leaping like a frog.

Even before I reached their home, I heard Auntie's laughter. His head down, Uncle sat in the room, and next to his feet was a large package whose wrapping was moist with fresh earth. Auntie was bending over looking at those things and chattering incessantly. Here were the things Uncle had taken away these last several years—all now unrecognizable, all ruined. Uncle seemed weary, and didn't look up.

"He lost the gold watch," Auntie said, "He threw it carelessly into this package of things, and it probably slipped out on the road. This guy—he's always careless."

Auntie looked happy. She wouldn't worry about the gold watch anymore. She thought, *Since he's brought back all the things he took away, that must mean that his peculiar hobby has become a thing of the past. Even though he lost a gold watch, still he himself has come back home and that's more important than anything.* So she was overjoyed.

Uncle's hobby had indeed become a thing of the past. He didn't take anything away again, but in fact his condition didn't allow for optimism. He was the same as before, but actually he became more and more unreasonable.

When I went to his home, he no longer greeted me. He seemed not to recognize me. Walking back and forth in front of me, he talked only with Auntie. Not only did he act like this with me, but also with his son, his daughter-in-law, and even his little grandson. One day, when I went to his home, I stood outside the door, and heard him say from inside:

"Why does that young guy keep staring at me? You said he went to the cemetery to find me, but that was just to satisfy his own despicable curiosity. That guy has been like this from childhood. I can see through him."

When I went in, Uncle looked embarrassed. He bent his head and didn't say a word. Distracted for a moment, Auntie soon regained control of herself, offered me a seat, and asked after me warmly. Just then, their son returned, a big guy, casual, and loose in his talk. He whispered to me:

"Pa says you lifted his gold watch. You're in real trouble. Haha!"

My face turned purplish with fury, and I stood up at once, intending to leave. Auntie insistently detained me.

"Don't believe what he says. Who can believe him? That old lunatic," she said.

It wasn't long before Uncle drove his son's whole family out. Auntie sobbed, while the son's wife stood at the door swearing that they would never set foot in this house again. Uncle charged out, and one of his slippers fell off. Pointing at his son's wife, he let out a torrent of abuse, and said harshly, "It's hard to guard against a thief inside the home." He was acting like an old scoundrel.

But what people couldn't figure out was that he didn't care about his property. He negligently threw his leather overcoat—the one that Auntie had bought for him—into the bathtub, and it became a complete mess. He also put the tape recorder on the floor of the lavatory—so he could listen to music, he said. Later he forgot about it, turned on the faucet, and the water dashed against it. As a result, the tape recorder was ruined. He told Auntie that in the past he had been terribly stupid to regard certain things as so important that he worried about them day after day.

When I went to his home again, he put on an act and shook hands with me, as if I were a guest he was seeing for the first time.

Auntie had grown old rapidly, the look in her eyes was empty and her memory had gotten worse and worse. The furnishings in the house were in quite a mess—all covered with dust. The dreary circumstances of her old age had already appeared. It seemed that she had resigned herself to fate. She said to me, "If I'd let him take the gold watch that time, and hadn't wrangled over it with him, things would surely be a lot better now." She said that she frequently understood things better in hindsight. She had never worked out any plan for the future. How could she win a fight with a complicated person like Uncle? Then she realized she'd made a slip of the tongue, and hastened to add that she certainly hadn't intended to fight with Uncle—she'd never thought that way before, she had just wanted to protect him.

"Did you say he dug a pit?" she asked me suddenly, her eyes flashing with a strange radiance.

Before I could answer, she said, "Just think. All along, he's buried the things he's used for years! That calls for a great deal of courage! I'd rather he were that way; at least, I can understand that. But now what's up? He dug everything up and flung it all into our home. He doesn't pay any attention to anything. He's suddenly turned against people. He keeps doing wild things. He's turned into an old oddball. How can a person live like this? Can you tell me how?"

She was beside herself with worry. She was up against a serious problem, but I had no way to comfort her. I could only keep quiet.

"Hello, young comrade!" Uncle walked over, his messy white hair standing straight up. This looked a little weird.

Recently, he always called me "young comrade." I told him I was forty years old, and he shouted in surprise, "Really? So fast? Truly, time flies like an arrow! Not long ago, you were still bare-bottomed. But I knew it would be hard for you to change your spots. You come here and you stare at this and you stare at that. Are you planning to take something?"

Auntie looked sad and miserable, wishing desperately that he would leave at once. But he didn't. Instead, he pulled up a chair, sat down facing me, and said he wanted to have a heart-to-heart talk.

"Hasn't this young fellow," he said, patting my shoulder, "been our neighbor for more than ten years? Back then, he went around bare-bottomed and got into everything, and I often beat the shit out of him . . . "

"He's your nephew," Auntie interrupted him coldly. "Don't put on an act."

"You didn't beat me. Just the opposite. You frequently let me sit on your shoulders and 'ride the high horse.' I liked you a lot." I was watching his expression scornfully.

"Bullshit! When did the two of you become just one person? In what you say, you're just alike. What do you talk about together? Haven't you come here intending to take some things away with you?" He stood up indignantly and went into the back room.

"You see, this is how he is. He makes it impossible for me to look anyone in the eye!" Auntie started crying again. As she wept, she stole a glance to see what Uncle was doing in the other room.

I said to Auntie, "Maybe Uncle is schizoid. You should ask the doctor to come and take a look. Maybe he's suffering from senile dementia. He's acting too abnormally. It worries me." But I wasn't very confident of myself. I wondered vaguely if there was something wrong with me, too. Why was it a certainty that Uncle was the one with a problem? When Auntie heard my suggestion, she stopped crying at once, and her face clouded over. She gave me a sudden look. The expression in her eyes made me start shaking all over.

"I'm leaving," I said, standing up in embarrassment.

Auntie's face was wooden. She didn't look at me.

In the bottom of her heart, she must have seen me as a complete villain! Crestfallen, I made up my mind that I would never again step into this troubled place. Exactly. I had to erase Uncle from my heart. I didn't want to play the role of the clown again. It was only now that I realized Auntie had been exaggerating her feelings all along. This kind of woman liked doing this; she found it satisfying. The two of them were really two peas in a pod.

I still ran into Uncle frequently on the street. Now he didn't evade me at all. He just charged along as if he hadn't seen me. Sometimes I thought, *Maybe he's becoming terribly nearsighted.* As for Auntie, she evaded me whenever she saw me. I knew she was nursing a hatred of me. People are always like this. You think you're doing a good deed, but you end up being hated. It would be better to play it cool from the outset—just be indifferent.

One day, I saw my uncle and his son fighting. Uncle grabbed his son by the chest. With a shove, his son pushed the old guy away. Uncle charged up again, intending to slap his son's face. His son didn't want to hurt him, so he took to his heels and ran off. Uncle chased him away, his white hair flying in the cold wind. Finally, he stood still and let loose a torrent of abuse. His fist tightly balled up, he shook it again and again—just like a hero of old—in his son's direction. The bystanders said the son had only paid a courtesy visit to maintain his relationship with his parents. But his father hadn't let him in, bellowing that a thief had come to his home. Not until Auntie opened the door did their son go inside. There, Uncle made oblique accusations all over again, picking quarrels and stirring up trouble. Unable to hold back his anger, the son said a few words in retort. Uncle picked up a club to strike his son. He didn't dream that he would end up striking Auntie who had rushed over to protect her son. At this, all three of them were crazy with anger. And the result was the scene that I had just witnessed. During the scuffle, Uncle sustained a slight injury to his face. He himself hadn't had a firm foothold, and had banged into the corner of a table. A bump on his forehead had bled a little. But Auntie, who had been hit by Uncle's club, had a lame left leg for several days.

After I made up my mind not to get involved in Uncle's family's doings, I went to the outskirts of the town to attend to something and went through the woods by chance. There, I suddenly saw Uncle walking in front of me. He must have fallen down, for his pants were completely mud-stained. His hair was disheveled, and he looked really old. He was walking into the woods, heading for the cemetery. Curious, I stole after him.

Uncle walked and stopped, walked and stopped, as if deep in thought, but also as if he hadn't made up his mind. He circled around among the tombs, and at last he reached the pit that I'd seen before.

I was watching from the edge of the woods. He was digging down, one shovelful after another, as if enlarging the pit. After he had dug for a while, he then packed the dug-up earth into a winnowing basket, and lifted it out of the pit. Backbreaking work. His shoes sank into the mud, and it seemed there were blisters on his hands, for I saw him constantly spitting into his palms. After working for a while, he was tired and climbed out of the pit. He sat on a large rock, with something weighing on his mind. Crows flew overhead, their *wa*————*wa* a strange call. My heart filled with pity, I walked over to him and placed my hands on his shoulders. He quivered a moment, then turned and looked at me, and with a condescending expression, he said:

"Ah, it's the young comrade! You never leave me alone. For sure, this place isn't far from home, but you should avoid it. If you come here, you can't go home. Eh, I misspoke. The one who can't go home is someone else. Whaddya think: How about the size of this pit? Will it pass muster? You must be thinking to yourself that I'm still acting, putting on an act for myself. I know, too, that this isn't good—that it's useless—but I can't change the way I am. Now, since you've sneaked a look, my fine drama has reached its denouement. Let's go."

All along the way, Uncle complained about Auntie. He said she hassled him so much that he ran off alone to this spot. In the past, he just stayed home doing nothing; now he had become a crow. This whole thing could be traced back to a long time ago. Not long after his son's birth, Auntie entrusted someone to buy a gold necklet to put around the child's neck. The more he looked at the gold necklet, the more offensive he found it. One day, when he took his son out to play, he hid it, and then later took it out on the sly and buried it in this pit. His wife had wept until her eyes swelled like garlic bulbs. From then on, he had often come to the cemetery to have a look, because he was afraid someone would open the pit and steal the necklet. Later, he had taken home all the things buried in the pit— all except the necklet, which he sold to a pawnshop on his way home. *If she's not to blame, who is?* Uncle surely wasn't saying this for my benefit. He was just talking to himself.

"You don't have anyone else to blame," I reminded him.

"Mind your own business! You're much too young to talk like this!" He was angry. "Why do you keep following me?"

The neighbors all said that Uncle's house was no longer like a home. Inside, it was a mess—things thrown all around, the kitchen heaped with unwashed dishes. Uncle had the most fantastic ideas. He raised chickens in the kitchen, and didn't coop them up, so their droppings were all over. Auntie became less and less enthusiastic about tidying up. Sometimes she even went out without washing her face. Her eyes were filled with a gummy substance. When she talked with people, she dug it out with her hands. She had changed completely. The two of them, though, got along quite well. It seemed they didn't quarrel much anymore.

Sometimes, I saw Uncle walking on the road out of town—preoccupied as he walked. When I greeted him, he said as usual:

"Ah, it's the young comrade!"

I thought to myself, *How long will he act out this drama before he stops? Who on earth is performing this play?*

I went to the cemetery again, and saw that Uncle's pit was already quite deep. This was to say that he'd been digging right along. He really was a hard worker. As I was going home, Uncle's son stopped me. He gestured, full of indignation:

"The old scoundrel wants my mother to be buried next to him, understand? He's already brought Mama to the point of collapse. She'll die soon! Now she can hardly recognize me, never mind her grandson. When I run into her on the street, I call her mama. She shakes her head; her face is cold and detached. What's this all about? Isn't it that old scoundrel who's brought her to this state? One time, from outside the kitchen window, I saw the old scoundrel thrash those chickens with a broom. Chicken feathers flew around everywhere! I've also gone to see that pit. He's dug it the depth of a person, and even wider. He probably wants to bury two people there. Whenever he has nothing to do, he digs the pit. He's very strong physically. He jumps up and down, and hums songs. This activity is disgusting! He's made this for everyone to see. What's the point of his working like this? What do you think?" He was staring at me, his hand grasping my arm and shaking it all the while.

"It doesn't make much sense," I had to reply.

I thought, *There are lots of pointless things in this world. Since Uncle is addicted to this, he surely has to finish what he has started. No one can interfere with him. Furthermore, who can judge which things are significant and which ones are insignificant?*

Auntie's eyesight grew worse and worse. She appeared to have cataracts, possibly brought on by her inattention to hygiene. Looking at the way she walked, one knew that her world had become hazy.

"Hello, Auntie!" I said.

"Do you still live here?" Her tone was reproachful, and I didn't know whether she recognized me.

Everyone knew about Uncle digging the pit, probably because his son had talked of it. Everyone went to the cemetery to have a look at the pit, and heaved sighs of perplexity. Before long, the pit was filled with accumulated rainwater, and someone saw Uncle jump in and stand neck-deep in the water. The weather was very cold, and he shivered uncontrollably.

"He's bathing in the cold water—this ridiculous old guy!" someone said.

Uncle was sick for a month. Auntie didn't call for a doctor, either. All day long, she boiled an herbal concoction for him to drink. It was said that after he drank it, Uncle's urine turned green.

When I went to their home, the two of them were sitting side by side on the edge of the bed, not moving. From their expressions, it seemed they couldn't recognize anyone. The odor in the room was enough to make a person throw up. In the kitchen, the chickens fluttered and flew around in confusion. I walked as lightly as possible, my shoes making a slight sound on the wooden floor, yet this sound alerted the two of them. Uncle began having convulsions, and Auntie jumped up and came after me with a broom. Pointing at me, she cursed loudly:

"Get out of here! Your being here could kill him! Don't you see? Are you blind?"

With her cloudy corneas, she certainly couldn't see me. She just saw a shadow coming into her home. I noticed she wasn't wearing slippers. She probably hadn't been able to find them easily.

As I hurriedly slipped out of Uncle's home, I heard Uncle's hoarse voice coming from the window. I stopped.

"Is it the thief again? It doesn't matter. Don't get angry with him. There's no way to avoid this kind of situation cropping up from time to time. I'm just trying hard to get used to it. Some people think I dug the pit for myself. They've walked into my trap. In the end, I won't be buried with those people. I want to be cremated. I've already stipulated that in my will. That fellow just now is really blind. He saw the two of us sitting in the room, and he still meant to steal something. Who knows what's going on in his head?"

*Uncle was pretending not to know what was going on in my head. Actually, it was I who didn't know what was going on in his head. Even if I made a desperate chase, I wouldn't be able to catch up with his thinking.*

# THE SPRING

SITTING IN THE KITCHEN, JIANYI WAS GAZING AT HER EYES IN THE mirror, and she saw something right away. Most days, the large, circular mirror was on the hearth. When Jianyi whisked the ash from it with a dust cloth, those dark haloes appeared from somewhere deep in the mirror. She followed them with her gaze, but she ended up seeing only her own eyes. And that something. Now Jianyi heard the frog singing. About three years earlier, a spring had suddenly gushed out from under a heap of rocks in the yard. It had gone gurgling through the weeds and flowed into the ditch. Later, an ugly frog had shown up. The sound of the frog was earthshaking, and Jianyi's hand trembled a little as she held the mirror. She immediately put it back on the hearth. As she sat there quietly, she thought, *Old Mai the butcher is a boor. How could he have appeared in that dream?* As she thought this, she smiled briefly; anyhow, being or not being a boor wasn't a reason for emerging in a dream.

There was a time when Jianyi wanted to make Old Mai talk a little. Carrying her shopping basket, she stood in front of Old Mai's chopping block and told him some local gossip. He went on boning the meat, his puffy eyelids drooping, while interacting with her in a perfunctory way. He appeared to have no interest in what she said. Jianyi realized it was fruitless to try to draw others into her business. But just as she was about to leave, Old Mai said, "Someone has been persecuting my dog. I just don't get it: How can anyone hate a dog so much?"

Jianyi thought maybe these words had a double meaning, but she just didn't know what that other meaning was. She began to feel uneasy somewhere deep in her heart, because if a boor like Old Mai could play with words, it was hard to tell what this world was coming to.

Of course, that something she saw wasn't unexpected. She was familiar with its atmosphere. It was just that there was something unique about the people who repeatedly appeared that way. One could describe their expressions with the words "beautiful sorrow." They reminded Jianyi a lot of a woman she had seen when she was a child. That woman had sat behind the door, with a large white cloth on her head. Her cloth shoes were also white. She had large hands that rested docilely on her knees. One day, when Jianyi got close to take a look, she saw bloodstains on the white cloth. All of a sudden, the cloth quivered for a moment. Jianyi was so scared that she backed away a few steps.

Jianyi didn't want other people to ask her about her experiences growing up. She wanted to be as she was at present in other people's eyes. No matter what she was doing, she was always unhurried: she combed her hair a little at a time with a wooden comb. When the comb bit into her scalp, the knots in her brain began to loosen. When she walked along the street, even the heels of her feet seemed filled with memories. In the early spring sunshine, she sometimes patiently spent an hour to get close to the frog. All these years, she was worried only once. That was the day that her landlords urged her to move. The landlords lived upstairs. It wasn't clear why, but for a long time, they hadn't wanted her to live there. With overcast faces, they had mentioned this to her twice, but each time, she pretended to be deaf and dumb. Later on, they came and moved her things. She rushed up, and bumped into the corner of the table, cracking her forehead and almost injuring her eyes. The old landlord and his wife were really freaked out, and never again suggested that she move out.

Jianyi had a job with a bogus company. She went to work every day, sat down at the typewriter, and typed appeals for help one after another. These letters were written to multifarious major corporations, begging them for donations. The letters were signed with the names of various charitable organizations. Jianyi's boss was a supremely self-confident old codger. Whenever he spoke, he claimed his company was "a busy little bee." He supervised everybody with a straight face. If someone wasn't working hard, he heaped abuse on that person, denouncing him as a "parasite." The company had been in business for a long time, and it was still in good shape. In the last two years, he had also opened a few branches. The company head-quarters, where Jianyi worked, was located downtown. It was a gray-colored two-story building. At the windows of each room hung dark curtains, which made people outside the building feel depressed. The entrance to the building was narrow: it would be difficult for two people to go through it shoulder to shoulder. Since only a few people worked here, the building looked desolate. In the middle of her work, Jianyi frequently went over to the window, gently raised the curtain a crack, and looked out. Sometimes, as luck would have it, her boss saw her, and he would make an odd complaint:

"If some hothead from the crowds outside comes in and takes our documents, what a disaster that would be!"

Containing her laughter, she would train her attention on his bald pate. With a dejected expression, she went back to her desk and typed a few lines. Then she turned around again and said to her boss, "The groundwater in our yard has found a place to break through. Boss, do you think the place where I live is a precious spot with good fengshui?"

Her boss frowned and thought, then departed without a word.

When she left the building and went back to where she lived, Jianyi always felt that her boss was hiding behind the curtains and gazing at her retreating figure. Maybe that's why her actions were unhurried. Her boss himself lived at the headquarters. Whenever she thought of this lonely old codger's life over the last years, she shuddered a little. When everyone else had left, what did the old codger do there? In the morning when she came to work, he always looked cachectic, as if he had had insomnia all night long. He complained of toothaches. And said some plaintive things, such as "I'd be better off dead." But before long, he pulled himself together, and was once again the strong-willed boss. No one had better think of being lazy on his watch. He didn't feel at all attracted to Jianyi. He seemed to look down on her a little.

When Jianyi boarded the commuter train and took a seat, it was already dark outside. She looked out the window at the superficial city. Those lights filled with foreboding were all blinking. For a while, her thoughts went deep under the ground. Those interlocking groundwaters were so vibrant. If they hadn't unexpectedly gushed to the surface, who would have paid any attention? When she was a child, she often imagined herself owning a well, so she had gone to the mountain behind the house to look. She hoped she would find the mouth of a spring. Someone told her, *If you dig straight down from any place on the surface, water will spurt from the hole that you've dug out.* She didn't have any tools then, so she couldn't dig a deep enough hole. She could only fantasize.

Later she had moved into the city, and given up this idea forever. The first time she had discovered the vibrant water under the heap of rocks in the yard, she was so excited that her heart—*ping-ping*—skipped a beat. That night, when no one was around, she lay on the ground next to the mouth of the spring, and listened intently for a long time. She felt it was incomprehensible. All these years, she had rented a room on the lower floor of this two-story building. It was a very old building, and its facilities were often in need of repair. The owners were an old couple—an eccentric couple. Still, she had never intended to move from here. Even at the outset, she hadn't gotten along well with the owners, and it had reached the point that they now wanted to drive her out. In her dreams, she imagined that the place where she lived had become a garden with springs everywhere, with the sounds of countless frogs shaking heaven and earth. After she woke up, she heard only one frog singing. She was infatuated with the mouth of the spring. Just then the landlord's old lady came to her room, and said to her haughtily, "The yard is a mess and steeped in dampness." Sometime she would have to "give it a thorough cleaning." Jianyi was terror-stricken, and hated that old woman as she had never hated anyone. Time kept rolling on, and the thorough cleaning never took place. It looked as if it would be difficult to carry out in the future, too, because the woman was so old that it was hard for her to do anything. Jianyi still remembered the way she felt the day she came to the city. That day, she was tingling with excitement! Even though there wasn't a sign of spring water in this kind of place, nonetheless at night she heard the hullabaloo underground. The best thing was that, before she went to sleep, a dove waited with her for the arrival of the spring water. At the beginning, she heard an almost imperceptible, remote disturbing echo, and then it became vigorous.

Back then, she was still living with her parents above a grocery store. Next door was a middle-aged man who recycled scrap material for a living. Her parents were staring at her morosely and kept repeating, "Jianyi, Jianyi, how will you ever grow up?" And so her heart sank. Sank, and became pitch-black. The town was dry as dust, and dusky, too. Her teacher called the malnourished Jianyi "the girl from above the grocery store." Although in general her life hadn't been bad, sometimes it was just terrible—especially when her parents announced they wanted to abandon her. Her terror persisted for some time, and then they finally went back to their old home in the northern countryside.

One evening, Jianyi walked into the courtyard, and saw that the landlord's old lady was sitting up straight at the door to her room. She seemed to be eating something. As Jianyi took out her key and opened the door, she said, "Grandma, please come in."

Turning on the light, Jianyi ran her eyes over the room. The old woman was still sitting motionless at the door. Jianyi grew a little uneasy, and walked quickly back to the door. In the dim lamplight, suspicious noises were coming from the old woman's teeth. It looked as if her flabby face would crumble. An awful idea came into Jianyi's head: could she be about to die? But then she heard the woman's woeful, feeble voice—a sound like a broken microphone.

"There's something stirring again in the backyard. Something—*hualahuala*—is coming up to the house. Weird things like this can occur in this kind of old house. A penny for your thoughts. When you go out in the morning, why don't you ever turn around to look at us? Of course, we've been behind the times for a long while."

"You always say that the yard needs to be cleaned up," Jianyi said lightly.

Her shoulders were shaking, as if she were laughing.

"The frog. It was my old man who brought it in."

"Hunh?"

Jianyi looked up and saw that the light in their bedroom was dazzling. Dazzling with white light. She heard lots of people going up the stairs. The sound of footfalls was non-stop.

"You have guests."

She heard herself saying this, and then she saw that the old woman had already taken off, leaving the date-red chair behind. The footfalls continued non-stop. She was puzzled: how could such a small house hold so many people? She looked up again: that light had gone out. No lights were on in the other rooms, either. It seemed to her that this evening was a little odd. Why had the landlord's old lady exerted herself so much to move a chair over to her door? Very likely, the old codger had helped her move it. She hadn't talked with them for two years. They'd been her enemies ever since they'd broached the issue of moving.

Jianyi went back to her room. She could still hear the faint sound of footfalls going up the stairs. She also remembered what the old woman had said about strange things in old houses. She couldn't help feeling a little tense. She took a shower to rid her mind of these depressing things. After blow-drying her hair, she sat on the sofa and remembered that, when talking with others, she always called this place her "home." And in fact, in the bottom of her heart, she really did think of it that way. Otherwise, why would she have resisted moving so strongly? A good many years had passed and her parents had long since become blurry shadows in her memories. Once in a while, they wrote her letters telling her of things at home. But Jianyi was here, and those things no longer claimed her interest.

Her mother wrote, "We're too old. Every day we go to the mountain in back to look at the tomb we've prepared. Once, your father noticed a hole you dug when you were little. The two of us thought it was quite interesting. That afternoon, we sat beside that hole and talked of you." Jianyi didn't buy it. She didn't think this was the least bit interesting. Then she thought, as well, of other things. When she looked at the clock, it was already ten p.m., but people were still going up and down the stairs.

Jianyi went over and looked through the glass door, and saw that a light was on in the stairwell. The sound of footsteps echoed from above. After a while, those footfalls came downstairs again. At first, she saw two really large pajama legs, so all along it had been the old codger of a landlord! He also saw her outside the door and hurried over to open it.

"Is something wrong?" he asked.

"Do you have guests?"

"No. It's just me doing my exercises."

He looked about to close the door, so she took off.

The old geezer's words startled her. And the *dengdeng* sound of footsteps above made her blood course faster. She tensed up for no reason and felt a little feverish. She washed her face with cold water. After that, the old man finally quieted down. "This home really bursts with vitality!" she sighed to herself. Without knowing why, she unexpectedly thought of her boss. Ordinarily, she didn't give him much thought. She wondered, *Does he also run up and down the stairs in that gray-colored tomb-like building? Or does he wander slowly from room to room like a ghost?* Her thoughts left her feeling faintly discomfited: had she also grown old so that she was finally paying attention to these things? She was only thirty-five, wasn't she? Why didn't she like the feeling of growing old? Wasn't there a saying that if you moved back a step, there would be a whole new world?

It was late. Someone rapped on her window unexpectedly. Standing there was Old Mai the butcher.

She vacillated about opening the door.

"You don't have to open the door, I'll just talk with you from here," the butcher said considerately. "Some kinds of persecution are really vile. I'm only a butcher. If I did what that sort of person did and put a little poison in the pork, there would be huge repercussions. We boors are never tempted by such traps."

Looking at him, Jianyi couldn't say a word. The butcher seemed disappointed. With a wave, he turned around and left. He had no sooner gone than Jianyi began recalling a lot of things about him. His appearance was coarse, perfectly matching his vocation. In the exact center of his left eyebrow was a fistula. Sometimes, the man was also in a trance, and then people stole his meat. Jianyi had seen him go after a thief with a butcher knife. The frightened thief had thrown the meat on the ground, and fled for his life. When he wasn't selling meat, he sunbathed on the flat roof of his home, which was at the entrance to the market. His dog also sunbathed, lazily gnawing on some bones. Jianyi had known him for years, but naturally had never given him much thought. She knew he didn't have a family, and she'd also seen him staring lustily at the women in the market. Sometimes he slyly threw a banana peel at a certain woman's tush. He seemed a little afraid of Jianyi. She had always felt superior in his presence. But now all of a sudden this superiority complex had vanished. She realized in astonishment that there was a black hole in her relationship with this crude man.

It was late. Since she had the next day off, Jianyi didn't intend to fall asleep so soon. She took a flashlight out of a drawer, and went into the yard. She shone the flashlight for a long time, finally shining it on the frog. It was squatting beneath a rock, as if paralyzed. Squatting down, Jianyi put out her hand to catch it, but it nimbly jumped out of reach. Beneath the rock, the mouth of the spring was hardly little. Now, the smaller part of the yard would soon turn into a pool of water. Jianyi noticed that someone—it must have been the old geezer—had dredged the muddy ditch so that the water would flow out more easily. She stepped on the rock, listened attentively to the sound of the water pouring into the ditch, and felt the joy of a dream coming true. The thing that she had wanted to find her whole life hadn't been in the countryside. It was right here. Right under this old house in the suburbs. And it was exactly like the one she'd imagined! Because of the force of the rushing water, the opening of the hole was getting bigger. The old landlord apparently was on her side, and here was the result. But it seemed his old lady didn't agree. Jianyi figured that the old woman was her chief antagonist. Jianyi thought haughtily: *This old woman: what can she do? She already moves with great difficulty.* Even so, in the bottom of her heart she had some faint misgivings. She remembered that today the old woman had actually sat at her door waiting for her, and she couldn't help but begin to worry. The window upstairs was dark. The old geezer must have gone to bed. His exercise just now had probably worn him out. While she was thinking this, the light upstairs went on. The dazzling white light hurt her eyes. She immediately noticed the water under her feet, and her head lowered, she took two hurried steps onto dry land. She said to herself, "This is really an exciting evening." She didn't want the old couple to see her from upstairs, so she circled lightly around to the back of the house. Behind the house, there was a low table under the locust tree. Standing on the low table was that wild cat, its eyes glistening like two lamps. It was unafraid of people, and waited until Jianyi walked up before jumping off. Sensing that she had encroached on its territory, Jianyi backtracked, turned around, and headed back toward her room. When she looked around, sure enough, it had jumped back onto the table, its silhouette looking stately in the moonlight.

After locking her door, Jianyi got ready for bed.

She lay in the dark, unable to get rid of a nagging worry. Every time her thinking dug down into an even blacker cavern, she imagined the mouth of the spring growing larger the more it gushed. It seemed as if it would turn into a torrential flood, scaring her so much that she instantly pulled back. What the hell was this about? She certainly wasn't dreaming, but the experience wasn't much different from a dream. Because of her anxiety, she got up and looked around the yard a couple of times. She noticed that the light upstairs had been on all along. Not until it was almost daylight did she fall exhaustedly into a confused sleep.

The first thing she did when she got up was to go out to the courtyard. The old geezer of a landlord was already standing there. Jianyi saw that the water had all dried up. There were just a few places with watery, mud. The mouth of the spring was no longer spouting water. The old landlord was lighting his pipe: he looked both weary and exultant. He turned around and saw Jianyi, her hair disheveled. Pointing at the jumbled rocks, he asked her, "What do you reckon has happened underground?"

"That's a real riddle," Jianyi said, shaking her head.

Not satisfied with this, the old geezer turned away coldly and ignored her.

Jianyi thought back on her sleepless night, thought back on the various impulses she'd felt all night long. None of this seemed real. Although the old geezer was now ignoring her, she still appreciated him. Just think, if it weren't for him, who would have caught the frog and brought it into the yard? Who was he? Maybe he was her grandfather? Was it because she was interested in the same thing that he was that he couldn't accept her? Jianyi shouted to his back, "The woman who wore white clothing and a white cloth on her head sat behind the door without making a sound. In fact, she heard everything. Our hometown didn't have enough water. It wasn't like it is here, where the groundwaters are so plentiful."

The old geezer smoked his pipe as if he hadn't heard her. A sound came from the window upstairs.

"Here, there is whatever one wants," Jianyi went on perversely.

"Except for one thing." The old geezer spat out these words slowly, and glanced at her sharply. Brushing past her, he went inside. His legs were a little lame.

A hail of confused sounds rained down from the upstairs window. Jianyi was afraid. She forced herself to stand where she was for another few seconds, and finally—feeling ashamed of herself—she shrank back to her own door. The sun told her that it was already afternoon, and—feeling at a loss—she absent-mindedly walked into the kitchen to wash up, brush her teeth, and cook. She had no sooner rinsed the rice and put it in the rice cooker than the telephone rang in her room.

It was her boss. In contrast to his usual arrogant manner, he was in a panic. "Something's gone wrong in the company. From now on, the company will no longer exist," he told her. Jianyi asked her boss if the company's fraudulent practices had been exposed. Her boss cursed her over the telephone, saying that she had "actually dared to smear the company" and that she "didn't have even minimal work ethics." He also cursed her for some other things. Jianyi asked what in fact had gone wrong with the company. Exasperated, he said, "If there were less scum like you, we'd all be better off!" And with that, he hung up. Jianyi felt rather numb as she returned to the kitchen and continued cooking.

She stood at the kitchen door, holding a big bowl of porridge. In the hall, the two old people were quarreling. The old woman's voice reached her ears: "If she doesn't pay the rent, then order her to get the hell out of here!" Jianyi blinked. It seemed she'd already forgotten the issue at hand. Her imagination began wandering in every room of that gray-colored building. In her mind, the door to the west-facing archives room was open, and inside, those phony documents had been thrown to the floor. The boss—sweat pouring down his back—was kneeling on the floor straightening them out. At one side, the women's restroom was crammed with employees talking about a popular movie. At the entrance, a police car was repeatedly sounding its horn, filling the atmosphere with terror. Inside the meeting room, several people with blurry-looking faces were whispering to each other. One of them stood up and hurried over to the window facing the street. He pulled the shade down quickly.

Jianyi spent the rest of that day in a trance. At night, she actually slept soundly. She didn't even dream. In the morning, she washed up and got dressed, ate breakfast, and then made up her mind to pretend nothing had happened and go to work as usual.

When she entered the building, she saw that the employees were all getting ready to start work. There wasn't any change in the room, either. Relieved, she continued with her unfinished work from the week before. After a while, she realized that everything was abnormally quiet in the office, and stood up to go and look for the boss. She looked all over, upstairs and downstairs, without finding him. All she could do was go back to her own office and resume her work.

When it was almost noon, someone knocked frantically on the door, and then opened it. It was Old Mai the butcher.

"I've come to see what kind of work you do!" He clamored, "You people are very good at keeping secrets. This building is like a fortress!"

Hands behind his back, he walked around the room several

times, and sat his ass down on Jianyi's desk.

Jianyi had never seen him look so barbaric, and she looked at him in surprise. She couldn't say anything for a long time. And because he was looking down on her from above, she lost her confidence.

"Let's have it. What's your work all about?"

Thinking that he already knew everything, Jianyi was so tense that her face paled.

"We really don't make any money. You know how careful I am with my daily expenditures."

"Right. How could you make money at this kind of work? Quick—Tell me about your work. I've wanted to know for a long time."

"What business is it of yours?" Jianyi felt relieved as she said this.

"None. I'm just curious."

Jianyi rose from her seat, stood in the center of the room, and gave a long-winded explanation of her work. She remembered that she used quite a lot of big words, such as "philanthropy," "sacrifice," "austerity," "tenacity," and so on. She might as well have been talking in her sleep. As she talked, she grew more and more excited, her face flushing red. Sometimes, for fear that the butcher wouldn't understand, she rapped her knuckles on the desk for emphasis. When she came to the tail end of her explanation, she felt that her manner had turned rather fierce.

As he listened, the butcher nodded his head. She couldn't tell if he'd understood her or not. His legs were swinging in the air. But when Jianyi finished talking, he got down from the desk and left without a backward glance.

Jianyi grew more and more uncomfortable sitting there. She headed to another office to scout things out. When she came to the corridor, she saw all her colleagues working in a disciplined fashion in their own offices. They all looked horrifically busy. She wasn't sure what to do next. While she was dithering, she heard the boss call her from downstairs.

"Great, great! You've saved the company!" The boss said jubilantly, "Old Mai told me everything. You've stood up to the test!"

"I don't get it," Jianyi said coldly.

"If you don't get it, don't try. Forget it. Who cares? Dreams often come true. Look at me, for example. At first, I would never have thought I could really manage such a large company. . ."

She gave him a sidelong glance—white foam was running out from the corners of his mouth—and she was sorry that she couldn't hit him.

"Confidence—confidence is the bloody foremost issue."

She walked away, the boss still shouting hoarsely behind her.

When she left work and went home, Jianyi saw right away that the heap of jumbled rocks had been moved away and some concrete had been spread on the ground sloppily where they had been. It was gloomy under the light of the streetlamp. She bolted her door and fell onto the sofa.

"We have to throw out that table in the backyard and spread out some concrete. Yesterday, water began seeping out from that piece of ground," the old woman said.

"Is there something wrong with our groundsill? What do you think? Will there be problems?" the old man asked the old woman.

"With such a deep subterranean area, who can possibly figure it out?"

"True enough. But we should do something about it, shouldn't we?"

"What should we do?"

As she was dreaming, Jianyi heard this dialogue and struggled to wake up. She tried for a long time, but she dropped into an even deeper dream. In that even deeper dream, she struggled again for a while. In the end, she couldn't hear anything.

# THE LITTLE MONSTER

IT WAS EARLY ONE MORNING WHEN I FIRST SAW IT. I WAS IN THE habit of getting up early and going out for a walk. When I came down to the third floor, something scurried out from the side and kept snapping at my leg. No one else in the building was up yet. It was barely daybreak; the light in the corridor was faint. I was terrified. Bending over, I saw a strange little dog. Or maybe it wasn't a dog, but some other species. It was repulsive: its hair had almost all come off, leaving its skin bare, pink, and smooth. There was still some filthy white hair left on its neck and head, both in serious shape from the invasion of bacteria. The thing was clinging to my pant leg. I could imagine eczema erupting all over my body. Suddenly, I kicked hard, kicking it down to the landing below. This little thing didn't even moan. It just went into the dark corner of a stack of old boxes used for packing electrical appliances. With one hand on the railing, I ran down the stairs in a hurry, rapidly reaching the road. Then I made my way along the road to a deserted field that was about to become a building site—a place where I often came to walk. I walked slowly along the perimeter of this semi-circular field, pondering the trivial details of my life, and figuring out ways to deal with them. As I walked, the fish-belly white of early dawn appeared in the east. More people were walking here now. The old man who came every-day to practice qigong also arrived: he had already taken up the qigong posture in the center of the field. It was time for me to go home. On the way, I bumped into two neighbors from my building who'd come out to buy breakfast. It wasn't until I went up the stairs that I remembered that little thing. I made a real effort to lighten my steps, but just when I reached the bend on the second floor I heard it whimpering. My heart was in my throat; I was quite terrified as I approached that stack of old packing boxes. Try as I might, I couldn't find its hiding place—I just heard it crying now and then. Maybe it had burrowed into a box. Thinking back to the kick I'd deployed earlier, I felt an inexplicable fear. I went up to my place on the fifth floor, changed into slippers, and calmed down right away. Surrounded by the familiar bed, sofa, and desk, I caught a whiff of the aroma of rice porridge cooking on the kitchen stove. It seemed to me that nothing out of the ordinary had happened after all. Reassured, I sat down and ate my breakfast.

I thanked my lucky stars that when I went downstairs to go to work, the dog didn't utter a sound. Maybe it had died. If it really had died, it would stink before long and the neighbors would clear it away. If it hadn't died, it would sooner or later. Soon, I reached the office, where everything was the same as usual—people drinking tea, joking and laughing, talking about some scurrilous rumors. All of a sudden, I blurted out, "I killed a little monster!"

"Really? Truly?" Everyone gathered around. "Is it really dead? Huh?"

My coworkers were shaking me by the shoulders. They were all questioning me at once, an urgent expression on each one's face.

Regretting that I'd said anything, I answered hesitantly, "I don't know. Maybe it died. I kicked it hard. Maybe it didn't die—a mangy little dog can't die so easily, can it? It looked really terrible!"

My answer disappointed my coworkers, because I'd just said I'd killed it and now I was saying maybe I hadn't. I seemed to be keeping them guessing. They weren't just disappointed, they were also quite angry. None of them would pay any attention to me. All I could do was sit there quietly, drinking tea, thinking about the little thing's fate, thinking about the way I'd kicked out rashly. Recently, I had less and less of a grip on myself. I never dreamed that my colleagues would be so interested in this incident. If I had, I wouldn't have said a word. Why the hell did I have to tell everyone about this irrelevant episode? I was supposed to be here to work: spread out in front of me were documents, newspapers, and a cup of tea. Yet, it seemed I had come here today only to talk about this episode! It was just too bizarre. I needed to deal with this incident right away; otherwise, tomorrow I'd make the same mistake.

What to do? Of course, first I had to find the little thing and see if it had died. If it had, I would throw it into the garbage can. If not, I'd hide it somewhere away from the apartment building. Either way, I couldn't leave it on the landing. But it was the third-floor neighbors who had put all those packing boxes there. We were strangers. Now if I suddenly straightened up their things, it was sure to surprise them. And I would have to repeatedly explain what had happened this morning. I really didn't want to do this.

Envisioning this, I could just imagine on the right side of the stairs the mean look of that guy whose face was scarred from a knife. He was a boor who loathed white-collar people like me. He'd be sure to keep a straight face as he listened to the long-winded story of my experience, and then he'd say something that I wouldn't know whether to laugh at or cry over. For example: "You're in a great mood!" or "Invite the little thing to your home, and raise it—that would be a genuinely magnanimous act," and so forth. It seemed I couldn't take care of this while my neighbors were on the scene. So I'd better wait until late at night when no one was around. I'd have to move lightly. If the little thing made any noise, I'd have to act decisively—for if there was too much commotion, everyone would think I was a burglar.

I went up the stairs with my ears pricked up, but to no avail, for I had no sooner taken a step than I heard a wild sob. The sound penetrated the whole building. I got the willies with each step I took. What I couldn't fathom was the neighbors' attitude. The people walking down the stairs all appeared very calm, talking about things—stocks and bonuses and such—as they walked. But then maybe they were only pretending to be calm. At last, I reached the stack of packing boxes. They were wobbling violently, and would soon collapse. The little thing's sobs were becoming sadder, and shriller.

I sprang over to the boxes. First, I moved the top one down, and then moved the others one by one—until the only box left was the one from which the clamor was coming. I looked at it up close, and saw the little fellow cowering in a corner. It was way too thin. It had shrunk to half its size since early this morning. A lot of wrinkles had appeared on its tender, red, diseased skin. The sparse hair on its head had also fallen out. Only its neck was ludicrously half-covered by hair. It was really quite strange that such a broken little thing could make such a powerful sound. I had unwittingly moved into its line of vision. It was watching me: not only did it not recoil, but it also seemed aggressive, unmistakably on guard. Its wrinkles turned an even deeper red. It seemed ready to pounce on me at any moment. Of course, there was no reason for me to be afraid. It seemed so sickly, and its body had

shrunk so much that it was no bigger than the palm of my hand. I felt
inexplicably queasy from looking at its diseased skin. I'd frequently
heard other people talking about mangy dogs. This was probably the
first time I'd seen one with my own eyes. Taking a closer look, I just
saw that its skin was covered with scarlet eczema the size of pinpoints.
It was this thicket of scales that made its skin appear scarlet. I'd never
heard that eczema was associated with mangy skin, so it was hard to say
if this was mangy or diseased skin. Maybe it was some kind of scary
contagious disease. But I couldn't linger: the sound of footsteps was
already coming from the first floor. I took a large towel out of my bag,
and with one quick motion I covered the little thing and held it tight.
Leaving this messy spot, I ran downstairs. The thing was struggling in
my grasp. As I ran, I covered it tight: I wasn't going to let it bore its
way out to be seen by others. When I got downstairs, I turned the corner. I knew that in the backyard there was an old work shed where construction equipment was piled up. I made a beeline for it.

I put it into an old cart. I didn't want to keep the towel. I just let
the dog lie on top of it. The thing collapsed on the towel; it wasn't
strong enough to stand up again. I thought I'd do the right thing
until the end: first, I'd go back and get some sausages so it could eat
its fill. Then I'd deal with it. For example, throw it into the adjacent
well and drown it. But it suddenly began making an uproar. It stood
on my towel, yapping at me ferociously. Its eyeballs were blood-red,
and the thicket of scales protruded from its skin. I was scared shitless.
The word "rabies" quickly came to mind. How could I dare approach
it? I just wanted to take cover and disappear then and there to avoid
looking anymore at this sick virus-carrying skin. My hands started
itching; I needed to disinfect them with alcohol right away. I ran a
long way away. When I reached the second floor, I could still hear its
tyrannical snarling.

Not yet over my fright, I swabbed my trembling hands with alcohol, and changed out of the clothes that had come in contact with the
dog. I was going to sterilize them with boiling water and then lie down.

Twilight had formed on the window, filling the house with a
dubious light. I grew uneasy again. I looked down from the window,
and at once I saw the scene that I least wanted to see: a lot of people
were walking toward the backyard. And then someone knocked on
my door. He was courteous, yet he kept knocking.

"I'd like to come in for a while. You won't say no, will you?"

It was that knife-scarred face and he was chewing betel nut.

I said he was welcome to come in and talk.

"Are you sure?" He gave me a probing look, and spat out the dregs of betel nut. "A boor like me—you could say it doesn't matter what it is, I'm always clumsy—I can't sweat the small stuff. Even if a volcano erupted outside the door, I'd be inside sound asleep as usual. Why on earth do you want to let me in for a talk?"

"It's not what you say. And besides, it's impossible for a person to think something through carefully by himself. You're a long-time neighbor. I'm happy if you want to visit. It's just that simple."

"But, if I do, I have to consider the ramifications. For example, if you made a big fuss, couldn't I still pretend that nothing had happened? Put yourself in my position, and think about it—okay?"

"Of course. Sure thing," I answered perfunctorily as I began trembling.

I glanced out the window inadvertently, and saw that it was completely dark. I thought, *At a time like this, such a person might want to make trouble for me. How should I deal with it? Could I shout for help? Wouldn't people just laugh their heads off? This guy is sitting there minding his manners: he certainly doesn't seem the sort to take action. He's merely come to tell me that I made him plunge off the deep end, that's all.* Inspecting my living room, he stopped at the window. He stuck his head out and looked several times. Then he drew back in. Unhappily, he asked me, "Is this all you can see from here?"

I nodded my head.

"What can you see? You can't see anything!"

Enraged, he left the window. He wanted to go.

I let out a sigh of relief. But when he got to the door, he turned around again and picked up the cloisonné vase from my desk. He said he wanted to teach me a lesson. That vase was the only valuable thing I owned. It was out of place on the shabby old desk, but it was my father's legacy. He left for a time, and I heard an enormous sharp sound: he had smashed the vase. I forced a smile. I wasn't all that sorry. There was another sudden knock on the door. I sluggishly headed over to open it. Knife Scar poked his foot in and opened the door. Once in, he slammed the door shut. His face was deathly pale.

"That beast scurried onto me from the stairs. My God!"

"Was it a little bald animal?" I tried my best to keep my voice calm.

"Bald? Who can say for sure? It apparently wanted to bite me to death. If it hadn't been for the sound of the vase scaring it off—just look at this pant leg!"

His pant leg had been ripped into shreds. It was too awful to look at. I didn't think I could go on standing there, but Knife Scar was still hanging on to me. He clutched me by my shirt and shook me hard, as if he wanted me to answer all his innermost doubts. All of a sudden, he let go of me and hid in the kitchen. The sound of claws digging into wood had been right there at the side of the door all along. I was looking around in confusion, but I couldn't find any weapon to defend myself. Luckily, the digging sound stopped after a while. As I turned around, I saw that Knife Scar had actually closed the kitchen door. His jumpy reaction made me wonder how terrifying the little thing's attack had really been. Quite a long time passed before he gingerly emerged from the kitchen. With both palms on his chest, he asked me, "Is the bed made up?"

"What bed?"

"Mine! Do I dare leave under these circumstances? I have to wait at least until tomorrow. If I did dare leave, as soon as the door was open, that monster would scurry in. Where would you hide?"

"And what if it still hasn't left by tomorrow morning?"

"Tomorrow is another day. Do you think you can plan your entire life?!" His eyes bulged.

Seeing my dismay, he spoke in a warmer tone. "It's your fault for running into this fierce and brutal monster. Now all we can do is pick up the pieces. You'd better not go to work tomorrow. For the time being, anyhow, you can't go out. I heard that you made a fool of yourself at the office today. Some people are coming after you, so tomorrow you'd better stay home. You're lucky to have me here for company."

I gave him my bed and made up a bed for myself on the floor. While I was busy with this, Knife Scar stood in a trance at the window, as though he'd forgotten what had happened. I didn't pay any attention to him. I just lay on the floor and read the newspaper. Then I went to the bathroom again, drank some cold homemade plum juice, and then was ready to fall asleep. I saw that Knife Scar was still in a trance. Although I was afraid, my nerves had relaxed by now. In a daze, I was shoved awake by Knife Scar. Looking at me, he said hesitantly, "I can't sleep. How can I sleep? I'm worrying about that little monster outside. Should I go out and take a look? Maybe it isn't biting people anymore? Are we too obsessed with this?"

"Just look at your pants! Do you still want to go out and look for it?!" I was angry and frightened. In an instant, I was sitting up—getting ready to hide.

"Hey, you, don't be so impetuous! I don't think hiding like this is the thing to do. Can you solve the problem by hiding? Just now, while you were asleep, I was putting all this in context. Even though I'm a boor, I do know the principle of the thing. When this began, the dog didn't provoke you. You're the one who provoked it. Search your soul and see if this is how it happened."

"Do you want to let it in?" I asked, glaring at him.

"Whaddya think?" he countered. "Shouldn't we be concerned about it? If you saw the desperate expression in its eyes. . . . It isn't after other people now. It's zeroing in on the two of us. Just think. If it can find us even on the fifth floor, where can you hide?"

"What if it commits homicide?" My tone of voice had changed.

He dropped his eyes, spread his hands out, and said, "We just have to trust to luck. You provoked it first."

When I saw him head for the door, I lost no time in shutting myself into the bedroom and locking the door. I also dragged the bed over to block the door. I heard him go out, and he didn't come back in. Then everything was quiet.

After a long time passed—it was already midnight—the outer room was still quiet. I made up my mind to open the door. I also turned on the light in the outer room. Strange—there was really nothing out of the ordinary. I swept my eyes over the table—indeed, the vase wasn't there. I decided to open the front door, too. I flung it open with all my strength. Sure enough, something fell on my foot, but it wasn't the little monster. Much like gossamer, this thing didn't move. I went back inside and got my flashlight. I shone it on an animal hide—the blood still sticking to it. It was the little thing's familiar skin. Probably Knife Scar had done it in. I hated this crazy lunatic with all my heart.

# MY BROTHER

M Y YOUNGER BROTHER MAJORED IN METALLURGY AT THE university. After graduating, he went to work in a distant frontier area. He was working in an office, but I'd never figured out what his job was. The first few years, he complained of his loneliness in several letters to me. At first, I answered every letter. Worried about him, I consoled him and pointed out several ways he could improve his situation. In my letters, I also recalled our childhood together. But, when all is said and done, he was far away, and words couldn't substitute for being together, as we had been in the past. As time gradually passed, I began feeling that my words were quite superficial, quite perfunctory—and finally quite hypocritical. Probably my brother also sensed these subtle changes. His letters grew few and far between—one every few months, one a year—and were limited to just saying everything was okay.

The last two years, he had been altogether silent. During that time, I made up several excuses for his silence. Later, I grew used to it. I thought, my brother finally has steady work and a decent salary. My chicken-hearted brother has found a place to settle down in this world, after all: this was really worth celebrating. As I was thinking this, I saw a pair of bitter eyes swaying before me, and I felt rather rocky inside. I pressed this uneasy feeling down, and made an effort to think about some good possibilities. For example: one day, he met a beautiful Uighur girl, and the two of them fell in love at first sight. He became part of a Uighur family, with lots of relatives to protect him. Or, he became good friends with someone at work—someone full of compassion and with a terrifically strong sense of justice. The two of them spent all their time together . . .

As I was imagining these scenarios, my son walked in. He glanced around the room, as if he had something he wanted to say to me, and also as if he didn't want to open his mouth. Picking up a book from the table, he flipped over a few pages, then feigned a careless manner and asked, "Why hasn't Uncle come back yet? You didn't have a falling-out, did you?"

"How could we? What are you thinking of?" I laughed artificially.

My son stared at me briefly and said, "That's good."

He put the book down and left the room.

It looked as if my son had picked up on the unnatural relationship between my brother and me. I say it was unnatural, but that doesn't mean there was any conflict between us. Still, for a brother and sister to have no communication for two or three years—well, one couldn't say that was normal. I began to blame myself, yet I felt I wasn't to blame for anything. Wasn't it just that I hadn't written? Why hadn't I? I'd been afraid to lie, afraid he'd see through my hypocrisy. My conscience was clear.

A few days later, a person surfaced from my brother's office, not at my home, but at the home of one of my husband's friends. There, he talked a lot about my brother. My husband's friend told him that my brother was doing quite well there. It was just that he was diffident and didn't talk much. It appeared he was sort of a loner there. When my husband told me this, I felt bad. After all, that person knew I was here, yet he had made a point of not visiting me. Maybe my brother had told him not to. What had happened to him? How could he have developed such an extreme attitude toward me? This wasn't like him, because he had always been tolerant and generous, intelligent and understanding.

I was fidgety for several days in a row. Observing this, my husband said, "Go see for yourself. It takes only four or five hours by plane. Seeing him will clear everything up."

I, too, felt I should go there and see for myself. It had already been five years since we'd seen each other, and especially considering his attitude now, I was even more restless. In my notepad, I had recorded that my brother had stopped writing first. But in my perception, I always felt I was the one who had stopped writing. Or maybe he hadn't received my last letter? My decision not to write showed that I had soon tired of staying connected this way: when all is said and done, he was the one who'd gone away.

A week later, I boarded the northbound plane. After the plane took off, I gradually began to unwind, because I would see my brother soon. No matter what he blamed me for, everything would be fine when we saw each other: he'd be surprised and happy to see me. Thinking this, I felt almost moved by what I was doing. Various words floated in my head: "If one even kisses blood ties away, what else can serve as our crutches through life?" "In the last five years, I've really been thinking of you all the time, but letters aren't a good way to communicate." Blah, blah, blah. As I was thinking, drowsiness overwhelmed me. The talk buzzing all around became distant. In my dream, someone jostled my elbow time after time. It was really annoying. I made an effort to open my eyes. I woke up and noticed that the little geezer next to me was smiling at me. He was the one who had shoved me just now.

"What do you want?" I asked angrily.

"Are you going to see him? There's no point. You won't see him," he said.

"Who are you?!" All at once, my drowsiness vanished.

"The other day, I told your husband's friend all about him. Why do you still have to make a headlong dash over there? Think about it: he hasn't even written you a letter. Doesn't that mean he's in hiding?" As he talked, the old geezer took his hat off and scratched his bald head with sharp fingernails. The sound made me want to throw up.

With a harrumph, I turned away and paid no more attention to him. An inexpressible depression arose in my heart. It appeared that this rotten old guy had wrecked the whole trip. How had he known who I was? Maybe he'd seen my photo at my brother's place. Maybe my brother had told him everything. Why had my brother chosen this sort of guy as a friend? But I still hadn't seen him. This was just the old guy's side of the story. Everything would be better when I saw him. After all, my brother and I had depended on each other for years. Was there anything we couldn't talk about? Swinging as I was between hope and despair, I wasn't the least bit drowsy anymore.

"Seeing each other won't make things any better, and furthermore, there's no chance of seeing him anyhow." The old guy had read my mind.

I glowered at him and noticed the traces of blood that his fingernails had scraped out on his bald head.

I really wanted to change seats, but the plane was full and there was nowhere else to sit. So I stood up and—under the old guy's surprised gaze—headed for the restroom. I dillydallied as long as I could, but finally I had to come out of there, because someone had been knocking on the door for a long time. When I emerged, the woman stared at me fiercely—just itching to gobble me up. Then she rammed me out of the way and went in. I had no choice but to return to my seat next to the old guy.

He'd put his hat on and was sneering at me from the corners of his eyes.

The plane was beginning its descent. Below, there was a large yellow desert. I squinted at the old guy. He seemed filled with joy— but not a pure joy. It seemed that a certain plan had been brewing in his mind, and he would now soon put it into action. He was elated. The closer the plane came to the ground, the less he could contain his inner delight.

"Look, we're already here!" Rubbing his fingertips, he said this joyfully.

A black sandstorm permeated this podunk town; you couldn't see a thing when you walked out of the airport. I waited a long time, but the bus to the city still hadn't come—never mind taxis. Looking behind me, I saw that all the passengers from the plane had disap-peared. Perhaps they'd gone to the waiting room to wait for the bus. In order to shake off the old guy, I went to the waiting room, too.

It was empty. The light was on. The only person here was a woman sweeping the room. Shocked and scared, I walked over and asked, "What time is the bus due?"

She looked up, took stock of me curiously, and answered with a question of her own: "How strange, didn't anyone come to meet you? Someone was here to meet each of the arriving passengers, and they all left a long time ago. See, not one person is here. There isn't any bus, because someone meets everyone here. Who have you come to visit? If you're not familiar with this place, you mustn't wander around alone. It's terribly dangerous when it's windy." She looked at me sympathetically, and put her broom down. Then she walked into her workroom and shut the door.

When I looked outside, I saw only a dense mass of sand striking the door and windows. It was so dark that you couldn't even see your fingers. To take even one stride out the door was risky. My brother had been living in this place all along. Why hadn't he written about the storms in his letters? Perhaps there was a long sandstorm season here. What did he do during this season—just hide out at home?

Dispirited, I sat down on a chair—scared and absolutely stupefied. Just this morning, I'd been in high spirits—planning how I'd while away my time after getting here. Life was hard to fathom. I blamed my brother for this, too. In his letters, he had described this city as an oasis in the desert, with beautiful scenery and clear air. "But it's lonely." It seemed he had lied because he was afraid I would worry about him. My poor brother: he had actually been exiled to this sort of place. If I'd known earlier, I certainly would have told him to come back to me. Even if he'd been out of work, still the hardships of a life unemployed would have been better than being in this kind of hole. As I thought these things, my eyes grew moist.

"Although the sandstorm is now covering the sky, tomorrow will be a beautiful day," said the old guy from behind me. I had no idea when he had come over here.

"Why is it like this? Will there be a bus tomorrow?" I asked him hesitantly as I thrust down my inner disgust.

"You don't have to wait 'til tomorrow. After a while, a pedicab will come for us," he said.

"Us?"

"Yes. Just you and me. If you don't go with me, where would you go? Or you could wait here. Tomorrow, there'll be a plane going back to D City. You could take that plane back." His eyes darted all over as he talked.

In an instant, I was feeling deep grief. After a while, I heard someone talking outside. A youth came in grumbling. His face was blue, his legs thin as stalks of hemp, his body wrapped in a hooded raincoat.

"The pedicab is here." The old guy said to me, "Take out all of your clothes and wrap them around yourself."

I opened my suitcase obediently, took out my few articles of clothing, and wrapped myself in them. I looked at the old guy again: he had also put his hooded raincoat on. He was even wearing sunglasses. He looked gloomy.

In the dark, we groped our way into the pedicab. The youth sat in the driver's seat in front, and pedaled ahead energetically. The pedicab started up slowly. Although sailcloth covered the roof and sides of the pedicab, it was open in front of the seats, so sand continually assaulted us. I had to cover my head tightly with my clothing. I didn't dare breathe. The storm howled like the sound of whistles in a playground. I'd never heard the wind sound like this. I was shaking from the tension. The old man sitting close to me didn't move: probably he was laughing to himself. It took a long time before I gradually became somewhat used to this. The pedicab moved extremely slowly. I imagined how the youth's hemp-stalk-skinny legs were struggling, and the incredible willpower required for him to press forward against the wind and sand on such a dark night. With every creak of the axle, my heart tightened. What was the connection between this youth and the old guy? And what was their connection with my brother? Where were we going? My head was crammed with doubts, but with my head covered tightly in clothing, there wasn't any way I could ask the old guy. And just then the old guy began snoring loudly.

The pedicab moved slower and slower. The youth seemed beat. Each time he pressed the pedal, he groaned. I couldn't bear it. Finally, he stopped struggling. The pedicab came to a complete stop, and he slumped over the handlebar and began sobbing. His sobs were drowned in the gale, but I could sense the violent twitches of his body. The poor guy! He swore abruptly and got down from the driver's seat.

"I have to trouble you to get down and walk. The pedicab is out of commission!" he shouted to me in the wind.

"Where can I go? I don't know the road, and the sandstorm is so awful! So dark!" I shouted. I trembled uncontrollably as if I'd fallen into an icy river.

"Not my problem. Go wherever you want! Anyhow, I have to take off." With that, he disappeared into the dark.

The old guy was still snoring. As soon as I remembered that someone was with me, I felt a little more sure of myself. What was I afraid of? I wasn't the only one left behind in the boondocks. The old guy was a local, familiar with the conditions here. If I was with him, there wouldn't be any danger. If he could fall sound asleep, he must not be worried. Since he had told me to come with him, he would have arranged everything. I just had to be patient. I changed my mind about the old guy. I wouldn't try to shake him off again: he had become a straw to clutch. If I stuck close to him, I wouldn't have a problem. And finally I would find my brother, and get him to understand: hadn't I made the long trip to be with him? Hadn't I put up with a lot of hardships on the way? Wouldn't all of this melt the ice in his heart, and make him recall the love between sister and brother? After thinking about it from all angles, I finally fell asleep. I dreamt that I was watching soccer: the referee's whistle was blowing constantly—as if perforating my eardrum.

It was already daybreak when I awoke with a start: the pedicab was moving again. Just now, I'd been awakened by the pedicab starting up. As soon as I looked up, I saw the youth pedaling hard. The storm had already died down a lot. It was still windy and dusty, yet you could distinguish the road clearly. A few people—all carrying heavy loads—were walking on the road. It seemed they were Uighurs. The women were wearing dazzling silver jewelry.

"Haven't you changed your mind yet?" The old guy began talking. I didn't know when he had awakened.

"Of course not. This is the reason I came here," I said. My disgust for him was rising again.

"You'd be better off if you didn't stick to your objective. Just imagine that you took the wrong flight and ended up here. That's certainly possible." His little eyes were staring at me craftily from inside the raincoat's hood.

"I came here to see my brother!" I said sharply, the blood rushing to my face with anger.

Along the way, I'd kept mum with him, and he with me. Would something happen now? Would the old guy retaliate for my rudeness?

The pedicab stopped. At the side of the road was a long two-story building, its veranda facing the road. Some men and women, holding onto the veranda's railing, were watching us. This was a typical dormitory. The old guy told me to get down, and said we had arrived.

I followed him into the building. The old guy opened the door to a room adjacent to the one for drinking water, and told me to go in.

"Whose room is this?" My head was filled with suspicion.

"His. Who else's? Wait here." He said coldly, "He went out."

With this, he made to leave, but I immediately held him back. "Hang on a second. Tell me, where did he go? When will he be back?"

"How would I know? I've been with you the whole time. You can ask his colleagues here in this dormitory."

After the old guy left, I began taking stock of my brother's room. The room was furnished austerely with a single bed, a desk, a bathroom. On the bed were the sheets, pillow, and quilt cover I'd given him when he took this job. After five years, these things were showing their age, but they were all clean. Seeing them tapped my feelings for him and I felt like crying. A series of self-accusations surged up in me. Raising my head again, I saw a lot of newspaper clippings stuck on the wall. The clippings were all about quite ordinary things. Some were even overly simple. One clipping talked about how to avoid getting diarrhea in the summertime. Another recommended ways to maintain electrical appliances. One provided guidance on getting along with one's family. Still another was the officials' message to the youth—urging them to exert themselves to be useful, to render service to the motherland, blah blah blah. Half the wall had clippings stuck to it. Some of the clippings bore a lot of heavy red marks. This wasn't the sort of thing my brother used to do. My brother—how can I put it?—generally kept his distance from politics. He didn't read newspapers very often, let alone clip articles from them. Why had he become like a little kid now? Had he lost his mind and started engaging in this kind of cheap trick because of the long, dark season of sandstorms? I read the clippings, then reread them. No matter how many times I read them, I couldn't figure out what had drawn his attention. But the marks were clearly his, because next to them were also words he'd written in red, such as "Brilliant!" or "The key point!" and so forth. It wasn't the way my brother used to react at all. It was as if he were another person. So, did he have a girlfriend? Was a girl influencing him? Changing his philosophy of life? I looked around the room. I didn't see any sign of a female presence. The room didn't have superfluous decorations, nor did it have signs of daily life. Everything was arranged just the way he always used to arrange things: absolutely precise, absolutely monotonous. And with the lonely air of a bachelor.

I sat down in front of the desk, where I saw the familiar, old-fashioned alarm clock. The tiny red hand was pointing at 3:30. Why 3:30? Did my brother wake up in the wee hours of the morning and then work on something secret? Or didn't he get up from his noon-time nap until 3:30? What time did he go to work? Looking at the clock, I let my imagination run wild for a while. Suddenly I heard the sound of little chicks. Right. There were chicks here in this room! I walked over to the corner at the head of the bed, where I saw three chicks in a large cardboard box. The top was covered with clear plastic film. There were a lot of holes in the sides of the box to give the chicks air. Inside the box were water and a bowl of chicken food such as chaff.

I thought, since he has chickens, he couldn't have gone far away. He would very likely come back at noon—or at the latest, in the evening. Now I seemed to understand a little: clipping these newspaper articles and keeping these chicks were hobbies he had developed during the long, dark season. In his genuine loneliness, he had backtracked. He must have been regressing for a good long time. When I thought back again to the perfunctory letters I'd written him about childhood memories, I felt ashamed to show my face. I lay down on my brother's single bed, inhaling the smell of his body and listening to the intermittent cheeps of the chicks. Thousands of thoughts were writhing in my mind.

The storm had passed. A little sunshine even appeared. The unfamiliar scent of the frontier filled the air.

People were talking in low voices on the veranda. It seemed they were quarreling in undertones. I got up and opened the door. A man and woman turned toward me at the same time. They were both very young, and they looked conceited. They were giving me chilly looks. Just then, the woman pushed the man, urging him to leave.

"Do you know where my brother Yiju went?" I asked politely.

Because I took two steps forward as I asked this, they retreated two steps.

"Yiju?" The man frowned, his eyes shooting ice at me—as if I were a thief. "Yiju?" he repeated, as though lost in recollection. He started fiddling with his finger.

I said, "Exactly! I want to locate Yiju. Just think, I've come such a long way, but he isn't here . . ."

The man suddenly jumped to. He slapped his ass, making a loud sound. Then he jabbed the woman, and said, "Look, he really did have a sister all along! That damn punk—I always thought he was lying! Haha!" He laughed fearsomely and threw his head back. Then his face took on a blank expression, and he said to me, "Yiju actually spoke of you."

The woman pushed the man again from behind, hinting that he should leave soon. She kicked him, too.

"You're Yiju's friends. You must know him well. Won't you come in for a while and talk with me about him?"

My words had an unexpected effect: as though afraid of the plague, the two of them retreated some distance away from me. The man kept saying, "No. You've made a mistake. Why would we be friends with him? We can't say we're even acquaintances. We just nod at one another. We've just heard a little about him. Can't say we know him. You mustn't expect that we can tell you anything." At this point, he shielded his girlfriend tightly with his hands—as if afraid I would attack them. "Yiju—how can I put it?—is a strange one. You certainly know him better than we do. If you really want to find out more about him right now, you can go to the third door over there and ask them."

With that, he and the woman took off in a hurry.

I didn't know where "over there" was, for he hadn't actually pointed it out to me. I didn't want to knock rashly on just any old door. I sighed. I'd better think things over carefully before doing anything. That man had said just now that Yiju "really did have a sister all along." He'd said, too, that he had "actually" spoken of me. Was it possible that Yiju had spoken to them about me frequently? Perhaps, in those dark days, his only topic of conversation was me. He had blathered on, talked too much—and in five years, I hadn't shown up even once, so everyone thought he was making it up. What the facts were, I had no way of knowing. I just knew that my brother was a very monotonous person. If he was chatting with his colleagues, for sure he wouldn't have been able to find any other topics of conversation. He was slow of speech and had a one-track mind. Who'd be interested in talking with this sort of person about his sister? I was visualizing my brother's plight: everybody disliked and avoided him. My heart was aching by fits and starts. My poor brother. In spite of everything, he really should have rushed back to me. He had put up with this for five years! He was like a fish at the bottom of the Dead Sea, the dark, boundless, toxic salt water on all sides. Five years. How much hatred would he have built up toward me over such a long time? Maybe the old guy had told him I was coming, and he had made himself scarce. His door wasn't locked: this showed that he had deliberately left it unlocked for me. He couldn't have gone far, because he still had to feed the chicks. Probably he had left in a huff because he felt wronged. Later, when his anger dissipated, he'd come back.

It was noon. I decided to look for a place to eat. I walked along the right side of the veranda, thinking I'd find someone to ask. Stopping at the third door, I hesitated a moment, and then knocked. Someone opened the door: a young, fine-featured woman. But her bearing was fierce.

She spoke first, glaring at me. "You're looking for Yiju? He's gone far away."

"Where—where did he go?" I began stammering. The feeling I'd had the night before during the sandstorm came back.

She didn't say anything at first. She was casting sidelong glances at me. Then she bustled around again tidying up her room, as though she had no intention of talking with me. Weary of waiting, I was about to leave when she came over again. The animosity on her face had vanished. She said:

"How would I know? And even if I knew, he wouldn't let me tell you. Why did you bother to come from so far away? Did you come to apologize to him? He did tell me that he would never forgive you. He also said if it hadn't been for you, he wouldn't have come to this sort of place. It was only because it was intolerable to be with you at home that he came to this rough, barren place. He's told a lot of people this. He said that you were his sister, but that you often put on airs in lecturing him. You were even stricter than a mother. He's told us this over and over. What's wrong?—you don't look well. Here, have a seat. You must be hungry. I'll fix some instant noodles for you. You're going back to his room? I didn't tell you anything new just now, did I? I really don't like to butt into other people's business."

I went back to my brother's room and lay down on his bed. Everything was black before my eyes. I was drenched in sweat. Was I coming down with something serious? In my confused state, I warned myself: *You cannot get sick here. Absolutely not!* Then I fainted.

When I awoke, my clothes were soaked, so I changed back into clothes that were filthy from the sandstorm. Peering into the little mirror on the wall, I saw an unkempt person who looked very old and terrified. I took a towel out of my suitcase, and went to the bathroom, where I washed my face and combed my hair. Then I felt a little better.

Outside the dormitory, in a low building next to this one, was a small shop. Sand heaped on its roof obscured the tiles. I walked in, asked for a glass of milk and a bowl of rice porridge, and began to eat halfheartedly. After finishing, I just sat there in a daze, not knowing what to do.

The old woman running the little shop noticed that I was sitting there too long, and struck up a conversation. "Everyone says you're Yiju's sister and that you've traveled a long way. Yiju drops in to visit frequently. Once, during the sandstorm season, he stayed in the storeroom in back for a week. I brought him food the whole time. Tell me one thing: are you really his sister? You aren't faking it? You can tell me who you are: I won't tell anyone else, I promise. To tell the truth, I never believed that Yiju had a sister." As she talked, the old woman came closer and looked me over.

"As it happens, I am his sister. It's true. Can you tell me where he went?"

The old woman sat down next to me, let out a long sigh, and said, "You probably can't see him. You don't understand your brother one little bit. If I were you, I wouldn't have come here."

"Why shouldn't I have come? He's my brother, isn't he?" I felt the blood rush to my head, and the big toe on my left foot itched something fierce—as if a poisonous insect had bitten it.

Ignoring manners, I bent down and took off my shoe, and scratched that toe for all I was worth. It began to swell inside my sock, and it throbbed with pain. When I looked up, I met the old woman's condescending gaze.

"Why get so stirred up? Hurry up and leave. You've been here too long. Everyone has seen you. They'll get suspicious of me." She was a little terror-stricken as she glanced all around. The four or five persons in the room all aimed their flashing eyes at this spot. "Just go. After a while, I'll come to your room. I still have to feed the chickens for your brother. You must do as I say."

"I'm not going." I was becoming desperate. "Please tell me what my brother said about me. If I did something wrong in the past, I'm determined to change. It'll be all right then, won't it? Why does he have to avoid me? Why are all of you helping him? Did I commit some unforgivable crime?"

"Oh, c'mon, don't make wild guesses. Nobody thinks you're at fault. Your brother doesn't think so, either, so there isn't anything to change. You always think you've done something wrong. I'm not very used to the way you think. Hey, how come you don't have a clue about your brother's worries? During the windstorms, he told me everything. Now since you've come here headlong, you might as well stay in his room. This is between you and him. Even if we wanted to help you, we couldn't." Her eyelids drooped. She seemed fed up with me.

On the dormitory's veranda, I once more ran head-on into that fierce-looking young woman. She was talking with an old man. As soon as they saw me, they stopped talking. When the old man turned around, I realized that he was the one who'd been on the plane with me. He'd changed clothes, so I hadn't recognized him at first.

"When do you plan to leave?" he asked me. He was scratching his head and looking unhappy.

"Leave? Why would I leave? I came to see my brother. Since he isn't dead, he'll come back in the end."

"You still think so? You've said this repeatedly. Everyone here knows why you came." He sketched a large circle in the air.

"So I'll say it again." I was staring at the two of them with hatred.

"It was only with great difficulty that he broke away from you. Why would he backtrack now?" the young woman said, glaring at me again.

I was itching to spit in the woman's face, but I had to endure the humiliation.

When I went back to my brother's room, the alarm clock suddenly began ringing, sinking my depression to its lowest level. The alarm clock rang two or three times longer than most alarm clocks. It was quite sad and shrill. God only knew what the clockwork springs were like. Staring at the clippings on the wall, I couldn't decide what to do next. All of a sudden, I caught sight of a headline on a clipping. Written in heavy black letters, it said, "Watch Out for the Enemy All Around Us." Panic-stricken, I scrutinized the article. It was a small article about air pollution. I thought the headline was offensively conspicuous. My brother had also drawn a heavy red circle around it, along with three exclamation points—each one larger than the previous one. The red exclamation points appearing before me made my brother seem terribly savage, I didn't know why. I couldn't stay on in the room. I leaned out the window and looked outside.

"You mustn't wander around here." I didn't know when the old man from the plane had come in. "Everyone is talking about you.

You've been too conspicuous. You must know that everyone here knows that Yiju has such a sister. It's easy for Yiju's emotions to run away with him. He babbled a little too much about his personal life. Of course, he painted the devil a little blacker than he really is. During the sandstorm season, people talk about everything, and as soon as something is said, it becomes an accomplished fact—everyone remembers it. It wasn't because of embarrassment over what he said that Yiju went into hiding, I don't mean to say this at all. He likely left out of fear that you'd tell him to go home. I have some advice for you: you'd better just stay inside and not move about. I'll bring you food. Look, the wind has risen again. What unpredictable weather! It's dark again. After a while, it'll be pitch-black. And anything can happen in the dark. You're a newcomer and not accustomed to these environs, so you mustn't move around."

After warning me, the old man was about to leave. I stood up and said to him, "Hang on a second. Tell me, is my brother hiding in this building? I have a kind of intuition: it seems he's somewhere in the vicinity. For sure he hasn't gone very far. Also with the storm rising once again, how could he have gone very far?"

"You're very bright, but you're wrong. He left here the day before yesterday, and went to another city. It was a nice day the day before yesterday."

"But how can he just leave whenever he wants? He has his work. Doesn't anyone here work? Is everyone a parasite? What the hell is this place all about?" I asked in alarm.

"You'll find out by and by. You mustn't get all worked up." He shut the door and left.

The sky grew dark, this time darker than night. It was black as ink. The wind was coming closer, howling strangely. And the sand was slamming against the windows like a rainstorm. I had never before seen such a raging wind. It was deafening. It was as if it would pluck this dormitory up from the ground. I was very frightened. I turned on the light at once, and hunkered down in a corner of the bed. The three little chicks hid their heads under their wings. I felt the wall swaying and creaking. Outside was the racket of people's voices; was this building going to collapse? I weighed the situation tensely. Eventually, the noisy crowd moved inside. The flashlights were glowing everywhere. I opened the door and leaned out toward the veranda. People covered from head to toe in raincoats were like ghosts as they went into the rooms. A dark figure shoved past me in a hurry, and I nearly fell down. It was the old woman from the little shop. She was also wearing a hooded raincoat. With one hand, she pushed me into my brother's room, and immediately hunkered down to look at the three little chicks. She fed them some cut-up greens that she took out of her raincoat. The little chickens cheeped happily. The old woman sat down against the wall. She seemed weary. The wall was still swaying gently. Sand was still battering the window.

I stepped up to the old woman. Sitting on the edge of the bed in distress, I said, "Why does Yiju hate me so much?"

"You really don't know?" A cunning light flashed from her eyes. "During the long nights in the storeroom, he spilled those long ago beans to me. The more the wind blew, the more his thoughts ran toward this ink-black, faraway cavern from long ago. And so he talked of what happened when he was nine years old. His tale was vague, filled with assumptions. In the dark, his laugh sounded like two bamboo blocks striking each other. Before he finished talking, I was scared witless and ran off."

Nine years old? What had happened the year he was nine? This wasn't hard to remember. That summer was so torrid. My brother's inclination toward world-weariness began to sprout. All day long, he wandered on the beach beside the river, exposed to the sun for a long time. One day, he fell and broke his neck at our front door. I saw him fall: he didn't fall heavily at all, he just lurched slowly downward. Finally he was on the ground, but he still broke his neck because he was so frail. After coming home from the hospital, he was immobilized and in bed for a year. The little guy even said, "It would have been better to die." Sitting next to his bed, I read stories to him. When he looked annoyed, I suggested that he and I make up a fantasy. I told him that he didn't have to think he had broken his neck. He could pretend he'd wanted to trade in his head, and now that he'd had an operation, his head had been exchanged for a cat's head. Now he could think like a cat. He had to pay something for this, so he had to lie in bed and nurse his injury. My brother laughed at what I said. We got through the roughest days by indulging our wild imaginations in fantasies. Later on, he recovered completely. He didn't suffer even a setback.

"That was when he began to get the idea of breaking loose from you," the old woman went on. "He said someone like you often made a big error in judgment without knowing it, so he had to get away from you. He also said that if he lived under the same roof with you, he would only become weaker and weaker."

"Perhaps he doesn't need me anymore, but why does he have to hate me?" I was looking hopelessly at the ink-black window. "In his letters, he said he was lonely here. He said it was boring. I never realized what it was like here—not until I came and saw for myself."

"And so you took him to mean that he wanted to go home to you, or that if you just said the word he would go with you for sure. You really are a dogmatic person!" She began laughing artificially.

"I miss him a lot." Flustered and exasperated, I said, "This isn't something you can understand."

"Of course. That goes without saying, because you were controlling him all along. Who wouldn't be nostalgic about being in such a good position? In the past, he was subordinate to your will. You did whatever you wanted with him. His soul was sobbing . . . Once he wanted to swim in the river. You wanted him to stay home and keep you company, so you wouldn't let him go."

"It wasn't like that at all. He hadn't recovered, so the doctor put physical activity off-limits. Why wouldn't I have let him go swimming? I loved swimming. Oh, what's wrong with this world? Did he actually tell you this?"

"He told everyone. So what? On windy days—you've seen how black it is all around. Listen carefully again. Everyone in the dorm is talking all the time. Why? This is the only way it can be. They have to talk endlessly—talk, talk, talk. You fish out everything. Your brother was the same way. Otherwise, how would I know about you? In fact, Yiju—this kid—was a little strange. As soon as the wind stopped, he didn't say another word. He usually shut himself up at home, clipping newspapers and feeding these little chicks."

"Is he somewhere around here?"

"Maybe. But he said he'd wait until you left before he came out. He also said that you couldn't possibly stay, because for sure you'd be concerned about your work and your family, and other—more vulgar—matters."

So it had all been part of his plot. He'd seen through me all along and played me for all he was worth. In an instant, it was as if a shaft of light was shining on my shabby self, but it immediately faded. Did my brother mean that he wanted me to cast off all "worldly things" and make up my mind to wait here forever, and then he would appear? Could this be another kind of bait? He certainly hadn't promised me this, and I couldn't cast off everything. I realized that since I'd come here, my desire to see him had grown more and more intense; in the past five years, for the most part I had never considered the possibility. I seldom thought ahead, and I wasn't sensitive enough. By and large, I was the very model of someone muddling through life. What kind of model was my brother? My impression was that he was effeminate, considerate, and generous. How had he developed this sort of incisive vision? Or, had he hidden this side of his nature in the past? I truly couldn't get a handle on any of it.

At about six o'clock, the old man brought me some food. I sat down and ate. With every bite, I seemed to also take in several grains of sand. I frowned and swallowed it. The terrifying wind was howling. The old man was watching me. The old woman was watching me, too. They seemed to be exchanging glances. Maybe something was brewing.

After I finished eating, I took the bowls to the bathroom to wash them. With the water running, I faintly heard them conversing in loud voices. When I turned the faucet off, they lowered their voices again, and with the wind also very close, I couldn't make out what they were saying. After washing the bowls, I went back to the room. The two of them closed their mouths simultaneously, and sat there with straight faces.

"When are you leaving?" the old man asked me.

"Do you want to drive me out?"

"Of course not. Why would we? It's all up to you. I was just asking, so I'd know what's going on—so I'd know the score, that's all. What you said is really offensive. Who'd want to drive you out?"

"I'm not planning to leave. I'm going to stay here."

"Liar." Staring at me, the old man said, "How can you stay here? Your feelings have been blown all out of proportion."

"Maybe, but I don't want to go now."

The two of them winked at each other, and, with stiff expressions, they headed outside. As soon as they opened the door, a great gust of dust and sand rolled in, landing on the tidy bedspread. Recalling my brother's cleanliness in the past, I closed the door at once, pulled off the bedspread, and shook the dust from it. Then I made up the bed again. When I looked up, I saw that another news clipping had been pasted on the wall. The paste wasn't yet dry. The old woman from the little shop must have just placed it there. The funny thing was that this clipping also had my brother's handwriting on it—and the ink was fresh, as though he had just written it. "Fallacious thinking"—my brother had commented in red ink. The title of the article was: "The Advantages and Disadvantages of Eating Raw Vegetables." The article was all in bold-faced letters—also unusual. I'd never seen a newspaper publish this sort of article in bold-faced letters, but this was unmistakably a news clipping. In the corner were the words "Science Daily." I wanted to read the article, but I had spots before my eyes. The instant I read one word, I became dizzy. I blinked and read on with an effort. After a while, I grew dizzy again. I'd been dozing all along.

I didn't dare turn the light off. I slept in my clothes in my brother's bed.

During the night, I was awakened by knocking on the door. I looked at the clock: it was just two o'clock.

The door opened. Three people in raincoats came in—two men and a woman. The woman was the old woman from the little shop. I didn't recognize either of the men. The old woman had no sooner come in than she put her ear against the wall and listened intently. Her expression was stern. Huddling in their raincoats as if afraid of the cold, the two men stood waiting to one side. After a while, the old woman left the wall and said to me, "You must come with us. This building could collapse at any time. It would be dangerous to stay."

She bent over, caught the little chicks, and put them into a bamboo basket she'd brought with her. Then she told me to follow her out the door. The three of them were all beaming flashlights back and forth. Lots of people came down the stairs, also shining flashlights. All of them were talking; it seemed they were talking about the same thing. Soon we were in the midst of a large group, walking in the same direction. I couldn't see a thing. I just felt we were walking inside the building, because the wind was blowing outside and sand wasn't hitting my face. But it also seemed that I wasn't in the building, because we walked a long time without reaching the other end of it.

"The year before last, we went to that place. Don't you remember? I didn't think you could forget it. There's a wooden bridge over there, yet there isn't a river under the bridge. Maybe there was a river a long time ago, and later it dried up . . . ," a woman said in a low voice.

"I'd forgotten that, but now that you mention it, I remember. We were muddleheaded as we charged into that place. We hadn't prepared," another woman said.

I took a few hurried steps, and clutched the old woman who was talking with the two men ahead of me. I asked her where we were.

"In a tunnel," she answered simply, flinging off my hand.

All around, the crowd was raising the roof. Someone was even whistling. I listened closely for a long time: people weren't conversing with each other any longer. Maybe by now they were talked out. Now they were expressionless. They were repeating themselves, talking and talking—not *with* each other, but at each other. Sometimes it was the same three or four sentences; sometimes, just one sentence. While one person talked, the one or two beside him nodded vigorously, and turning their heads, responded with "Uh, huh." They would also hug the one who was talking. When one person tired of talking, a listener started talking again, still repeating what the previous one had said. And that person also responded with "Uh, huh," a fervent expression on his face as he earnestly hoped that the more the other said the better it would be.

Finally everyone stopped walking and sat on the ground. I glanced all around, and saw that this was an underground plaza. I was the only one without someone to talk to. I sat all alone among the others. The old woman was talking in front of me, but she had long since forgotten me. Listening to the talking next to me—sounds like the chanting of sutras—I was imagining what it was like when my brother was here. Maybe once or twice, he would have sat silently over to one side like me, but how could he have gotten through five years? If he hadn't learned how to talk the way they did, what could he possibly have done? The old woman had said he told her everything. Under what circumstances had he told her? He had moved about among these people—fretting, isolated, afraid, and so that conversation had taken place. I felt I was gradually drawing close to the crux of the matter.

"Wednesday, I visited a Uighur family," the old woman said to those two men. "They have a large wooden cupboard that holds many bottles of old vintage wine. Wednesday, I visited a Uighur family. They have . . . "

Eyes half-closed, the two men nodded contentedly. They opened their mouths like infants and murmured, "Ah, ah. . . ," their fingers restlessly clawing at the fronts of their garments.

I stood up and wandered about in the wavering light of the flashlights. This place was huge. I walked a long time. Everywhere, people in raincoats were sitting on the ground. Everyone was either absorbed in talking or in listening to the same kind of words. Where had these people flooded out from? Maybe my brother was among them. I stepped on some people quite a few times, thus leading to little altercations. Each time I scurried away in fright, but actually no one chased me. After this brief commotion, the one who'd been stepped on resumed talking.

Someone tapped me on the back. It was the old man from the plane.

"You mustn't look for him everywhere. I'll take you to see someone." With that, he shone his flashlight on my face. I saw spots before my eyes. Just as I felt I was about to be seized by spasms, he dragged me over toward the wall.

His back toward us, that person was thinking aloud. He was also wrapped inside a raincoat. When he turned around, I almost made a mistake and shouted.

Naturally it wasn't my brother. But he was familiar. In the past, I'd seen him almost every day. His right cheek bore a birthmark that I'd never forget. But who in the world was he? His name was on the tip of my tongue, but then it was blocked. And the various links between him and me were like many strands of gossamer that I couldn't get hold of—wafting away before my eyes.

He was looking at me intently. An elusive expression skimmed over his face.

"You're—," I said.

He laughed dryly, and said, "Don't you recognize me? You're so forgetful. Have a seat. I want to talk with you about Yiju."

I turned around: the old man had long since left.

"Yiju generally disguises himself well. You must think you rushed over here of your own volition, don't you? Have you connected all the dots and thought it all through?" He narrowed his eyes. He seemed to be mocking me.

"Are you suggesting that Yiju set a trap to lure me here?"

"Could be. But now, from your point of view, it shouldn't make any difference. Nor from his point of view."

"Are you one of my neighbors? We used to see each other all the time, didn't we? How come I just can't call it to mind?"

"It doesn't matter. Take it easy. Don't worry about it. Just think of me as your neighbor. Look, I'm sitting here absorbed in listening. I'm not taking part in these conversations. This has been going on a long time. Don't be impatient and wander all over. If you sit down without moving, you can realize something. Let me ask you: why don't you just forget your brother here and now? In any case, he's been away from you for a long time. You don't live together; each of you has his own life. You can't think of him every day, he can't think of you every day. So why are you here?"

"Because I fell into his trap," I said in a bad humor.

"Yes indeed, but that's only his side of it. Look, in the stillness of the night, who is he? He doesn't exist. What the hell was it that gave you insomnia and made you decide to travel thousands of miles to look for traces of him? This beats the hell out of me!" Shutting his eyes, he sank into deep thought.

He and I both remained silent. The hullabaloo around us gathered more and more steam. I seemed to be bobbing in billows of chant-like talk. In this strange underground plaza, one could faintly hear the distant battle of wind and thunder. My acquaintance sat facing the wall and mumbling.

I don't know how much time passed before the crowd began moving. I was also swept ahead. When I looked around, I saw only strangers. They were all talking the same way. The flashlights were wavering like innumerable little lights. I started trying to make some sounds. Of course, I didn't have an audience. I was just one person trying hard to produce a sound. This sort of practice didn't bring any surge of happiness. We walked on and on. On and on. Later, I didn't make any more sounds. I walked on dizzily. Slowly. I was almost sleepwalking. And so the people behind me pushed, and I nearly fell. Then I did produce a sound: I shouted.

But no one noticed. My shout was immediately drowned out. I was like a wooden marionette being forced to stride ahead. I was tottering from tiredness.

It was almost dawn when I got to my brother's dorm room. I

looked at the clock: it was seven in the morning. I opened the window: a puff of white fog laced with the scent of the frontier floated in. Two Uighur girls passed in front of the window. The silver jewelry on their chests gleamed in the fog. The storm had subsided earlier. I had no idea how I had made it back to this dormitory from the tunnel during the night, because afterward I'd been muddle-headed.

I sat down on my brother's bed, intending to get a good sleep, but I sat on someone's leg.

"Go ahead and lie down. I still have to talk with you about him," the old woman from the little shop said from under the quilt.

I didn't have the slightest interest in sleeping in the same bed with her, but I was feeling more and more drowsy. I fell back on the bed involuntarily. At first, I thought it would be crowded with two people sleeping in a single bed. Not until I was falling asleep did I discover that the old woman was as thin as a fish fillet: she took up scarcely any space. What's more, she did her best to curl up, as though to give me more room. She slept against the wall. In the shadows, I heard her talking intermittently:

". . . When he first arrived, he wasn't used to the sandstorm season. He was a little on edge. And so I helped him out by bringing him these chicks. The point was to give him some spiritual sustenance. He and I didn't always go into the tunnel with everyone else. He stayed over there with me, and we sat together in the storehouse. From then on, he chattered to me about things between you and him. He mentioned a wooden building—an abandoned outhouse. When he was six, he took a crap there. It was raining outside. You left him there and ran off. As he crapped, he was sweating from irritation. It was raining so hard that when he came out, all he saw were reflecting, floating loblollies. Afterwards, he thought, when he grew up he would make you experience the same thing. Hunh, are you sleeping? No? Your brother was steeped in his memories . . . Okay, no one here has to work. We enjoy a special government subsidy, similar to the one the government provides for lepers. Think about it: with this kind of treatment, would your brother still go home? . . . Hey, are you listening to me? You don't have to worry about him. I've looked after him all along. He and I are as close as a mother and son. He told me you'd be coming. . . ."

When I woke up, I heard her still running on at the mouth. I shoved her and sat up, asking, "Is Yiju hiding out near here?"

"You can ask Old Wang—the bald guy from the plane. Didn't you talk about this on the plane? The last few days, he and Yiju have been up to something. Very secret. We've all been puzzled: what on earth is this about?"

The old woman had just finished speaking when Old Wang came in. He'd brought us food. He sat at the table, his bald pate covered with traces of blood from his scratching fingernails.

"She wants to get to the bottom of the matter!" Pointing at me, the old woman began yelling, "She wants to know everything! Tell her a little something."

I blushed, and took some things to the bathroom to wash up. Old Wang talked with the old woman as she lay on the bed. The old woman's behavior was strange: she certainly wasn't sleeping, so why was she staying in bed? Why wasn't she getting up?

After I'd finished washing up, I sat on the edge of the bed and ate the breakfast that Old Wang had brought. Just then, the old woman finally started stretching lazily a few times. Her eyes clouded with sleep, she grabbed some bread. There was dirt under her fingernails. She had no sooner eaten two bites than she spat it out on the floor and said it tasted bad. She fed the bread to the little chicks. Hunkering in front of the cardboard box, she broke off bits of the bread and flung them in. Old Wang winked at me and said, "Let's go talk in the vacant room next door." My heart skipped a beat, and I went with him to the next room.

This certainly wasn't the vacant room he'd said it was; a family lived here. They were eating breakfast. The people's faces were all hidden in the steam rising from the hot pot on the table. I couldn't make them out. Old Wang took me into the hallway, and said to me earnestly, "You mustn't believe anything that old woman says. She has a persecution complex. Five years ago, as soon as your weak-willed brother arrived here, she started badgering him. You've seen that: he raises little chicks and he puts news clippings up on the wall. He sets the alarm for three o'clock. The alarm goes off in the middle of the night before he's had a good night's sleep. That old bitch has forced him to do all of this. You want to see him now because you don't know what he's become. If you saw him, you'd regret it. This is all that old bitch's doing. Were you surprised to see her sleeping proudly on your brother's bed? This has been going on for the last five years. Your brother gave her the bed, while he himself paced on the veranda—right up until dawn."

"What on earth has happened to my brother? Please tell me where he is."

"Oh, if I were you, I wouldn't ask such things. It's much too late for this kind of question. Think about it: at first, when you drove him to this sort of place, it couldn't have been without some mental conflict, could it? Now you haven't seen him for five years. Why do you have to come back to this? Just act as if this hadn't happened. Go home with a sense of relief. . . "

"You are so vile! It's clear as day that you lured me here. What did you hope to achieve?"

My raving startled the people at the table. They all dashed over to see what was going on. Their eyes showed their scorn. I felt myself recoiling.

"Just look at yourself. Look at what you've done," Old Wang said, scratching energetically at his scalp. He scratched open one spot, and a drop of blood slid down—like a slender red ribbon—from his head. "When you act so fierce, how can other people help you? It was Yiju's wish not to see you. No one can do anything about it. If you knew the facts, you'd thank him. He's been a considerate child all along, hasn't he?"

As Old Wang was talking, that family crowded up close and stood between him and me. I couldn't hear what he was saying. The two little girls next to me tugged at my sleeve and forced me to take a stand. The middle-aged woman, probably the mother of the family, smelled my sleeve and said, "She lives in the room with those chickens, so she smells like chicken shit. Her brother does, too."

Pushing them out of my way, I went back to my brother's room. I had no sooner gotten there than Old Wang also came back in. He had scratched two spots on his scalp, so now two red ribbons ran down his face. It was absurd.

The woman was putting a new clipping up on the wall.

"Okay, this guy Yiju is back, and has actually gone so far as to pull the wool over my eyes!" Old Wang said loudly as he pointed at the clipping. Then he turned to me. "See: it's in his handwriting. He's back, and he doesn't want to see you. He's even deceiving me."

After she put up the clipping, the old woman, her face glum, turned to rewind the clock.

Was my brother hiding upstairs? I recalled that when I'd just gotten here, a lot of people on the second-floor veranda were looking at me. Maybe he was hiding among them. Why hadn't I thought of looking for him in this building? Perhaps the old man had seized control of my thoughts: he'd said my brother wasn't in this city, and I had believed him. But if I had searched every room in this dorm, I probably would have found him. Of course, this didn't exclude the possibility that he was hiding in the tunnel. I had to feel out the situation, scout around, and locate the entrance to the tunnel.

Just then, Old Wang and the old woman exchanged glances without saying a word. They took stock of me with pitying eyes. I flared up.

"You can't wander around here. Without us as guides, you can't do anything," Old Wang said.

"I have to find him." I spat these words out one by one from the cracks between my teeth, and looked desperately at the two of them. I was filled with hatred.

"You talk a big game! Where are you going to look? Do you think he's on the second floor? Do you think you can go up there from the landing here? No. You can't go up. The first and second floors are two separate worlds. If you want to go upstairs, you have to take a big detour, go into a very long tunnel, and on the way—" He stopped and scratched his scalp again. "On the way, there are numerous turnoffs. You'd probably take a wrong turn, and then wouldn't be able to get back. So, you mustn't wander around here. Think back for a moment: ever since you were on the plane, I've been with you—I've been your guide. Why? If you were buried in a pile of sand, you couldn't get out. Yiju was buried in the sand one time. He had a narrow escape."

I looked in the corridor for a long time. Sure enough, there weren't any stairs going up. But I also clearly heard noisy talking coming from upstairs. Those people had gone upstairs through a passageway—the tunnel Old Wang had mentioned, probably the very tunnel I'd been to during the night. I looked around in the nearby courtyard. It was empty. It had neither trees nor grass. Sand was everywhere. I remembered my brother's first description of this place: "an oasis in the desert." This is the way he'd described it in his letter, but what kind of symbol or metaphor was that? Where had that unknown passageway taken him? Old Wang and the old woman could go into that tunnel anytime, just as though it was their own home. Last night, they'd been like ducks taking to water. As I looked out from this plateau, there was sand all around as far as the eye could see. The highway was a blurry belt. Our blue-tiled building was the only thing standing in the middle of the sand that was everywhere. On the distant horizon were firm, unmoving clouds—also yellow. Only after a long time did I see one tiny beetle crawling past on the highway. It was a truck. It went by our building and headed toward the faraway horizon. Compared with the hullabaloo in the building, it was deathly still outside. Of course, it was different during storms. I didn't dare walk far away, because—apart from this dorm—I didn't have any point of reference. I circled around the building twice, and then went resentfully back to the veranda. Was the entrance to the tunnel perhaps in a certain room on the first floor of the dorm?

I walked into my brother's room, and saw that those two had left and that they'd taken the chickens with them. The wall was bare: all of the clippings had been torn down. I stood questioningly in the middle of the room. The alarm clock suddenly rang loudly. It went on for a full minute, much like an ominous hint.

Dispiritedly, I sat down on the edge of the bed, with thousands of things on my mind. I was confused. I remembered what I'd said to my husband before I came here. At the time, I thought I'd made a momentous decision. Not until now did it occur to me that my brother had manipulated everything. But what if he was the one who had been manipulated? For instance, had he been manipulated by Old Wang? And had Old Wang perhaps been manipulated by the old woman from the little shop?

Someone knocked on the door: it was the acquaintance I'd seen in the plaza of the tunnel.

He wasn't wearing a raincoat, but a long black coat like a uniform. Seating himself at the desk, he lit a cigarette.

"It's boring here. Why don't you go home?" he said.

"I agree that it's boring, but I'm still not reconciled to going. I feel I've come here for nothing, and I'm plenty upset about it," I said aggrievedly.

"Is it because they took the little chicks away that you're in such a rotten mood? How about if I bring you two more?" He was looking at me with concern.

"It isn't that."

"I didn't think you'd be angry about such a small thing. A place like this has insignificant things like this happening the whole day long. If one got angry over everything, it would be enough to drive a person crazy, wouldn't it? I have a friend who always hangs his laundry up to dry on the outside veranda. If someone passes by and knocks his clothes down, he starts kicking and cursing. He's out of his mind with anger. But, the next time, he hangs his laundry out on the veranda again, gets angry, and curses people all over again. And so on and so on. I don't think you're that sort of person." He took a drag on his cigarette and swallowed all the smoke.

"Maybe I really should go."

"Good. Who wants to stay long in a place like this? Tomorrow, I'll ask Young Wu to take you to the airport. This is the second time you and I have met. Guess who I am?" He took another drag on his cigarette.

"I can't guess. I always think your name is on the tip of my tongue, but I can't come up with it." I tapped my head a few times in annoyance.

"If you can't guess, then don't." His tone was gentle and soft.

He stood up and walked out. On his way, he turned off the light for me.

The night was long and chaotic. In the inky darkness, I heard countless cavalrymen fighting at close range in the desert. Yet, the camels they rode stood motionless. The sound of the weapons vibrated so much that I almost fainted. No one could hear my weeping.

It was the same young man who gave me a ride to the airport in his pedicab. It was a fine day. The air was filled with the scent of the frontier—a scent a little like sand, a little like watermelon. Now and then there were a few Uighur girls on the road: their steps were light, as if floating in air.

On the airplane I kept thinking maybe my brother had really vanished. The handwriting on the newspaper clippings didn't mean a thing. Back at home, I seldom thought of him. Old Wang and the others had all said: "Just act as if you didn't have a brother." When you don't think of a person anymore, isn't that the same as his not existing? I'd gone there only because habit drove me. In those long five years, my brother had gradually gotten over his former ways, and

had become a person without substance. As I saw it, for sure, he had
no entity. In other words, he would never have any more worries. He
would still think and feel, but his thoughts were all fantasies. No one,
including me, could ever arouse his interest.

# TOP FLOOR

"**D**O PEOPLE LIVING ON THE TOP FLOOR OF A THIRTY-STORY BUILDING worry at bedtime?" I used to ponder this question frequently. I live in an office in the bustling city center. It's the mailroom, with a table, three folding chairs, and a bed. I receive and dispatch letters at the table; I sleep in the bed at night. I keep watch over this thirty-story apartment block, where all the people know me: they call me Old Zhu.

These familiar faces come and go in front of me every day: they're all rather dreary people. Even the children walk as if they were adults—heads drooping, backs weighed down and bent by their book bags. After they've left and walked off into the distance, I feel liberated.

Once at midnight I couldn't sleep, so I got up and took the elevator to the top floor. I stood in the narrow corridor. There were six households, each door tightly closed. I looked out the window: the city below was flickering with light, like lots of fireflies hidden in a thicket. It was truly a wonderland. When I was about to go back downstairs, a door on the right opened slowly, and a young person looked out. He wasn't the least bit surprised to see me (at midnight!). Indeed, he took stock of me with reproachful eyes (I don't know what he was dissatisfied about). He was about thirty years old, Ma by name. His gaze was clouded, stagnant. Although I saw him every day in the mailroom, for some reason I still was a little afraid. I did my best to squeeze out a smile, and said hurriedly, "Ah, excuse me, I have to go downstairs. 'Bye!"

"Stay where you are!!" he ordered.

He was now standing completely outside his door. In the corridor light, he looked excited. He was wearing only undershorts and an undershirt. Although it was early summer, the draft in this building was plenty cold.

"Now that you're here, you have to keep me company," he said bluntly, taking a few steps toward me.

"Can't you sleep? Are you worried about something? You're feeling bad even living in a transcendent place like this?"

I took out a pack of cigarettes and handed one to him, but he turned it down.

"There's something scary going on." He squeezed out the sentence a word at a time. Suddenly, he blew his stack, "How can anyone live in this kind of place? There's no way to sleep! There's just endless torment!"

A gust of wind blew past, chilling him so that he shrank into himself, but he persisted in standing there. I knew he was a bachelor, and I'd never seen him bring a girlfriend back, so I suggested that we go into his room for a while. In any case, I couldn't sleep, either. Looking at me hesitantly, he was unwilling to open the door. Instead, he said again, "Scary! Scary!"

"Try talking about it. You'll feel better if you talk about what's on your mind," I said sympathetically, patting him on the shoulder.

The moment my hand touched his shoulder, he jumped back a step, and looked at me in alarm.

"I don't like it when people touch me! But, anyhow, you can go in and have a look at the scary thing."

Facing me, he backed up, retreated to the door, stuck out a hand, and opened it. His manner made me uncomfortable.

"Come on in, come on in." Standing to one side of the door, he grabbed me and pushed me inside with one hand.

It was a two-room apartment. The light wasn't on. The room where we were standing was probably the one he used for a dining room. Behind it was the bedroom. The darkness was filled with the smells of leftover rice and other dishes. Ma said that the light was burned out, took out a flashlight, and shone it randomly a few times on the ceiling. I sat down on a chair that he had casually kicked over to me. I felt really oppressed, but I also felt a rising curiosity. This person had been so excruciatingly terrified in the middle of the night. He couldn't have called me in just for fun. He stood for a while in front of the dining table, and told me that right then he didn't have the nerve to show me the scary thing: he'd already gone without sleep for two nights, and he was beat. Now that I was here, I might as well serve as his guard for a while to prevent anything from happening while he slept in the back room. With that, he went into the other room, and made a special point of bolting the door. I noticed that the light in his room went dark, then light again. This happened three times, as though he were signaling someone. Then everything was silent.

What garbage. I was sitting here like an idiot in this filthy room, while he was sleeping in the bedroom. Sure, I could leave: this young guy just couldn't sleep at night and had suddenly called me in on a whim. I couldn't take this too seriously. Although that's what I was thinking, I still sat there motionless as if possessed by something. Probably the guy inside his room had figured I wouldn't leave. Damn. How could he have guessed? I stood up and stretched, then walked over to the window and opened it to let the breeze blow on my face. I looked down: how strange, everything was grayish white. I couldn't distinguish anything. It was absolutely different from what I'd seen from the window in the corridor. I didn't get a good feeling from this grayish-white scene. I shut the window at once, and retreated to the chair. I understood a little: probably people living so high up felt uneasy when they looked at the night scene below. No wonder Young Ma was losing sleep. I pressed my ear against his bedroom door, and listened for a while. He was snoring. It seemed I actually should leave. I circled around the table lightly, but the sound I made opening the door woke him up. The bedroom door opened wide, and the light was also on . . .

"Stop!" he said from behind me. "Come over here!"

I turned around and went into his bedroom. His bed was even messier than a doghouse. Signs of insomnia were everywhere: the blanket was drooping down to the floor, and next to the pillow were two apples, each with one bite gnawed out of it. There was even a shoe on the bed. He gestured, indicating that I should follow him to the rear of the bureau. Standing in the corner was a large metal pail filled with dirty clothes.

"Move this pail out of the way," he ordered, "and then look down."

I bent over and did as I was told. Under the pail was a hole. I took a look, and immediately sprang back. Drained of strength, I sat down on the floor. In a split second, I had the profound feeling that I was a weak-willed person. The saying "hanging by a hair" kept going through my mind. The vision I saw was too difficult to describe. In a word, I saw the inner structure of this large building—from the thirtieth floor straight down to the first floor. But the situation was extremely critical: this multi-storied building's collapse was imminent. Now my legs had gone mushy: it was impossible for me to even walk out of this apartment. I had definitely lost my wits; otherwise, I should have figured out that what I saw was certainly a hallucination. What I saw was absolutely impossible.

When I got over my dizziness, I discovered that Ma was sticking his head into the hole to take a careful look. After a while, he turned back to me, and shouted, "Ah, this sort of agony is like a saw! Who can put up with it?! Ah, this grisly thing: yiiiiiikes!" He pulled a long face, calling to mind a skull. A whispering sound came from the floor, and the floor began wobbling. I shut my eyes, waiting for that inescapable thing to come. I waited for a while: the shaking continued lightly. If you didn't pay attention, you couldn't feel it. Still bent over on the floor, Young Ma was nattering—as if he were talking to a lover down there: "Why aren't you the least bit relaxed? You strut back and forth like a slut. What the hell are you doing? Do you think I can't leave you? It was clear to me quite a while ago that you intended to block my way out. Humph! What the hell: you're making that sound again, just like an echo in a graveyard. Has the ceiling on the fifteenth floor started to collapse? Ah, I am truly worried . . ."

I gradually got hold of myself. I figured I'd take advantage of his talking to the monster in the cave or hole, and just leave without a word. I walked lightly toward the door, but he was too quick: you couldn't slip anything past him.

"Stop! Do you just come when you want to, and leave when you want to?" He twisted his neck around and spoke to me gravely, but then he became fed up quite quickly. With a wave of his hand, he said, "Hurry off! Hurry off! I'm not in the mood to deal with you."

As the elevator was descending, I thought doomsday was approaching, and I actually began sobbing. I couldn't think of anything at the moment—not my son in the countryside, not my retirement pension, not my bankbook hidden in a hole in the wall, not the fifty yuan the resident on the thirteenth floor had borrowed from me, not anything that used to be important to me. With undivided attention, I was waiting for the ultimate tragic roar. But the elevator was just the same as always—going down with just a slight sound. The indicator light reminded me that I'd reached the first floor. I entered the office restlessly, flopped down on the bed, and went to sleep.

The morning rush hour came all too quickly: one after another, people went past the office window, and in surprise, they stuck their heads in to take stock of me. Their little heads looked a lot like camels' heads. I went on sleeping, not paying attention to much at all: who cared what they were saying?

The worst thing was my insomnia. The scenes I saw that night were too terrifying. That hole came all the way through to my office. Maybe that guy named Ma was looking at me right this minute. Was there anything he hadn't seen? I smacked my lips. Was there any meaning in life? The people living in this large building were all muddleheaded. The only clearheaded one was a noctivagous freak. When we die here, we aren't even aware where the death comes from. Is there anything more tragic? Yet, I can't leave this place. My son is waiting in the countryside for me to get him to the city. My hometown is on the sands of the Gobi, where the sunset's afterglow is splendid but you have to walk miles to find a tree. Every time I write my son, I admonish him not to go outside for *anything*, lest he be buried by a sandstorm. I tossed and turned in bed like a biscuit being fried.

I stayed in bed for three days. On the table, the newspapers and books delivered by the mailman were piled up like a mountain. The residents looked in on me from the window—daring to be angry, but not daring to say anything. Let them look. These fools couldn't find anyone to replace me. Who else could keep watch here twenty-four hours a day for rock-bottom wages? It was because they knew this much that they didn't dare reprimand me. Now, even if they fired me, I wouldn't care; maybe it would even be a way to break away from this building. Otherwise, wouldn't I be buried under it? The afternoon of the third day, I noticed that the residents were beginning to whisper to each other. I guessed they couldn't take this situation any longer. At this point, I suddenly felt sentimentally attached to this building once more. I'd worked here twenty years. Everyone knew me. Almost every day, I rode the elevator upstairs to keep an eye on things. I didn't go into anyone's apartment, just stood in the corridor taking in the city landscape. Downstairs, I also sorted the mail, and arranged the letters on the window glass for people to pick up. I read the name and address on each letter very carefully, and memorized them: they were lined up in my brain. If a stranger showed up, I would detain him and ask all kinds of questions to get him to give himself away. This was also a good way to show my authority. From the bottom of my heart, I was content with this kind of life. I had this feeling right up until three days ago. So now how was it that everything had changed? Was it because my brain had been muddled that night when Young Ma had enticed me into his home on the top floor and told me to look at the weird scene from his apartment? Probably that was a deception he had contrived. How could such a grotto appear on the thirtieth floor? For all I knew, he'd taken advantage of my not thinking clearly and played a mind game; he had somehow caused my brain to produce this wacky picture. Thinking this, I sat up with a start. Just as I sat up, it so happened that Young Ma walked into my office. His appearance had changed a lot: he was wearing a business suit, a gaudy floral tie, and spanking new shoes. His hair was gleaming. At first sight, I thought it must be his brother!

"You old fart, you actually pretended to be sick and wasted a hell of a lot of time!" He smacked me hard on the back.

"You're all dressed up. Do you have a date?"

"Sure thing." He whispered to me: "None of us has much time. We have to enjoy life while we can."

All of a sudden, he thought of something, and glancing at his watch, he quickly turned around. In grand high spirits, he headed for the street. As soon as he left, I went back to my normal work, and the apartment residents were naturally very relieved.

It was the middle of the night before Young Ma returned from his carousing. Somebody had torn his new suit, and there were four purple fingerprints on his right cheek. One eye was swollen. When he came in, he collapsed on my bed, and kept saying in a tear-laden voice, "I'm a loser, a hopeless loser. I might as well die, might as well just die. . ." Taking in his appearance, I recalled the scene when he had bent over on the floor and conversed with that grotto. I sensed something vaguely.

"Will you go with me to look at that cave?" he suddenly asked in an absolutely composed voice.

As we rode the elevator, his hands took turns thumping his head. He was also stamping his feet in desperation, as if he were itching to stamp out a hole that he could drop through. I left the elevator with him and went into his bedroom again. I was really surprised to see that it was now as neat as a pin. But he didn't value his work: he flopped down on the bed, kicking off his shoes. The shoes fell onto the bed.

"Go on over and move that pail again. Take another look," he bantered, his hands pillowing his head.

I walked over to the place with the deep hole next to the bureau, and tried to pick up the metal pail. It never occurred to me that this pail would have put down roots: it couldn't be moved. I looked carefully at the lower edge of the pail, but I didn't see anything like screws riveting it there. What the hell had happened to it? I kicked it a few times, but it still wouldn't be moved. It covered the hole beneath it very tightly.

"You never guessed," he sneered, "that the hole has a strong magnetic force which has gripped the metal pail. It can't be moved just with the little strength that humans have. It's only when I take a devil-may-care attitude that the magnetic force vanishes of its own accord—like last time. But now I'm too much on edge, so it rejects me. Now you know: it isn't any comfort; it can't console people. This word 'comfort' is too philistine."

I thought he was completely mixed up: this deep scary hole, this monster's den that frightened him so much his face was drained of color, in truth *was* a comfort to him. When you came up against this kind of thing, how should you deal with it? Hadn't it also reeled me in? He was solemn, watching me dejectedly.

"Where did you go today for entertainment?" I wanted to distract him.

"Where could I go except over to my parents' place? This morning, a passing whim took hold of me—to start afresh. That was fine for the first half hour, but then I betrayed myself: I don't know why, but I started fighting with my parents. They thrashed me within an inch of my life. They said they had to 'teach me a lesson.' Later on, the neighbors called the police. Since I was the one who'd been beaten and lost face, the police couldn't very well take me into custody. If they had, I'd be in jail now. I've been lying here giving it a lot of thought: how did I turn bad? I thought the starting point was this hole. Every time I look at the scene in the hole, courage flows through every pore of my body; I'm as strong as an ox. But then, it's merely a hallucination. As soon as I come up against something, I turn into a black turtle. The views in the hole give the turtle the courage of a lion—a fruitless valor. Can you understand this kind of thing?"

"No, but it's really interesting."

"Sure, it's interesting to stand on the dry shore and make sarcastic remarks to someone who's fallen into the water. Come around again tonight. Now I need to calm down."

That night, I went up to the top floor again, but Young Ma's door was tightly closed. The third time I rapped on the door, the door next to it opened, and a man whose eyes were exploding with fury hurled abuse at me. He said I was just like Young Ma: we were both pederasts. He said if we went on disturbing people like this, the residents of this building would never have any peace.

"When I saw that you were pretending to be sick, I knew you were in cahoots with the guy next door," he said fiercely.

I couldn't do anything but return to my place and go to sleep. I woke up twice more during the night, both times startled awake by shouting. Someone in the building was shouting for help. Both times, I acted reflexively: I ran out to the street, but then I just saw the building standing securely in front of me. After this happened twice, I was wiped out. I was too tired to respond again to the shouts for help, desperate though they were. I just went on sleeping.

It's been more than six months since all of this happened. Now, Young Ma still goes past my office every day. He's changed again—back to the way he always was: lazy and sluggish, careless with his appearance. When he sees me, he looks down. When I see him, I turn my head away. The two of us understand each other too well: we're just like two enemies all too familiar with the same machinations.

# MOSQUITOES AND MOUNTAIN BALLADS

I HAD TO PAY ANOTHER CALL ON THIRD UNCLE, A SIMPLE AND unsophisticated old man.

In the open field, from a long way away, I saw that navy-blue undershirt of his. After washing the mud off his feet on the ridge of the field, he led me toward his home. As usual, none of the villagers we ran into along the way, men or women, old or young, greeted him, but simply walked on. Some turned around and stood there looking at Third Uncle's receding figure. The villagers were weighed down with worries.

Looking at Third Uncle's rather decrepit appearance, I felt a little sick at heart. His stride wasn't as brisk as before, either; he shuffled a little now. Walking with me, his old shortcomings resurfaced: he was constrained as he tugged at my arm. He wanted me to listen closely to a sound coming from the mountain. At times like this, I sometimes had absolutely no faith in my own judgment. I responded only vaguely, and so Third Uncle grew angry and went on by himself. After walking a while, he forgot his anger, and once more told me to listen attentively. But I listened for a long time, still without hearing anything. And so, by the time we reached his home, we were both peeved.

Third Uncle's home was sadly simple: it was just a one-room tiled lean-to in the foothills, with the hillside acting as one wall, as if the place were a dying old man leaning against the slope. Inside was a large coal stove taking up a third of the space. Next to it was a large storage cabinet that served as Third Uncle's bed at night.

Third Uncle had no sooner entered the house than he took a small copper kettle out of the cupboard so he could boil tea for me. After the tea had boiled for a while, he poured it into a large cup. The brown liquid smelled smoky. Frowning, I drank it. Beside me, Third Uncle said, "It's an herb tea—good for curing all kinds of ailments."

Well, I certainly didn't need to cure any ailments, so after one mouthful, I set it aside. Third Uncle was not at all pleased.

After a while, something stirred outside. A weak smile began floating on Third Uncle's face, and his rough old skin softened a lot. His eyelids drooped: he was waiting.

The one who came in was Awei, the village bum, a renowned blackguard in these parts. I had never understood the connection between him and Third Uncle. Given Third Uncle's seriousness and worldly ways, he ought to have put distance between himself and this sort of person, but contrary to all expectations, the two of them were close.

As soon as Awei sat down next to the stove, he picked up the copper kettle and poured himself some tea. Tipping his head back, he downed a large cup of it. He smacked my thigh with his dirty hand, and told me not to pretend to be refined. Disgusted, I moved a little way away from him, but—not one to let me off so easily—he crowded even closer.

"Hey, Awei, have you examined your feelings today?" Third Uncle asked.

"Yup. I think I have more and more antipathy for you. This morning, when you were walking in front of me, I nearly cut you down with my hoe. Just think what a great scene it would've been if I'd done that," Awei replied humorlessly.

"He's just bluffing, isn't he?" Third Uncle turned and fixed his eyes on me.

I didn't understand anything they were saying.

"Hey, Third Uncle, the amaranth oughtta be cut. I'll help you do it." With that, Awei rose and went out the door carrying a basket.

The door shut. The only light in the gloomy house came from a tiny tuft of light falling on the stove from the skylight. I felt a little antsy, and decided to find an excuse to slip away. From inside the storage cabinet I was sitting on came the sound of claws scratching on the wood. It was the black cat sharpening its claws inside: the sound made it seem that it was scratching my ass. I glanced furtively at Third Uncle: his expression had turned apathetic. Suddenly, from the field in front of us, we heard Awei singing mountain ballads. The dreary, melancholy sound came intermittently. I hadn't known that Awei could sing, and I was mesmerized by the sound. Awei sang several songs, and then the sound gradually grew distant and finally faded away. It was obvious that Third Uncle was also listening, but he kept his composure: no one could penetrate his innermost feelings. In more than three decades, I'd never seen through to his heart, had I? As we were sitting there face to face in silence, I recalled bygone days.

Back then, when I was maybe five or six, I always loved tagging along with Third Uncle when he went to the mountain to chop firewood. After we got to the mountain, Third Uncle told me to sit on a flat stump and wait for him. Then he disappeared into the woods. He might be gone for a short time or a long time. He might come back after half an hour, or I might be waiting for him from morning until afternoon. How could I while away so much time? And I would for sure be afraid. So I learned how to find things to do. I racked my brains during those endless days. It was way back then that I began to realize that Third Uncle had cast a spell. About once an hour, I could hear Third Uncle hoarsely singing mountain ballads: he was deliberately circling back to this vicinity, chopping firewood in order to reassure me. The strange thing was that he wasn't the least bit worried that I might be in danger. He was very confident of this.

Looking back, I thought that Third Uncle's mountain ballads somewhat resembled what Awei was singing today. Was Awei singing in order to reassure Third Uncle? Could it be that Third Uncle was just as scared as I used to be? Considering this, I stole another furtive glance at him. He was sitting absolutely still and erect, clearly not the least bit afraid. I couldn't understand how a person like Third Uncle could be part of this world. For all I knew, as time passed, there would be fewer and fewer of his sort.

I never could rub away my childhood memories. After Third Uncle had finished chopping firewood, he and I would come down the mountain together. After leaving the mountain, he always turned around to look back. Sometimes, he also put down his load, and pricked up his ears and listened attentively. He kept prattling along the lines of "I'm getting old. I have to be a little careful about this kind of thing." It was as if he had become a different person from the one on the mountain. It was obvious that there were things that Third Uncle was afraid of, too.

I'd left the village years ago. Meanwhile, Awei had taken my place in Third Uncle's life. According to Third Uncle, back then, Awei couldn't go on drifting in the village. His mother was living in his elder brother's home. As for Awei, he never had enough to eat. One evening, when Awei had nothing to eat, he was dazed with hunger and he charged into Third Uncle's home. From then on, he was a frequent guest.

When I first returned to the village, I meant to get back on the same old terms with Third Uncle; later, I realized this was no longer possible. With Awei squeezed in between us, I always felt that words couldn't express meaning very well. The two of them always understood one another tacitly. At first, I was jealous of Awei. Later, when I saw that Awei was the one Third Uncle thought a lot of, I gave up.

Now, Third Uncle's relationship with me has become delicate. Every few days, I come to see him. I just come and go, that's it. He never asks me questions, nor does he care about anything I'm doing. Sometimes, I bring up our time together when I was a child. He just says I used to love "making trouble" for him. With a word, he dampens my enthusiasm. Nonetheless, I always remember the endless waits in the woods, the movements of shadows cast by sunlight through cracks in the trees, the torment and the terror, the isolation and the helplessness I felt. Despair alternated with hope until delight and relief finally set in: I would remember all of this until the end of my life. With his mountain ballads, Third Uncle divided my time into segments. Was this because he felt compassion for my youth and innocence?

Time has rolled on: am I the one who has changed, or is it he who has changed? Third Uncle hasn't chopped firewood on the mountain for a long time. Now he just needs to get a little brushwood or straw to start the fire, because the village switched to cooking with coal long ago. Since coming back, I haven't heard him singing mountain ballads, either. Third Uncle's memory is worsening, too: he sometimes forgets to water the vegetables and fertilize the plants. He's a lonely old guy, without anyone to remind him. It's easy to imagine what will happen to him.

Now he's especially enamored of a senseless activity: battling with the mosquitoes at night. Third Uncle is sensitive to mosquitoes, but he doesn't bother to sleep under a mosquito net. Third Uncle has good eyesight: once he's awakened by a mosquito bite, he gets up and swats the mosquito with his hand. He also keeps track of the number he's killed—writes it down in a little notebook. According to him, one time he killed 137 mosquitoes in one night. I've seen the way he chases mosquitoes: he's overcome with excitement then—not at all like the average seventy-year-old. In the front and back of his home are some loblollies, particularly good for nurturing mosquitoes. I urged him to fill in these loblollies. He sneered slightly and said, "You don't understand anything." That depressed me for much of the day. Mosquitoes are active at dusk. If you go to Third Uncle's home at that time of day, from a distance you can hear him smacking mosquitoes with his hand. As you get closer, you can see the fresh bloodstains all over his hands. He tries to explain things away by saying, "I'm sort of thin, but I guess my blood tastes okay."

Every year, he has a bout of malaria. It's hard to look at him when he's sick and his illness drags on for a long time. One time, I thought he was going to die. Awei also thought he wasn't going to make it. But the next day, we saw him actually creep along on the floor and drink water from the cat's bowl, because he'd already finished the last drop of water we'd given him the night before. By afternoon, he was gradually getting better. Three or four days later, he could wobble his way out the door. Third Uncle had lived seventy years, but it was as if he hadn't lived long enough. He began to value his life even more. As I was thinking of this, I was sitting on the cabinet, and the black cat made its way out of a hole in it. It leapt across the teapot, and bumped Third Uncle's teacup to the floor, where it splintered into several pieces.

As he stooped to sweep up the bits of porcelain, Third Uncle finally opened his mouth: "What else do you want to know?"

"Was the forest actually dangerous?" I asked.

"Probably."

"Weren't you afraid to leave me alone?"

"Of course I was afraid, you silly youngster."

As I left Third Uncle's home, I was rather distracted. I always felt the color of dusk was murky, and I walked aimlessly in my confusion. Suddenly I heard singing coming from the mountain. It was Awei, but I also thought it couldn't be Awei. After all, he had just been in the vegetable garden: even if he were fleet of foot, he couldn't have reached the mountain so swiftly. A light breeze carried the singing to me: it was certainly Awei. Could there be another voice like his? While I was working this out, I saw Awei sitting at the door of his home playing with a black rooster. What a rascal! I couldn't hear anything now. Awei's mother came out. Lifting a bamboo rod, she meant to strike Awei with it, but the rod hit the doorsill with a ringing *dang* sound. Awei had long since lobbed along, into thin air.

The old woman squatted on the ground, and broke into noiseless tears. I got away from this scene in a hurry.

So Third Uncle had figured out a long time ago that the forest was dangerous! This discovery seemed terrifically important. He was like everyone else after all—merely an ordinary old farmer: where had this hunch come from? I recalled people saying that his aunt had brought him to the village. The aunt hadn't stayed long, but had left Third Uncle in the village. Back then, Third Uncle was terribly emaciated: no one thought he would grow up. Of course, everyone was wrong. What had things been like for Third Uncle before he came to the village? I had never gotten a reliable answer to this question—not from him and not from anyone else, either.

My association with Third Uncle began very early. I was just five. One morning, I was playing alone at fishing for shrimp next to a small creek when Third Uncle's tall, thin shadow fell across the water. From above, he said, "Hey, little guy, want to go with me to the mountain?" I jumped up and went with him.

We kept up our relationship for years. What had attracted me to Third Uncle? After all, he was taciturn. The path to the forest was long and lonely. When he abandoned me to go off and cut firewood, it was even harder for me. Yet, I went to the mountain with him time after time. Sometimes, I simply couldn't wait to go. I heard the howling of wolves, and from a distance I saw a wild boar. The time I saw the wild boar, I fainted from fear. Or maybe I purposely fainted. At that moment, I was terrified: I was sure I was done for. When I came to, I heard Third Uncle singing nearby. The wild boar had vanished. I've always thought that I might have imagined the boar—that it might have been a hallucination born of the extreme strain I was under. Back then, when I told Third Uncle about the wild boar, he pondered for a long time. Finally, though, he didn't say anything—he just hoisted up his load of firewood and left.

The year I was fifteen, I left the village. I had a consuming sense of weariness. A few years before, I had stopped going with Third Uncle to the mountain to cut firewood. Naturally, we were still on close terms with one another. When I had nothing to do, I lent a hand in his vegetable garden—just as Awei did now. Bored beyond belief, I decided to change my lifestyle. Sitting atop the newly made storage cabinet in Third Uncle's house, I said, "Tell me where I should go." I recall Third Uncle saying, "How can I tell you where to go? I don't even know where I am going myself. Just go off with no direction, and don't look back." "Are you speaking from experience?" I asked. "Naturally," he said.

It wasn't until I turned thirty that I came back to the village. In the meantime, I'd been wandering aimlessly—right up until the day I once again saw the old camphor tree at one end of the village.

I was almost home, and someone rushed from behind to catch up with me. It was Awei. Awei wasn't shouting as usual, but was in low spirits.

"Your singing was great," I said.

"Hmmm." Head down, he seemed to be full of worries.

When I went inside, he did, too, and sat in the doorway.

"Well, in the end, Awei is sometimes also depressed," I couldn't keep from saying.

"You don't know shit. Third Uncle intends to slough us both off. What will I do? I sing because of the despair in my heart."

"It's really strange that you can't leave him. Aren't you annoyed with him?"

"It has nothing to do with whether he annoys me or not. You must know that. Let me ask you: do you hear the singing on the mountain over there? You must have heard it once, and probably not just once. Me, too. But what good is that? Neither of us can be like Third Uncle, who can hear it whenever he wants. It's we who've been truly muddleheaded."

"This really doesn't sound like Awei talking."

"And what's Awei all about? Awei is a bum all right: can't a bum think about his problems? I never thought you were such a vulgar person."

"How on earth did you figure out that Third Uncle means to cast us off?"

"We've both heard the singing on the mountain over there. This is the reason he wants to cast us off. Hey, talking with you has really worn me out. Can I sleep here for a while?" He toppled over against the doorsill, his face showing anguish and fatigue.

In August, Third Uncle refused to see Awei and me. We kept watch outside the door, and looked in through the window. We saw a swarm of mosquitoes besieging his spare frame. He lay on top of the storage cabinet, lingering on in a steadily worsening condition. Now and then, he still swatted feebly at his face. At last, we ourselves were bitten by mosquitoes until we couldn't take it anymore. Our faces began to swell. Awei said if I wanted to go, I should just go. He could keep watch here by himself. He wasn't afraid of mosquitoes. He was just afraid of one thing. When he said this, he looked at me with eyes that were red and swollen. I wanted to stay, but in fact I was unable to. My nerves were too fragile.

I had to leave. On the way home, I heard again the singing I hadn't heard for so long. It was the same voice; some coquettish elements had been added to the song, bringing to mind a seductive fox spirit. Ahead of me were shadows. Going home, I seemed to run into quite a lot of villagers, but looking down, they didn't greet me—they walked straight on by. Could it be that my face was so swollen that they couldn't recognize me? All of a sudden, I thought of the many mosquito eggs in my blood. This was really enough to drive a guy crazy. Maybe these mosquitoes could also hum this kind of mountain ballad: this was the sweet, joyous music Third Uncle was hearing as he lay dying. Awei certainly knew everything: that was why he had finally looked at me like that. Did he want me to know these things, too? If it began raining tonight, would he force his way into Third Uncle's house?

# AFTERWORD BY CAN XUE
# A PARTICULAR SORT OF STORY

THE PARTICULAR CHARACTERISTICS OF MY STORIES HAVE NOW BEEN acknowledged. Nevertheless, when someone asks me directly, "What is really going on in your stories? How do you write them?," I'm profoundly afraid of being misunderstood, so all I can say is, "I don't know." From any earthly perspective, in truth I do not know. When I write, I intentionally erase any knowledge from my mind.

I believe in the grandness of the original power. The only thing I can do is to devoutly, bring it into play in a manmade, blind atmosphere. Thus, I can break loose from the fetters of platitudes and conventions, and allow the mighty logos to melt into the omnipresent suggestions that inspire and urge me to keep going ahead. I don't know what I will write tomorrow, or even in the next few minutes. Nor do I know what is most related to the "inspiration" that has produced my works in an unending stream for more than two decades. But I know one thing with certainty: no matter what hardships I face, I must preserve the spiritual quality of my life. For if I were to lose it, I would lose my entire foundation.

In this world, subsistence is like a huge rolling wheel crushing everything. If a person wants to preserve the integrity of his innermost being, he has to endlessly break his self apart, endlessly undergo "exercises" that set the opposed parts of one's soul at war with one another. In my exercises, while my self is planted in the world, at the same time my gaze—from beginning to end—is unswervingly fixed on heaven; this is forcing a division between soul and flesh. By enduring the pain from this splitting of the soul, I gain a force of tension—conquering the libido and letting it erupt anew on the rebound. Through this writing, where the self is split apart, one achieves the greatest joy in the midst of an infinitude of keen feelings. As for the world, it constantly exhibits an unprecedented godly purity.

It isn't possible for people to live in pure spirit, because we are situated in a world that is highly filtered and conglutinated. The birthplace of pure spirit is situated in our dark flesh and blood. Perhaps my stories simply return to the old haunt: while pushing forward the dark abyss, they liberate the binding desires and crystallize them into pure spirit. The impetus for this kind of writing lies with the unending desires that make up ordinary life. While the conglutination decomposes wondrously and while the wide-awake imagination receives a clear message from profound restlessness, my pen achieves its own spiritual power. If one is in pursuit of the very purest language, one has to encounter grime, filth, violence, the smell of blood. While writing, you have to endure everything, you have to give up all worldly things. If you still care about being graceful, concerned with your posture and stance, you can't write this kind of story. In this sense, I exist only after my stories exist.

Stories with this kind of unusual language open another life for me. These stories and my ordinary life pervade each other, are interdependent. Because of their intervention, all commonplace vulgarities are imbued with secret significance; human feelings become the greatest enigma of them all. Therefore, daily anguish is no longer something that can't be endured, because the unending source of inspiration lies precisely in this. Perhaps it's from the boundary which is between melting and blending that artists are able to derive truth in a split second, the result being a coagulation into a work of art.

I believe that art is instinctive in human beings. Artists are simply those who are able—via mighty restraints—to exert their instincts to the utmost. My realm is one shared with all artists. When I enter this realm, the first thing I do is to remove the stone foundation from under my feet, and suspend my body in a semi-free state. Not until then is there an acceleration of mystery. And that is only in spurts. Years of repeated practice have gradually made me aware that success benefits from the mighty logos, inside myself, that is like a murderous machine. The more rigorous the sanction of reason, the more ferocious the rebounding of flesh and blood. Only in this way can the stories have a powerful, unconstrained style and fantasy, yet also have a rigorous and profound level of logic.

I certainly did not painstakingly set out to write this kind of story. From the beginning, as I practiced, I heard the faint drumbeats of fate. Afterwards, my life naturally evolved in pursuit of that summons. From my experience, one can see how great the power of art is to transform a person's life. Whether or not a person is a writer, if he maintains the sensitivity of art, his humanity can be greatly increased. So, art very much harmonizes with human nature and humanism. Art is the most universal pursuit of what it means to be human. Its essence is love.

Some people say that my stories aren't useful: they can't change anything, nor do people understand them. As time goes by, I've become increasingly confident about this. First, the production of twenty years' worth of stories has changed me to the core. I've spoken of this above. Next, from my reading experience, this kind of story, which indeed isn't very "useful," that not all people can read— for those few very sensitive readers, there is a decisive impact. Perhaps this wasn't at all the writer's original intent. I think what this kind of story must change is the soul instead of something superficial. There will always be some readers who will respond—those readers who are especially interested in the strengthening force of art and exploring the soul. With its unusual style, this kind of story will communicate with those readers, stimulating them and calling to them, spurring them on to join in the exploration of the soul.

Self-reflection is the magic formula for creation, a particular self-reflection different from passive self-examination. This kind of self-reflection brings all one's strength to bear on entering the profound world of the soul, and makes what one has seen there appear again through a special kind of language. Thus, it opposes the scenes of the spiritual world with the exterior world we're accustomed to, so that we can deepen our understanding. So artistic self-reflection is virtually an active process: it is taking the initiative to go down into hell, to establish oppositions, to strengthen self-contradictions. And in the brutality of fighting closely with oneself, one achieves a unified, highly conscious creation. This dynamic process comes from the longing of the artist to deny his worldly, carnal existence.

To satisfy this innermost desire, I put into effect this sort of drill every day. I bring into play my energy to seek out ancient memories that faded long ago. I feel instinctively that there's no way to stop this kind of exercise. Beginning a long time ago and continuing until today, it is my purpose for living. When I face this world that is filled with material desire and immerse myself fully in the worldly roles, it is precisely what endows my worldly life with meaning. Without it, I would be ashamed to show my face, I would have no foothold. Now, every day, I put into effect artistic activity and restrict my daily life to serve my artistic calling. I feel that I am mightier than ever!

In essence, there's no way for modern art to consider its viewers. Modern art cannot "consider" who its observers are. It can only provide information and summon people, inducing them to stop in their busy lives to think and self-consciously make time for a certain kind of spiritual activity. And so we can say that modern art—approaching human instincts ever more closely—as a spiritual pursuit, can only be an adventurous activity filled with initiative. The relationship between a successful work and its readers is described by the priest in Kafka's *The Trial* when he says to K, "It receives you when you come and it dismisses you when you go."

What I try hard to reach in my stories is this realm of freedom. I believe, when writers create their uncertain imaginary world, they are restless; their eyes are blurred, their hearts startled. But only when it receives affirmation from perceptive readers does this world exist. There must be this kind of reader. I deeply believe that humankind's soul is a shared place: humans are those who can reason, who are good at self-criticism. In the process of deepening their understanding of the self, people, uninterruptedly, have developed a high level of reason, and have begun to construct a spiritual mechanism forever at odds with "jungle culture."